UKRAINIAN FOLK STORIES

DIXON'S BOOKS
383 Water Street,
Peterborough, ont. K9H 3L7
Comics for Collectors

MARKO VOVCHOK

UKRAINIAN FOLK STORIES

By
MARKO VOVCHOK

Translated by N. Pedan-Popil
Edited by H. B. Timothy

Western Producer Prairie Books
Saskatoon, Saskatchewan

English translation copyright © 1983 N. Pedan-Popil
Western Producer Prairie Books
Saskatoon, Saskatchewan

All rights reserved. No part of this publication may be reproduced, stored in a retrieval system, or transmitted, in any form or by any means, electronic, mechanical, photocopying, recording or otherwise, without the prior written permission of the publisher.

Cover design by John Luckhurst, GDL

Printed and bound in Canada by
Modern Press
Saskatoon, Saskatchewan

Western Producer Prairie Books publications are produced and manufactured in the middle of western Canada by a unique publishing venture owned by a group of prairie farmers who are members of Saskatchewan Wheat Pool. From the first book in 1954, a reprint of a serial originally carried in the weekly newspaper, *The Western Producer*, to the book before you now, the tradition of providing enjoyable and informative reading for all Canadians is continued.

Illustrations, with the exception of the photograph of Marko Vovchok, are reproduced from Marko Vovchok, *Povisti ta opovidannia* (Kyiv: Vydavnytstvo khudozhn'oi literatury 'Dnipro' publishers, 1966).

Canadian Cataloguing in Publication Data
    Main entry under

Vovchok, Marko.
    Ukrainian folk stories

Translation of: Povisti ta opovidannia. Kyiv:
    Dnipro, 1966.
ISBN 0-88833-103-7

I. Title.
PG3948.V66P613   891.7'93'012   C83-091273-8

CONTENTS

Acknowledgments	vii
Translator's Note	ix
Introduction	1
The Sister	9
The Kozak Girl	25
The Chumak	40
Odarka	44
The Spell	50
The Dream	57
Horpyna	64
Redemption	68
The Mother-in-law	77
Father Andriy	81
Maksym Hrymach	85
Danylo Hourch	91
Instytutka	97
The Slacker	135
Two Sons	149
Mismatched	155

ACKNOWLEDGMENTS

I would like to express my thanks to all those who, by their help and encouragement, have made this translation possible. A special word of thanks is due to my son R. E. Popil, for assisting in the preparation of this book and for contributing the first draft of the Marko Vovchok story, "Instytutka." I would also like to convey my gratitude to those of my University of Regina students in Ukrainian who participated one way or another in the production of this translation which, it is my sincere hope, may be of service to them and to many others.

N. P.-P.

TRANSLATOR'S NOTE

Marko Vovchok, *Povisti ta opovidannia* (Kyiv: Vydavnytstvo khudozhn'oi literatury 'Dnipro' publishers, 1966), was the text used for this translation, which is faithful to the original except in the few cases of Ukrainian folk sayings and proverbs which have no exact equivalents in English, and are, therefore, replaced by the closest English substitutes or translated loosely.

The system of modified transliteration of the Library of Congress has been followed throughout the book. Correct transliteration of Ukrainian geographical names such as Kyiv, Dnipro, Krym into English is used instead of Kiev, Dnieper, Crimea, etc.

The portrait of Marko Vovchok owes a considerable debt to *Marko Vovchok, statti i doslidzhennia* (Kyiv: Vydavnytstvo Akademii Nauk Ukrains'koi RSR, 1957).

From "Instytutka"

INTRODUCTION

Marko Vovchok, the outstanding Ukrainian prose writer of the second half of the nineteenth century, began her literary career at the time when most of Ukrainian territory was under the power of the Russian Empire and the cultural and political life of the country was subject to all kinds of oppressive governmental measures.

The most severe situation calling for immediate remedy was the plight of the peasantry, who constituted the greater part of the Ukrainian population and remained serfs with no elementary human rights until 1861. Their future was bleak and their status in society degrading. There were numerous peasant uprisings, especially in the Kyiv area, but in every case they were repressed. In the last decades of serfdom, the government put into effect a series of laws to end some severe abuses to which the serfs were subjected, but this did not correct the situation. The interests of the serfs were ignored; they continued to be treated as the property of their masters and were obliged to do unpaid labor for them three and in some areas even six days a week, the system of serfdom becoming in consequence a truly unbearable hell.

The worst set-back experienced by Ukraine in her political and cultural life was the suppression by the Russian government in 1847 at Kyiv of the Brotherhood of SS Cyril and Methodious, a secret political organization in which most Ukrainian intellectuals of that time participated. Its main objectives were independence and equal rights for all Slavic nations and abolition of serfdom. All participants in the Brotherhood were arrested and banished from Ukraine. Among the arrested was the great Ukrainian poet and thinker, Taras Shevchenko who was already known in Ukraine through such markedly revolutionary poems as "The Dream" (1844), "My Testament" (1845), "The Caucasus" (1845), "The Epistle" (1845), in which he advocated national independence for Ukraine and openly condemned the Russian Empire for its retention of serfdom and its encroachment on the lands of other nationalities.

Ukraine, which always represented a direct threat to the Russian Empire because of its drive for national independence, came, after the 1847 affair, under the special scrutiny of the Tsar Nicholas I government, literature and the periodical press subject to the harshest censorship ever recorded. With the accession to the throne of Alexander II in 1855, there was a noticeable lessening in autocratic pressures. The Tsar, known to history as the "Liberator," started his reign with an appearance of liberality. An amnesty was granted to many of those who had incurred the displeasure of his father; there was an easing of restrictions on the printed word; the members of the Brotherhood and even Shevchenko were released and allowed to resume their work in St. Petersburg. The easing of governmental policies, the milder censorship in particular, immediately brought about a considerable revival of Ukrainian literary life to which Marko Vovchok's collection of stories was the most valuable contribution. Unfortunately, this revival in the literary and social life was short-lived. In June 1863 a special decree was issued prohibiting the printing of Ukrainian schoolbooks and popular reading material; and in June 1876, in order to put an end once and for all to the "Ukrainophile danger," yet another decree, "Emsky Ukaz," was issued, which repeated in more severe terms the law of 1863. For several decades thereafter Ukrainian literature in the Russian Empire lived an underground existence, in a complete state of decay.

Marko Vovchok witnessed all of the sad moments of Ukrainian social, political, and cultural life of that period and her writings reveal, in a most realistic and telling fashion, one of the saddest — serfdom. Her stories effectively exposed the harsh realities of serfdom and added to the growing resentment of it among all thinking members of society.

Marko Vovchok (pseudonym of Maria Vilins'ka) was born on 22 January 1833 into a Russianized landowning family of Ukrainian descent in the Orel region in Russia. She completed her final education in Ukraine (1845-1848) at the Kharkiv school for daughters of the nobility. In 1851, while in Orel, she married Opanas Markovych, a Ukrainian ethnographer, and the same year the young couple moved to Ukraine where they lived for almost a decade (1851-1858) in Chernihiv, Kyiv, and Nemyriv.

In the course of assisting her husband in his studies, Maria Markovych developed a keen interest in Ukrainian ethnography. While collecting Ukrainian folk songs and all kinds of ethnographic material in Ukrainian villages, she got very close to the peasant-folk. Speaking to them and learning more about their life, strengthened her interest in them and aroused her sympathy for the inhuman conditions.

It is not known exactly when she began writing her short stories, probably at the end of 1855 or at the beginning of 1856 when she was living in Nemyriv.[1] Her first collection of eleven short tales under the title *Narodni opovidannia (Folk Stories)* was published in St. Petersburg on

---

[1] *Marko Vovchok, statti i doslidzhennia* (Kyiv: Vydavnytstvo Akademii Nauk Ukrains'koi RSR, 1957), p. 19.

11 December 1857 (dated 1858 on the cover) by P. Kulish, the well known Ukrainian writer and literary critic. It included: "The Sister," "The Kozak Girl," "The Chumak," "Odarka," "The Dream," "Horpyna," "Redemption," "The Mother-in-Law," "Father Andriy," "Maksym Hrymach," and "Danylo Hourch." The stories were immediately acclaimed by P. Kulish who warmly congratulated her and predicted for her stories a great future in Ukrainian literature. Five of them were on the subject of serfdom.

The appearance of her anti-serfdom stories on the eve of the emancipation of the serfs in the Russian Empire, created widespread discussion, first among Ukrainian intellectuals and, after the Russian novelist Ivan Turgenev's translation of them in 1859, among Russians as well. In his introduction to the translation, Turgenev praised the originality and poetic grace of Marko Vovchok's stories. Ukrainian readers, he said, had enjoyed reading her stories for some time now, and her name had become dear to all Ukrainians. By translating her stories into Russian he wished to introduce her to Russian readers and make her name equally dear to them.[2] There was opposition to the stories, however, the strongest coming in 1859 from O. Druzhinin, editor of the Russian periodical *The Library for Readings*, who accused Marko Vovchok of "laying on the dark tones too thick" and of "a deliberate heaping up of disgusting, repulsive events."[3] Shevchenko, in contrast, greeted the new talent in Ukrainian literature with great joy and fatherly blessings. He compared her stories to the French George Sand's writings on peasant life and evaluated them more highly from the social point of view.[4] In 1859 Shevchenko, seeing in Marko Vovchok a disciple of his own sacred ideals, dedicated to her his poem on serfdom, "A Dream," beginning, "Toiling in serfdom, she was reaping wheat."[5] Marko Vovchok in turn dedicated to Shevchenko her most powerful anti-serfdom story "Instytutka" which she finished in St. Petersburg in 1859. It was there, on 24 January 1859, that they met, and, in memory of this meeting, Shevchenko on 15 February of that year wrote a poem entitled "To Marko Vovchok," in which he displayed his deep admiration for her work, and hailed her as "a gentle prophet" sent to the Ukrainian people by God and "a revealer of the insatiable fierce souls of cruel men."[6]

From then on Marko Vovchok produced several stories in Ukrainian and also wrote a few long novels in Russian. In 1859 her series of tales in Russian was published under the title *Stories From the Folk Life of Russia*.

---

[2] I. S. Turgenev, *Sochineniya* (Moskva-Leningrad: Izdatel'stvo "Nauka," 1968), Vol. 15, p. 80.

[3] *Istoria ukrains'koi literatury* (Kyiv: Vydavnytstvo Akademii Nauk Ukrains'koi RSR, 1954), vol. I, p. 350.

[4] B. B. Lobach-Zhuchenko, *Litopys zhyttya i tvorchosti Marka Vovchka* (Kyiv: Vydavnytstvo khudozhn'oi literatury 'Dnipro', 1969), p. 37.

[5] *The Poetical Works of Taras Shevchenko, The Kobzar*. Translated by C. H. Andrusyshen and Watson Kirkconnell (Toronto: Published for the Ukrainian Committee by University of Toronto Press, 1964).

[6] Ibid, p. 508.

However, it was her Ukrainian literary achievement that brought her fame and recognition. Her writings in Russian, which were probably produced mainly because of the restrictions imposed on the Ukrainian written word, have received scant attention in Russian literature.

During the greater part of the 1860s (1859-1867), Marko Vovchok resided in Paris, from which she traveled to England, Switzerland, Germany, and Italy. While living abroad, she devoted much of her attention to acquiring foreign languages. She learned to speak English, German, and Italian, in addition to the Russian, Ukrainian, and French of her childhood.

Marko Vovchok came to be considered one of the best translators of her time. Through the 1860s and 1870s she translated many French, English, and German literary works into Russian, French works foremost. Her translations of sixteen of Jules Verne's fantasy novels still remain the best standard translations in Russian. She was also very popular in France as the authoress of several stories for children, one of which, "Marusia," became prescribed reading in French schools, went into its hundredth printing at Paris in 1967,[7] and was translated into several languages. From French it was translated into English by Sarah Herrick Kidder in the late 1880s (exact date unknown); by Cornelia W. Cyr (New York, 1890); and by Edward Arnold (London, 1926).

In May 1862 appeared a second volume of Marko Vovchok's stories, including "Two Sons," "Mismatched," "The Spell," "The Slacker," and "The Three Fates." The year 1865 marked the appearance of the third volume of her Ukrainian collection comprising fables and other stories and legendary tales for children. In February 1867 she returned to St. Petersburg, visiting France again on several occasions, primarily to see Jules Verne about her translations of his works. While at St. Petersburg she edited her short-lived (January 1971 — May 1872) literary magazine *Translations from the Best Foreign Writers.*

After Marko Vovchok's husband died in 1867, she married in January 1878 a former navy officer, M. Lobach-Zhuchenko, and in the spring of the same year they moved to the Caucasus where she lived in seclusion and for some years in complete isolation from the literary life. Between 1885 and 1893 she resumed her interest in Ukrainian ethnographic studies and in 1900 renewed her connections with several Ukrainian publishers. Her last story, "The Devil's Adventure," was published in 1902 at Kyiv in *Kievan Antiquity,* a scholarly journal of Ukrainian studies. On the whole, however, the closing period of her life was not markedly productive. She died in Nal'chyk (Northern Caucasus) on 10 August 1907.

Marko Vovchok enriched Ukrainian prose with a new narrative form that differed in language and style from previous Ukrainian prose writings. Her style is characterized by simplicity of expression, compactness of narration, and closeness to the Ukrainian vernacular,

---

[7] Evhen Brandis, *Marko Vovchok* (Kyiv: Vydavnytstvo khudozhn'oi literatury "Dnipro", 1975), p. 312.

polished by her to a markedly high degree. Faithful reproduction of the vernacular made it possible for her to establish close rapport with her literary characters, especially her peasant heroes. Her stories are very simple in content, the events narrated by the characters themselves, mostly by peasant women. The language of the narratives is extremely melodious and rich in folklore elements, particularly proverbs and folk sayings. Some stories have traces of old superstitions; some present thoughts about God, truth, and justice; some give evaluation of a person's capacity and character, views on people's feelings, freedom, and justice. They are marked by rhythmic structure, picturesque language and reflect the life of Ukrainian people, surrounding nature, and the agricultural way of life of her heroes. Some plots of her stories, like "The Chumak," "The Spell," "The Dream," "The Mother-in-law" and others, bear a strong resemblance to the motifs of Ukrainian folk songs about everyday life, about the bitter fate of hired hands, landless peasants, vagabond-kozaks, the loneliness and moods of melancholy of the chumaks (the salt carters), the position of a wife in the family, etc. Others draw on motifs in folk songs, like happy and unhappy love, obstacles to love, jealousy, etc. Extensive use of epithets, metaphors, and comparisons taken from the oral folk literature gives her narratives a strong native coloring and beauty.

A young girl, for example, in her stories is always compared to a "bright star," "little dove," "little quail;" she is happy and merry as a "poppy flower;" she is young and beautiful like a "ripe berry" or a "little cucumber." Young men are always compared to the "brave eaglets," "young hawks," "strong young oaks," "daring falcons," etc. Her stories too are extremely rich in traditional Ukrainian diminutives of affectionate address, such as "little heart," "little bird," "little pigeon," "little sister" or "brother" (to a friend).

Her first publisher, P. Kulish declared that she had "drunk all the succulence and fragrance from the Ukrainian language."[8] On Ivan Turgenev's asking what author should he read in order to learn Ukrainian, Shevchenko replied: "Marko Vovchok! — She is the one who is most powerful in our language!"[9] Ivan Franko, the most outstanding Ukrainian novelist, poet, and literary critic of the Western Ukraine, affirmed that the best feature of Marko Vovchok's writings is "undoubtedly" her Ukrainian language. "In all its simplicity and popularity," he wrote, "it is very rich in its vocabulary and is incomparably melodious."[10] In this respect Marko Vovchok is considered to be an important contributor to the development of the Ukrainian literary language in the new era of Ukrainian prose — the era of realism — synthesizing as she does the folkloric with the realistic themes from rural life under serfdom.

---

[8] *Marko Vovchok v krytytsi* (Kyiv: Derzhavne vydavnytstvo khudozhn'oi literatury, 1955), p. 264.
[9] B. B. Lobach-Zhuchenko, *Litopys zhyttya i tvorchosti Marka Vovchoka*, p. 46.
[10] *Marko Vovchok v krytytsi,* p. 265.

Marko Vovchok's Ukrainian writings can be roughly divided into three groups, according to their subject-matter: (1) stories depicting serfdom, (2) stories depicting the life of free Ukrainian peasants, and (3) fables, historical tales, and other stories for children.

In the stories depicting serfdom, Marko Vovchok skilfully captured the main trends of her time by describing in a forthright, realistic manner and in a simple but most dramatic way, the hardships of the defenseless peasants and the cruelty of their masters. She presents numerous examples of the everyday humiliations to which the serfs were exposed. The French writer Prosper Merimée compared her stories to Harriet Beecher Stowe's *Uncle Tom's Cabin*. In a letter to Turgenev he commented that her stories made one sad, and that he felt in them "the power to stimulate the slaves to rise against their oppressors!"[11]

In the stories "Odarka," "The Kozak Girl," "The Slacker," and "Instytutka," Marko Vovchok describes the degrading position of the serfs who lived in the households of their owners, at the mercy of the landlords' whims. The story "Odarka" relates the tragic fate of a young girl seduced by her master, then given away to another household. On the other hand, the peasants of Kozak descent lived as free people on their homesteads or in special villages free of interference by the landlords. The striking difference between the two ways of life is forcibly depicted in "The Kozak Girl," where a serf village and a Kozak village are contrasted.

Contrast is also the main artistic device whereby Marko Vovchok reveals two opposing social worlds in the story, "Instytutka," the central figure in which is the young mistress, so lovely to look at, yet so cruel and despotic. The contrast between her angelic outward beauty and her evil disposition is most striking. Ivan Franko was loud in his praise of the story, which, in his opinion, "penetrated the most deeply into the core of the disastrous times of serfdom" and truly "belongs to the finest pearls of Ukrainian literature."[12]

Marko Vovchok gives vivid examples of the bitter fate of the peasants of Kozak descent who had lost their Kozak rights and been made serfs. In "The Kozak Girl," a free girl Olesia falls in love with a serf and marries him. She and her children automatically become serfs. In "The Slacker" a once free Kozak woman Chaichykha, who has been made a serf by some illegal means or other, lives a life full of hatred towards her owner, while her daughter Nastia constantly dreams of their former freedom and determines to free herself at any cost.

Not all of Marko Vovchok's serfs bear their unfortunate lot silently and submissively. In "Instytutka" Justine's husband Prokip can no longer tolerate the everyday cruelty of the lords and the urge to protest rises in

---

[11] Oleksa Zasenko, *Marko Vovchok i zarubizhni literatury* (Kyiv: Vydavnytstvo Akademii Nauk Ukrains'koi RSR, 1959), p. 26.

[12] Evhen Shabliovsky, *Ukrainian Literature Through the Ages* (Kyiv: 'Mystetstvo' publishers, 1970), p. 124.

him. As a result of his rebellious behavior, he is forced by his master into lengthy military service. In the same story, the master's coachman Nazar, unable to bear the misery of his lot, runs away from the lord's estate to find freedom in the far steppes. Chaichykha's daughter Nastia in "The Slacker," in order to gain her freedom, stops at nothing and finally through drink drives herself to destruction.

Marko Vovchok's stories about the free peasants embrace different periods of Ukrainian history and focus upon aspects of their domestic life with all its joys and sorrows. In most cases there is poverty and human suffering, but there are no landlords. These stories are all accessible and their subjects are based largely on the popular folk themes with strong tendencies in most of them to Romanticism.

"The Mother-in-law" illustrates the conflict between a mother-in-law and an unloved daughter-in-law. "Mismatched" portrays an unhappily married couple who, owing to their different personalities and interests, grow apart. "The Sister" describes the love and unbounded devotion of a sister toward her brother and his children. "The Spell," based on the popular belief in witchcraft, depicts the sad consequences of unrestrained jealousy. A vivid example of fatherly rigidity and stern patriarchal ways is given in the story "Maksym Hrymach." Strong will and self-destructive character are depicted in "Danylo Hourch."

All of Marko Vovchok's stories show her deep concern for the fate of the Ukrainian peasant woman of whose feelings and problems she wrote with great understanding and respect. In highly emotional fashion she reveals her heroines' hard lives as serfs and their sometimes difficult position in the family as housewives and mothers. She pities the unhappy lot of young peasant girls made victims of the dissolute behavior of their lords, and, in matters dealing strictly with peasant family relations, she stresses their fate under the prevailing stern patriarchal traditions.

Marko Vovchok's fables and other stories for children are based mostly on Ukrainian folklore material: historical legends, traditional tales, and folk songs. To this category belong "Karmeliuk," "The Slave Girl," "Marusia," "Nine Brothers and Their Sister Halia," "A Bear," "The Devil's Adventure," and others. All of these stories are marked by their high moral quality and in most of them reality is skilfully blended with the fantasy world of the folk tales and legends. Keen observation of people's feelings and moods, high examples of heroism, love of freedom, and the triumph of truth and justice are their main features.

The artistic, as well as the social, significance of Marko Vovchok's stories extended its influence to many Ukrainian and non-Ukrainian writers of the second half of the nineteenth and beginning of the twentieth century. Her works were noted abroad as early as the 1860s, especially in the Slavic countries, and in France and Germany, many of them being translated there at one time or another. Popularization of her stories in English translation is practically negligible. Turgenev probably tried to introduce her work in England. While visiting Alexander

Herzen[13] in London in June 1859, Turgenev gave him his Russian translation of the *Folk Stories*. Herzen's correspondence reveals his desire to meet the authoress and his enthusiasm for her stories. Writing to his step-sister, M. K. Reikhel on 14 June 1859, he praised the great social and artistic value of the stories and suggested translating them into English.[14] There is no evidence that it was ever done. The only other stories translated into English besides "Marusia," already mentioned, are "The Guest of the Steppes" (probably "The Chumak") by A. Hunter (published in *Ukrainian Review*, London 1931); "The Sister" by P. Cundy (published in *Ukrainian Weekly*, Jersey City, 1946 and 1955 issues); and "Lymerivna" by T. Wissotsky-Kuntz (published in *Ukrainian Weekly*, July 1951).

The present translation, consisting of sixteen narratives from Marko Vovchok's Ukrainian collection, includes all the stories on the subject of serfdom and most of the stories on the family life of the free peasants. It does not include the fables and stories for children.

N. P.-P.

---

[13] Alexander Herzen — Russian political writer and journalist of the nineteenth century. Herzen had left Russia during the regime of Nicholas I. *The Bell* (Kolokol), a journal published by him in London (1857-67), served as an organ of liberal opinion.

[14] B. Lobach-Zhuchenko, *Litopys zhyttya i tvorchosti Marka Vovchoka* (Kyiv: Vydavnytstvo khudozhn'oi literatury "Dnipro", 1969), p. 58.

THE SISTER

I was still young when my mother died, and I do not remember this time very well, except for my dreams, when I dream of someone rocking me in my cradle and singing quietly over me.

After my mother's death father had no inclination to remarry. "There will never be another better than my first dear one," he said. "God has received her into His kingdom, so now let my children manage the farm."

Our father was very good to us. His affection was bestowed equally on both my brother and me. We lived in comfort; there was nothing that we lacked. Whatever I planned for myself, I achieved. I was free to do anything. My girlhood was full and happy, and I remember it with affection, may my dear father rest in peace!

For almost three years I enjoyed my girlhood; then offers of marriage came my way. I kept refusing them and father did not put any pressure on me, even though some of the suitors were rich and handsome. Heaven at last sent me the one who was the perfect match for me. My suitor was a fine man, a very fine man indeed! He was dark and handsome. He certainly caught my fancy! I thought of nothing but Pavlo, and of how soon I could see him! He was from another village. Seeing him was happiness! But if I did not see him, I was so overcome with sadness, so overwhelmed with sorrow that life itself no longer mattered to me! If he was late for our meeting, I would cry my eyes out waiting for him. "Maybe," I would think to myself, "he has another girl!" One day, after the feast of Semen, when I least expected it, not as much as dreamed of it, he asked me to marry him. Father gave us his blessing. It did not matter that he was from a far-away village; he was such a good worker, and managed his farm so well, that he was known and liked by everyone in the area.

My husband took me to his farm. Dear God, how lovingly we lived! However, the Lord did not grant him long life. We had only two years together. He loved me very dearly! Our home was like a garland of flowers; it was a pleasure to behold. Whether we sat, worked, or just talked, we did everything together.

Then all of a sudden — misfortune dealt me a heavy blow! My Pavlo began ailing. I went to sorcerers, and to doctors, but nobody could do anything about it! As they say: "There is no cure for death" ... Pavlo died ...

My father came for me and took me back with him. We sold my husband's house and all the cattle.

"Live with me, daughter! Why should you live in a far-off village, all by yourself! God preserve us, you're no orphan!"

II

In the meantime my brother got married. His bride was a girl from our village. She was so lively and orderly! They had a baby, a little girl, as fresh and chubby as a little cucumber.

I had been scarcely six months in mourning for my Pavlo, when my father died. "Misfortunes never come single," people say — and they are right! For some time we lived well, but soon my brother became poor. The harvest gave a poor yield; the livestock perished; and God had given them five children to bring up: two girls and three boys. My brother worried to the point of collapse. His wife went about sadly, and even the children became sad. It was now so bad that they did not even have enough money to buy bread.

"Sister," my brother said, "do me a favor and lend me some money if you can! If I live long enough to earn some money, I will pay you back — if not, God somehow will repay you!"

So I loaned him the money that I got for the house and cattle, and things got better in our home: my brother would talk, his wife would smile, and the children would chatter merrily and laugh. I was happy. "The Lord be praised that everything is fine with us, as with other people!" I thought. My brother bought some cattle, and his farm began prospering again.

My brother and I had loved each other since we were children. We never fought or offended one another. We always made up if we fell out over anything and forgave each other.

My brother's children as well cared for me so much that they used to vie with each other for my affection. "This is my aunt!" one would say — and the other would pull at me and say: "She is mine!" Clinging to me and kissing me, they would tear what I was doing from my hands.

Only my sister-in-law looked down on me. I tried to please her as I would a small child, but there was no satisfying her. "Dear sister-in-law," I would suggest to her, "let us do this this way, and everything will be fine." But, oh no! Never in her life would she listen to me! Even although everyone could see that harm would result, if we followed her ideas, she would insist that her decision was the right one. I fell in with her wishes by keeping silent to save my brother worry. I would cry in secret, and that would be that! But afterwards I would approach her again with pleasing words.

One day when we were planting seedlings in the garden, I spoke to her. Acting as if she had not heard me, she walked away. My heart grew sad, and I began to sing softly to myself. I sang, and the tears flowed. . . . Suddenly I heard: "May God be with you, and a good day to you!" I looked up — it was our neighbor. She leaned over the fence and greeted me.

I quickly wiped away my tears.

"Good day, neighbor!" I said.

"I am on my way to see you," said she.

"You are welcome anytime!"

"Would you please sell me a few seedlings?"

"Selling is a word for strangers; to a neighbor one should give."

"If you would be so kind, dear!" and she held a jar out towards me.

I put some seedlings into the jar and gave it to her. The woman thanked me and left.

Right away my sister-in-law pounced on me:

"If everyone started to run my farm as you do, I would have nothing left at all! People like you could scatter even a mountain of gold!"

When she got started, she got started in style . . . Dear Mother of God! What could I do but cry bitterly.

"Sister-in-law," I said, "I never grudged anything that I gave you while I had it! It would be a sin for you to grudge a piece of bread that you have given me!"

I stopped what I was doing and left the garden.

I found this painful and hard to bear. Then an idea struck me: "I will leave them! I will go and find some work." I gathered together all my belongings. I packed some of them into a little bundle, and the rest I divided among my brother's girls. I had a lot of clothing, all of it good and new. There was much linen material, there were kerchiefs, plakhtas,[1] and ordinary skirts. The children were delighted; the girls immediately began trying them on. "Does this look well on me, auntie?" "How about me?" "When I get married, I am going to wear this red kerchief," one of the girls said, even although she herself was just a tiny bundle. They chattered round me, and I became so sad that I could not even speak a word and through my tears I could not see a thing! The children noticed it and felt sorry for me: "Dear auntie! Why are you so worried? Has someone offended you? You are ill, perhaps?" They gathered round me, like little birds. "Do not cry!" they begged me, as they tried closing my eyes with their hands to stop my tears.

III

Around evening, I heard my brother coming into the house. I moved out of his way and sat in the corner. He was happy as he entered.

---

[1] plakhta — traditional Ukrainian garb; a hand woven wrap-around skirt with stripes or checks.

"How are you, my children, and you, my sister?"

His wife followed him into the house. They sat down to eat supper with the children.

"And why are you not coming to eat, sister?"

"Thank you, brother, but I am not hungry."

He looked very attentively at me, then into his wife's eyes, and shook his head.

"I see, wife, that this is all a whim of yours. Do not harm my sister. It is a sin you will have to answer for," he said.

"Oh, this is an evil and unfortunate hour for me!" she cried. "Who do you think I am in this house, a maid, that I am not allowed to speak my mind? Am I pestering your sister, or what? I spoke the truth to her!"

She stopped eating, and walked out of the house.

Then the oldest girl asked:

"Father, why is it that auntie is always crying? My God, how she cries! What did mother say to her?"

My brother said nothing, but patted the girl on the head.

After supper, he came over to me and said:

"My sister, my little dove, do not worry. We have lived lovingly together for a long time, and I hope that we remain so for all time coming. There are only the two of us in the world. Forgive my wife for her harsh words. Do me this big favor, my beloved sister!"

"My dearly beloved brother! God knows I would never quarrel with you. I will forgive your wife for the poor way she has treated me, but my heart is heavy, my dear brother! Let me cry — it will ease the pain!"

"Do not cry, dearest sister! Please, do not!"

"Brother, I want to leave you."

Startled, he replied, "Where will you go?"

"I will go and find some work!"

"Oh God, what sort of thoughts are these for you to have, sister?"

He started to plead with me and convince me to stay. He fetched his wife, and she asked me to stay as well.

"Do not leave us!" she said.

The children heard this and ran to me in tears.

"Our loving auntie! Why do you want to leave us? Do not leave us! We will please you, we will respect you!"

What I held against the others, I could not hold against the children. I drew them toward me, held them close to my heart, and all I could do was cry.

My brother thought I had changed my mind and began thanking me.

"Thank you, sister, that you have pity on my children! Without you, they would feel like orphans!"

I still had my mind set, however, on going out to work. Everyone went to bed. As for me, I did not even close my eyes. Thoughts, memories, and worries overwhelmed me. It was hard for me even to imagine myself as a maid-servant somewhere. I had livestock, a farm of my own, I grew up in wealth. How could I bring myself to become a servant, I reflected, working for a morsel of bread, maybe to please some evil or idle person or to put up with all kinds of injustices and restrictions. I may live through all kinds of sorrow and distress. No one will worry about me, and there will be no one to utter a sincere, loving word to me! Strangers are strangers! They might be good people but, still, they would not know what sort of person I am, and I would not know what sort of people they are either.

IV

I got up very early. Everyone was asleep. The dawn star had not yet risen; mist enshrouded everything. I looked for the last time at the children and my brother. My heart went out even to my sister-in-law. I took my bundle of clothes and quietly left the house.

I kept on walking without casting a backward glance. Up yonder, round the bend, there was a large green mound. I made for the top of it and looked back on my village. The sun was just coming up. The village was clearly spread out before me, as if on the palm of a hand. The white houses and the well-tops came in view. The orchards in blossom and the gardens glimmered before my eyes. I saw my father's yard and the bushy branchy willow tree under which I played when I was still a little girl. Lost in wonder, I stood and gazed, without stirring from the spot. Every path and bush was very familiar to me and, as I gazed on what lay before me, I saw my childhood, my luxurious girlhood, my wonderful marriage, and my bitter widowhood — everything was there as if written down in front of me.

Where was I to go? I did not know anyone or anything. Sadness and unsettledness were getting the better of me. A long time ago I had heard from my deceased father that in the village of Demyanivka there lived some sort of relatives of ours. My mother's niece had married a blacksmith Lyashch, from this village. "I will go to them," I reflected. "It will be more desirable for me to work where I have kinsfolk."

I continued to follow the road — and, Mother of God, I was so scared! I was glad when I saw people moving to and fro. And it was a busy road, with one meeting me here, another meeting me there, another driving past in a wagon, and yet another walking by. I had already passed so many villages, Kozak villages and serf villages. I pushed ahead avoiding talk with anyone, keeping to myself. I would ask for directions to Demyanivka, thank people for their kindness, and move on.

The next day I became very weary, so I sat down to rest in the shade of a willow tree. Around me the rye fields were turning yellow and, among the rye, clumps of blue flax were in flower. The barley was beginning to ear. In the distance a copse showed blue, and a sandy road wound its way up a hill like a golden thread. It was a hot day and there was not a puff of wind. Nothing could be heard but the bees buzzing over the fragrant buckwheat, and the twittering of a solitary bird nearby which reminded me of the loneliness and forlornness of my soul.

I looked up — some people were walking along in a group, old and young folk, and children. They came up to where I was, hailing me with words of greeting. "Good day!" I said to them too. "Sit down and rest a while." I saw that they were very tired.

"Where have you come from?" I asked a young, dark, pretty woman who was cuddling a baby in her arms.

"We have been on a pilgrimage to Kyiv," she said. "And where are you heading?"

"To Demyanivka, if you know the place."

"How should we not know it. We are from Demyanivka! It seems that we are going the same way as you are; let us walk together!"

"Perhaps, then, you know a blacksmith named Lyashch?"

"Lyashch? What blacksmith by the name of Lyashch? No, dear, I do not know him, and have never heard of him. There are some people by the name of Lyashch in our village, but they are not blacksmiths, just simple farmers, like ourselves."

"Ask me, woman," spoke up an old granny. She glanced at me tender-heartedly as she handed out bread among the children crowded about her. "I was acquainted with that blacksmith Lyashch, and with his wife as well — may they both rest in peace! They were very good people!"

"How long ago did they die, granny?"

"A long time, my dear, almost nineteen years ago. They both died the same week. They so truly loved each other that the one could not live without the other. First he died, and then she followed him. They were buried together, side by side. The house became deserted, for they had no family or relatives. Were you going to them, by any chance? Are they relatives of yours? I knew that she came from a far-away village."

"It was them I was going to, granny. How unfortunate for me."

"Heaven help you! What has happened to you, dear?"

"I was looking for work and I thought that my kinsfolk would be able to advise me where to find some, but, oh God, now, what am I to do!"

"It is not worth worrying about, young woman! Worry gets you nowhere! I will advise you about a job. Go to our priest, Father Ivan, and work for him. I was baptized and married by him; I am in service with him now and will probably end my days there. They are very good people, simple and old-fashioned! There are only the two of them, both of them getting on in years. They had a daughter, and she got married, but she had not long had a home of her own when she died. She left a little girl behind, so the old couple now have the granddaughter to look after. She is such a pretty little thing! Father Ivan is now very old and has been blind for almost nine years, but that does not keep him from saying Mass. When the Bishop found out that the old blind priest was still saying Mass, he ordered him to stop, but the village folk pleaded for his return. 'My good people,' said the Bishop, 'since you love him so much, I will not forbid him to stand before the altar of God, as long as he lives. All I need is proof that this blind priest can still conduct the Mass with due solemnity.' The Bishop, therefore, came and gave God thanks that the blind priest was strong and made no mistakes in the conduct of the Mass, so he gave him his blessing. . . . Go to them, young woman. The work will not amount to much. If my strength permits, I will help you."

"Thank you, kind-hearted granny! May the Lord always give you everything that is good!"

"Well, let us now have lunch, and be on our way. Tonight, if God wills, we will sleep at home."

V

Demyanivka lay nestled in a small valley. The village was large and prosperous. There were two churches, one a tall stone structure, the other an old, wooden affair that had sunk into the ground and tilted to one side. Father Ivan lived a little way behind the stone church; he had a little house, an orchard and a garden — it was not so very big but it was a fine homestead.

We entered the village toward evening, and the pilgrims went their several ways. Everyone was hurrying to his own home, while I followed the old granny. For some reason I was so downcast and afraid that my heart sank within me. It used to be that I was happy and eager to go anywhere, but now I could not even look straight in front of me. I went indoors with her and just stood there, as if not my own self. I heard the granny explaining all about me.

"Come on in and rest, my child," someone said in a very quiet and dignified tone of voice.

I raised my eyes, and there before me, on a lindenwood bench, was an old, old man. His eyes were blind, but in those eyes there was such a peace and kindness as I had never seen before. His white beard curled below his belt; he was sitting in the shadow, and the rays of the evening sun in red and gold hues fell on him.

When I heard these kind words, my heart filled. Tears streamed from my eyes. He stretched out his hand and gave me his blessing. Then his wife came in. She was old and shrunken, but still lively and loquacious.

"Stay with us, and God keep you, young woman," she said. "You are young, and will brighten up our home and make my grandchild happy. Come over here to us, Marusenka! Come along, do not be shy! She is as shy as if she were a promised bride."

She took by the hand a small, pretty, dark girl who was just then peeping out from behind the door with her sparkling eyes, and led her into the house.

"Be nice to the young woman; bow and show your respect."

So she bowed and greeted me politely. I thought to myself: "I wonder how my dear little darlings are now? Do they still think of me?"

So I stayed with them — one month, two months. Life was good for me there! They were very good to me as if I had been their own child. I would tidy up the house, then we would have lunch, and afterward go and sit under a cherry tree in the orchard. The priest would sit quietly and meditate, or pray in a whisper, or sing psalms. God! How beautiful it all was! The granny and the priest's wife would chat about this and that; I would stay close to them and listen. Their granddaughter would be rolling about the orchard like a ball of white yarn, sometimes bounding up to us, then disappearing again into a green thicket. The day would pass quietly and serenely. I wished that my whole life could be like this, but I was still lonesome. They tried to console and comfort me.

"Do not be sad," they said, "that is a great sin. The young child cries, because it does not understand, but a grown-up should be able to handle the situation. Think of the good there may be in this world; if you lose your health, what kind of life will you have then? Enough of this, my dear, listen to us old folk! Look at what a beautiful evening God has given us!"

The sun was setting. Between its green banks the river flowed like a stream of gold; the curly willow trees bathed their branches in the water; the garden poppies were in bloom and the tall hemp was turning green; by the white house the thickly-clustered cherry trees were ripening; a tall cranberry shrub, propped up against the thatched roof, completely covered the white wall; and, in the midst of this blossomy garden, the house lay as if in a nest of flowers. And all around the house there was green, and red, and azure, and white, and blue, and pink. Quiet and warm it was, and there was a red glow everywhere: in the sky, on the hills, and on the water. Dear God!

"This world is like a poppy flower — I wonder what the other world will be like!" the old granny would say, shaking her head.

"My God, my God!" the priest's wife would reply quietly.

The priest would just raise his blind eyes to the sky and say:

"Glory be to God!"

VI

One day, early in the morning, I was carrying water when a man approached me. I glanced at him — why, it was Trokhym Rybets from my village! Good Lord! I almost dropped the yoke I was carrying, from which the pails were suspended, and stood there, tongue-tied — very happy! And then he said:

"So, you are really living here? We heard so, but did not believe it. Your brother is very worried about you. 'If you go to Demyanivka' (and it so happens I am here to get some wheels), 'maybe you will see my sister,' he said to me. 'Tell her that she has grieved me greatly and that I beg her to return to us.'"

"Are they all well there?" I asked tearfully. "How are the children? Maybe they have forgotten me?"

"Forgotten you! They are still crying because you left them. What am I to tell your brother?"

"Tell him that I miss him also very much, and that my heart wilts when I think of the children. But, I will not return to him! It is a waste of time to try and convince me and to force me!"

"And is life good for you here?"

"So good that I cannot even describe it!" And I went on to tell him about where I was working.

"Come with me," I said, "and I will send something back for the children. You can tell them that their aunt sent it."

I got some money, and bought one or two things, which I sent to them. As I conveyed the man through the village I could not stop crying.

"Tell them that for the rest of my life I will never stop loving them, and that I think of them every hour and every minute. Wherever I look, whatever I say, I am always thinking of them!"

"Fine! Why not? That is what I will tell them. Goodbye! May God help you in your work for your masters. They are such good people! They welcome me, a stranger, as if I were a member of their family. What marvelous folk!"

"It is God's grace that has made them love and cherish everyone," I told him.

"That is true, they are God's people!" the man readily agreed.

I saw him to the outskirts of the village, and wept. A week passed by. On Saturday I was white-washing the house, when my Marusenka ran up to me.

"You have company!"

"Who?" I asked, and my heart warmed.

"There is some man or other, tall and dark, a pretty young woman, and children with them. They are asking for you."

I could not think what she meant — I just stood there. Then I saw my brother entering the house with his wife and the children. My God! I almost fainted: first of all, from my overwhelming happiness at seeing them, and again, when I reflected on my misery.

They began to plead with me:

"Come on, come with us. If you will not listen to me or to my wife," (and she also pleaded with me, but she did not look too happy about it) "then listen to the pleas of our children; they cry for you every day."

When the children finally began clinging to me with their arms around my neck, they would not leave; they kept on kissing me and begging me:

"Come with us, dear auntie, do come!"

"No, I will not come."

They began to cry, my little doves. Oh, how the tears fell from their eyes! When they pressed close to me, I could not free myself. I kept on refusing to be swayed by them, but in the end I had to give in.

I went to say goodbye to my employers, and thanked them for their kindness and their generosity. Even though they were sad because I was leaving them, they were happy for me, because God had helped me to return to my brother and my own house. They saw me off and gave me their blessing, and Marusenka cried because I was leaving her.

Once more I entered the house where I grew up and where I spent my girlhood. It seemed that every corner smiled back happily at me, and it had such an effect on me that I even felt younger. I saw myself running round the yard with the children. I glanced out onto the street, and then ran into the orchard. I was home! But I was not happy for long.

My sister-in-law started bothering me again. Now she would not leave me in peace for a moment. She was after me for everything I did. This thing was not good enough, and that thing was not right! When she got wound up — well, Lord preserve us! I was eating and drinking them out of house and home! She even mentioned the money which I had once loaned to them: "You think that we owe you money? We should be taking more money from you! You have already eaten more of our food than that money could buy!"

And I had lent my brother all my savings, everything that I had received for my livestock — and I had had more than one pair of nice oxen, and cows, and a flock of sheep, and I had sold my house — the entire proceeds I gave to him.

"Well," I said, "if I have eaten my money's worth already, then heaven help you! Why did you persuade me to come back? It was as good for me at the other place as it was when I lived with my own father!"

She became silent when she saw she had insulted me greatly, and perhaps frightened that my brother would be angry with her.

VII

That very day I left them without even saying goodbye. My brother was not home at the time. "No matter how difficult things ahead of me may be," I thought, "I will not go back again! I will go where no one can find me to plead with me to come back, because I am so soft-hearted that I would not be able to resist any pleading and entreating." With that, I made up my mind to go to Kyiv.

I went first to Demyanivka. It was out of my way, but I had a great desire to see my former employers. I cried when I saw them, and they shared in my sorrow.

"I am going to Kyiv," I said to them. "If I am far away, they will forget about me, and maybe I will forget my misery too."

"God be with you! Goodbye! Come back to us if ever you wish to. We will be happy to see you, and will welcome you to our home again, if we are still alive."

It was a warm morning when I left them. I proceeded on my way, feeling much happier.

No one paid any attention to me, a passer-by, a traveler. Thank God for that! From time to time a Muscovite on foot would pass me, a merchandizing wagon would thunder by, or a wealthy man would drive past with a team of four horses, leaving me behind in a cloud of dust; and then the wind would blow again from the fields, and I could see again the green valleys and the steppes. Once in a while I would catch sight of a lake glistening or a river, level with its banks. From time to time I would meet groups of wagoners going by, and was more than happy to hear them greet me with "God be with you!", or to ask for directions. They were all our good, simple folk, who have known the pitfalls of life, and whose hearts, because of that, go out to other people's sorrow.

In a week I arrived in Kyiv. Heavens! How lovely it was! The holy churches were so indescribably beautiful! And people everywhere! Countless people, all strangers, passed on without noticing you. I rested near St. Lavra's,[2] and then set off to find myself a place to work. I kept on and on through streets and crosswalks.

Finally I arrived at the Podolsky market place. There I came upon a group of young women and girls.

"God be with you" I said.

"Thank you!"

They looked me over, trying to make out who I was and where I hailed from.

"Do you know," I said, "where I could find work hereabout?"

"Why! We ourselves are looking for the same thing, young woman!"

You see, they had also gathered to offer themselves for work. It was the way of doing things here.

"If you do not mind very much," I said, "I will also stand here with you."

"By all means, join us! We have nothing against it."

I stood and looked about me. People were buzzing around like insects, getting in one another's way, coming and going, talking and shouting — wealthy people, and regular city folk. There was much noise and milling about, one selling, the other striking a bargain. Two young women were chatting together pleasantly; and there was a group of children quarreling about not getting share and share alike. A market woman, with a face as red as a fire, stood in the sun rattling beads and calling out: "Hey! I have good coral beads here! Look, young woman! Buy them, my dear, buy them — try them against you! Well, well now, do not be shy!" She was talking to a pretty young woman in a white blouse and green kerchief. She did not want to buy the beads, but the market woman put them round her neck and began shouting:

"Look, look, good people, how these beads suit her. She is as pretty as a guelder rose, like an apple, like a young gentlewoman!"

"For heaven's sake, let me go," responded the young woman, "or I will break your necklace. Really! Why are you pestering me?"

With that she went as red as a cherry, blushing bashfully; and, although she was annoyed, her eyes were sparkling and she was laughing.

A Muscovite who was selling old scrap iron stood staring at her with a smile on his face, captivated, not even noticing the lively townsman poking him and saying:

"Moscow, Moscow! Are you selling iron?"

We stood there for about an hour or maybe more. Then a somewhat elderly lady came towards us.

---

[2] St. Lavra — Kyivan Caves Monastery.

"Is there, by chance, a woman here who would agree to work for me on a monthly basis?"

"Why not?" everyone answered. "No trouble at all!"

They started bargaining. The lady then said: "Do this, that and the other thing for me: paint, sew, cook, and wash. I will pay you one ruble a month!"

"Look somewhere else," they told her, backing away from her. Then she asked me whether I would work for her.

"All right, my lady!"

So I went with her. "Come what may," I thought, "I will earn some money. I am not afraid of work: one must live, so one must work. There is no idle bread! If one does not want to offend God or be shamed by honest people, one must earn one's living."

VIII

The lady conveyed me to her home. It was a small house with little low-roofed rooms. Nevertheless, it contained all kinds of tiny tables ranged against the walls; there were curtains on the windows; on one wall there hung a small mirror which was in such a condition that probably if you had looked into it, your features would have been so badly distorted that you would not have recognized yourself, but there it was. We were met by a young lady, already quite grown up, and rather stout.

"Did you hire anyone, mother dear?" she asked.

"She is right behind me. A village girl agreed to take the job."

"Oh mother! Whatever you do, you never do it properly! What do we need a village girl for? She does not know anything! She knows neither how to iron, nor how to serve properly. What are we to do with her! Use her as a pretty picture to look at?"

And she left the room, slamming the door so hard that the little tables jumped as if alive.

I could see that it was not going to be good for me here! Wherever has anyone heard of a child acting so disrespectfully to its mother?

The mother did not say a word to her daughter.

"Cook, woman," she said, "get the dinner ready!"

She explained a few things to me, showed me how to go about my work, and left me alone in the house.

Soon her husband came home for lunch. He was a tall dark man, with smiling, penetrating eyes. He was dressed in a dark blue coat. He bowed to me and said:

"Attend to your duties, woman, be respectful, and we will be good friends!"

I was thankful for the kind words with which he greeted me. I worked hard — God knows how hard! All day long I was occupied; before I had finished one thing another would be waiting for me. The old lady herself never wasted one minute idling. And the daughter was so fussy, Lord preserve us! From sunrise to sunset there was no pleasing her. This was not good — that was not right or in order — and do not talk like that — and you walk the wrong way ... if she had bothered only me, but she sounded off at her own mother as well. "Why," she would say, "is it not the same here in our home as with Ivanenko's family? Everything there is in the style of the nobility — lovely and pleasing; and here everything is so much peasant-style. I just cannot live like this!" And with that she would sit down and cry. Her mother talked to her, entreating her earnestly: "Do not cry, daughter, do not cry! God will help us, and some day we, too, will live in the style of the nobility!"

The father spoke right to the point: "Don't make a fool of yourself, daughter! What are you complaining about now? You always have one kind of expensive notion or another at the back of your head. You had better behave or sensible folk will laugh at you!"

She would get angry and run out.

"What have we here?" he would say to his wife. "God will punish for spoiling our daughter like that! She will suffer for it in life, if she continues as she is. Do not put up with her or you will be sorry for it later! Why don't you knock some sense into her head? You are her mother, her first advisor. She spends God's whole day doing absolutely nothing. You yourself are always trying to keep up with the rich folk; just take a good look and you will see that there is nothing there worth reaching for. All that glitters nowadays is not gold. If you have any affection for your child, restrain her with threats, if you cannot do it with pleas."

But the daughter was not too eager to listen to her mother. She would toss her head, like a well-trained horse, and leave the room.

God visited misfortune on the family. The master became very ill and soon died. As he lay dying he called his daughter to his side and said:

My dear, darling daughter! Many times you have worried me, God forgive you! At least, listen to me now. Do not try to live up to the nobility, do not look down on your background. It is a fine and respectable one. It has not produced thieves, or murderers, as have other families that are wealthy. Live, my daughter, the way God planned for you, and respect your old mother. It would be better if you looked after her, instead of her, in her old age, watching over a capricious girl like you! Mark my words, daughter!"

The daughter just cried, and kissed his hand. He gave her his blessing; and said again:

"Well then, daughter, you will not forget my dying request?"

"I will not forget, dear father!"

They buried him at Skavytsi cemetery. Many city people attended the funeral, all sorts of people. What a crush — a hazel nut could not have been squeezed in! I did not hear an evil word said of him; everyone wished him happiness in heaven. Such a good man was he!

IX

So the girl came a little to her senses. She would help her mother with a few things, and even spoke to me like a human being. Then some sort of presumptuous, superficial girlfriends started to visit her and she fell under their influence. She could not settle at home. She got bored with work; she wanted to gad about and have new, expensive clothes. Any time she was at home she would spend half a day dressing up, piling on all sorts of adornments, as one might do on a clothes-peg! If she knew that her mother had some money, she would insist right away on getting it, and her mother was the kind that would listen and give in to her demands. That was the hardest time for me, because the old lady wanted to recover all that her daughter had wasted — so, at such times, I hardly had as much as a chance to breathe. It was then nothing but work, work, for me!

Spring came. The warm wind blew, water dripped from the roofs, and the sun shone cheerfully. The snow melted, little streams rippled down the streets, the orchards were turning green. Pilgrims were beginning to gather. Every spring they came from almost everywhere to Kyiv. People from my village also came. They somehow spotted me in the market place and recognized me.

"How has it been with you?" they asked. "Your brother is very angry with you. He traveled to Demyanivka after you, and there he found out that you were already in Kyiv. 'If she wants to be like that, to leave me as if I were a wicked lord, and have no pity for me,' he said, 'I, too, in that case want nothing to do with her!'"

"How are they doing?" I asked. "Are the children all alive and well? Is everything all right with them at home?"

"Oh no! They have become as poor as a church mouse. For some reason things are not going very well for them. God only knows what has happened! Maybe your tears are punishing them. They are now so poor that sometimes they have to borrow bread."

"My dear villagers," I said to them, "is there some way in which I can see you again? Will you not drop in at my place? I have a few things to send to my brother, so do me a favor, and take them for me."

"All right," they said, "have them ready in the morning, and we will take them."

I had by then earned five rubles and got myself a small clothes-chest. In it I had a kerchief and a couple of shirts that I had already bought for myself.

So, I sent four rubles to my brother, and with the fifth I bought necklaces and earrings for the girls, crosses for the boys, and some ribbons and a skirt for the oldest niece — let the dear children think of me!

As I said goodbye to the village folk my brother's poverty was constantly on my mind. Dear God! Maybe it was true — maybe my tears were punishing them. May the Mother of God forgive me, a sinner, for bringing this misfortune on my own brother by shedding so many tears! It is not right for me to weep, I felt. There are more unfortunate, more miserable people than I, and they get along; as for me, I am well enough, thank God, and earn enough for food and clothing. If I am to weep, let it be, not for myself, but for my brother, his wife, and his children.

I thought about it, and my work seemed to become more agreeable. I could now even bear the young lady's fussiness. "Maybe, if I am condescending and more submissive, I will be able to calm her down," I reflected. But she was not like that! She saw that I was giving in to her and began still more to put me down and eventually to beat me.

"Heaven help you — Goodbye!" I said, "let someone else work for you; I have had enough. Never in my life has anyone beaten me, and, with God's help, no one will as long as I live!"

"We will not give you any money! Wait until the end of the month. You are not permitted to leave your work until you have finished your period of service. We shall not pay you!"

"You will not grow rich by keeping my money, and I shall not be any the poorer for not receiving it. If you don't give it to me, God will."

The old lady began pleading with me. Stay, stay! She felt sorry about it because I had worked faithfully for her, never losing a minute, always obeying her commands, and doing whatever I was told.

X

While we were arguing and making up, someone drove through the gates with a wagon. I looked out, and could not believe my eyes. It was my own dear brother!

I ran out to him.

"Brother dear! They told me that you were very angry with me!"

"No, my dear sister!" he said. "I have come to the point where I cannot be angry with anyone nor complain about anyone! Poverty has aged and withered me."

I saw at first glance that all the vitality had gone from his features which were almost ashen. And what a handsome young man he had been, how jolly, how radiant, like the full moon. Tears gushed out of my eyes.

"How do you happen to be here, dear brother?"

"I took the notion to, so I came," he said. "I was overcome with great sorrow! I wanted to see you and the outside world."

We sat at the gateway. We talked and we worried and the time just flew by. He described to me how poverty had come upon him, how very petulant his wife had been, even though she loved him, and how the children were growing up and thinking about me. When they heard from some of the village-folk where I was, what I was doing, and how I was living, they were extremely happy!

I said to him then:

"My dear brother! You are the only person I have in the whole world. You are father, child and family to me. I will work for you and your children as long as I am able to. I will work for you and your children as long as I am able to. I have no money now, except for two rubles which I earned at my place of work, but I don't know if they will give them to me. I would like to arrange to work another year for them. If they want me to stay on, they should pay me in advance. You may take this advance, then, and buy what you need most."

"Thank you, sister!"

He was bent in humiliation.

I went to my employers. I had barely reached the front door when the old lady asked me:

"Will you stay on? Why bring up that unfortunate incident?" she said. "My daughter will never again mistreat you. She is like this because of the poor state of her health."

"If you are so touchy," said the daughter, "I will not lay a finger on you."

"And why should I not be touchy? Have you, young lady, ever shown me any pity or consideration, that I should feel grateful to you?"

"That is enough!" butted in the old lady. "Agree to stay for a year. How much?"

"I want twenty rubles," I said. "If you give me that, I will stay. If not, I will find another place. I also would like my money in advance."

They began to argue. That was too much, and they could not give me the money all at once. But I had stated my terms and had no intention of going back on my word.

"Well," they said, "we have no other choice! We will give you twenty rubles, but not all at once. Give us your papers and here are your fifteen rubles."

"I will take it," I reflected, "even though it is only fifteen rubles; he very badly needs the money right away."

I gave them the paper which the priest had given me, took my money, thanked them, and went to my brother.

"Here, my dear brother!" I said. "May this help you toward a better living!"

He stayed with me for two days. I felt happy to wake up, knowing that I would see and speak to him. That is what having a family meant to me!

To this day I am working for the same people. I have two months to go before I complete one year. Lord! It is hard to please the idle! I have been hired, which is like being sold — I have to work! And, when I have completed my year here, maybe then God will grant me to find a better place to work in. There is always work for willing hands!

THE KOZAK GIRL

Once there lived in our village a Kozak named Khmara. What a rich man he was! Such livestock he had! He had so many acres of land and all kinds of riches! The Lord did not give him many children: only one girl was born to him, like the one sun in the sky. They pampered her and raised her to be beautiful, smart, and sensible. Sixteen years had already passed for Olesya and matchmakers had begun to visit the house. The parents thanked them for the honor and paid them the customary attentions, but did not give away their daughter: "Let her enjoy herself as a girl a little longer. She will have something to remember her girlhood by. It is too early for her young head to be bothered with housekeeping responsibilities; let her enjoy herself yet."

What a girl she was! How many admirers she had! Wherever she went they would be buzzing around her like a swam of bees! She was gracious, beautiful, and kind; she would talk, smile, and joke with everyone; and, when she noticed anything out of place, she would immediately show her disapproval by a cold look and take her leave.

She lived with her parents, knowing neither misfortune nor grief. It is said that, when one is young, all that one thinks about is fun. But, no matter how merry and gay her life was, the time came for her to learn what sorrow is as well. To begin with, her mother's strength began to fail — she was by that time quite old; she ailed for two weeks or so, then died. After the mother, the father died from loneliness and from grieving for his devoted wife with whom he had spent all his days.

Olesya was left an orphan. She cried her eyes out, but had to make the most of it. The good people did not forget her: an old aunt would call to cheer her up, or the girls would come to chat, sometimes even to make her go out with them.

Autumn arrived. The matchmakers kept coming one after another to Olesya's house. But she simply expressed her thanks and for one reason or another refused them.

"Why are you not getting married, Olesya?" the old aunt would ask. "You have as many suitors, God be thanked, as a garden has flowers.

Why should you be so haughty? The young lads we have here are like eaglets! All of them energetic and in the springtime of life. Even an old heart rejoices at the sight of them, but I do not know what the world has come to when a young girl like you does not take a liking to any of them."

"Dearest aunt! Leave me to enjoy myself for a while longer as I am!"

"But it is time, time, my child! Listen to the advice of an old woman. You are happy by yourself, but with a loving husband to keep you company, you will be happier still. And as regards housekeeping worries — do not be afraid of that! You will not be working for anyone but yourself. It is even nice to be troubled in that way. You are not a serf, thank God, your work will not be in vain."

"Not a serf! As if, were I a serf, the whole world would come to an end! Others live on in spite of being serfs."

"They live on, Olesya, but what a life they have!"

"If the landlords are good, their people benefit thereby."

"And what of it, if the landlords are good? What will the young landlords after them be like? You have to please even the good ones, and even in their case, all you earn by the sweat of your brow is three feet of ground for a grave! In the case of the bad ones ... Lord forbid that we should even hear tell of it! The very mention of it is enough! Take my advice, Olesya, and we will have a good time at the wedding! In no time then, the Lord will bless you with a family and I will be most content and happy to see the little ones around you humming like bees in a full-blown flower.

"I would still like to enjoy my girlhood, auntie!"

II

Then came the matchmakers from Ivan Zolotarenko. Olesya paid her respects to the honored guests and accepted the proposal of marriage.

This Ivan Zolotarenko was a serf. So handsome and sprightly was he that no one could have recognized him as one who had grown up in bitter serfdom. Everyone had now guessed for whom Olesya was waiting and why she had refused the others. The talk got up in the village, like the babbling of a brook: "How is it possible! Who ever heard of a free Kozak girl marrying a serf!"

The old aunt heard about it and slapped the sides of her skirt in astonishment.

"It would have been better had I not lived so long as to hear this! My child, Olesya! Come to your senses! If your father or mother were alive they would rather drown you in a deep well! Why, their very bones, from sheer dismay and sorrow, will tremble in the ground! What are you up to? You must have been bewitched!"

So she tried to talk some sense into her; she pleaded with her, and wept.

"No, my dear aunt," said Olesya, "it cannot be helped; I will marry Ivan!"

The old woman went to Petro Shostozub, but he was not at home; he had gone to the fair. What tough luck! Petro Shostozub was the most respected elder in the community.

She went to Andriy Honta — he, too, was not at home. Then she went to Mykhailo Didych — he was from home as well; they were all at the fair.

"Oh, woe is me for this unhappy hour! I shall hurry, then, to Opanas Bobryk, perhaps he is at home."

He was. He was lying in the orchard under a pear tree, puffing on his pipe. Seeing Olesya's aunt, he called out to her: "Good health to you! Why are you running? Is there a fire somewhere?"

"God be with you, sir! I have come to you for help. Please assist me. An unexpected misfortune has taken place! Call a council meeting!"

"Call a council meeting for women? What for? What a community that would be — as senseless as a tomtit! You had better get together by yourselves, and the one who outshouts the other will win the day."

"O, dear sir! These are not women's fancies. A great misfortune has befallen us!"

And she told him the whole story. Even he, although always merry and carefree, became worried over this mishap.

"Oh!" he said, "what a stupid little girl! What a misfortune she has brought upon herself!"

"Come, sir, perhaps she will listen to you. And if she will not listen, we will order her to! Here is your cap, let us go!"

They set off. The streets were full of people. They were all coming to Olesya's — the old, the young, and even the little ones were running to her house. All of them tried to stop her, and pleaded with her:

"Do not marry a serf! Do not! One might as well drown oneself!"

The young lads surrounded the house and shouted:

"We will not let the girl go!" they shouted. "We will not give her away! We will not allow a free Kozak girl to be made a laughingstock by becoming a serf, and to put her village to shame!"

Nothing helped, no matter how they pleaded with Olesya. They only saddened the girl more. Although Olesya listened to their honest and wise advice, she told them over and over again that she did not care for the livestock, because she was not poor herself, nor for freedom, for, she said: "What would life with a free man be without love?" — still the tears kept streaming from her eyes and grief overwhelmed her.

"I see, my girl, that it would take more than a year to convince you; and listening to your reasoning might take even more than that," said Opanas Bobryk. "As they say: 'What good is a woman's reasoning?' The only thing I hear from you is: 'I love him! I love him!' And who your love is, and what position he is in you care nothing about! You do not even listen to me! And this way, I know, we will not be any further ahead than we are now! So, farewell then ... All I can say is: 'Look before you leap!' "

Having said that, the old man went back home, to his place under the pear tree.

Later, the other people also began to disperse. Only the old aunt was left crying in the house.

III

Night had embraced the land. The moon came out and cast its bright rays on the white houses. Olesya, sad and upset, opened a window and looked out. The young lads were sitting round her house; some were talking, others sat dejectedly with their heads drooping. Olesya looked at them, thought a little, shut the window, and came out with her aunt behind her.

Standing on the doorstep, she spoke these words to the Kozaks:

"Young Kozaks, I have known you from childhood. You have always been considerate and courteous! I would never have suspected that you could show me such disrespect. Why do you guard me as though you were my enemies? Why do you disgrace an orphan in this way? You should fight against your equals and not against a helpless girl! You, men, will not gain any glory this way!"

"We also never expected this of you, Olexandra," answered a tall, sturdy youth. "We did not expect that old Khmara's daughter would marry a serf!"

"When our young lads were not to your liking, you should have let us know," another Kozak, handsome like a bolt of lightning, said. "Then we would have found someone for you ourselves! We would have searched all Ukraine and found!"

"It is a waste to search now, when God has already sent me one that I do love. My fate will be what it will be. I will not blame anyone. Even if you were to guard me for a whole year, I will marry the next, and none other than Ivan Zolotarenko. Go now, Kozaks, I beseech you, do not sadden me more! Listen to my aunt, heed her sober words of wisdom!"

"Please leave, my young hawks!" said the old woman, in tears. "You cannot help our misfortune any more! It is God's will, my children!"

The young lads talked among themselves for a while and dispersed.

Now, Zolotarenko's matchmakers became angry:

"We have never heard the like in all our lives!" they said. "After having given us their consent and entered into the betrothal, they now take it into their heads to dispute it! You are Kozaks, but you do not know the customs! We know how to defend our honor, even though we are serfs!"

"But who is to advise the orphan, if not us?" retorted the old Kozak women. "It would be for us a great sin against God, if we did not try to do something to prevent this misfortune. If she pays no heed to us — God help her! The silly girl will have a miserable time repenting — then she will remember us!"

IV

In the morning Olesya went to ask the girls to be her bridesmaids. Wherever she went all declined; others even wept. To some girls, mothers refused them permission to be bridesmaids; other girls refused to take part. The ones who did agree to, sighed sorrowfully saying: "It is a sad maiden's night for our bride!"

Olesya and Ivan finally did get married and went through the village to invite folk to the wedding feast. Just then, all the other villagers were returning from the fair: Petro Shostozub, Andriy Honta, Mykhailo Didych, and the others. Petro, with his carriage drawn by gray oxen, was plodding on ahead of the others. He was already old and gray, but he was still as tall and erect as a maple tree. His eyes shone like stars. He rode on slowly and asked the first man he met:

"What wedding is it that has taken place here?"

"The marriage of the late Khmara's daughter to Ivan Zolotarenko," someone said.

"To Zolotarenko? Who is this Zolotarenko?"

"A serf, sir, a subject of Sukhomlynsky's landlord."

Old Shostozub became sad, very sad, but said nothing. The others cried out in disappointment.

Just then the newlyweds came up to them and, in keeping with tradition, it was necessary to greet them. The newlyweds bowed and invited them to the wedding feast.

Petro raised his high cap. "May God be your helper!" he bellowed. "May God bless you with happiness and health!"

The newlyweds thanked him.

"We invite you, dear sir, to the wedding feast!"

"No, young princess, I will not go; it is not fitting for an old man like me to revel at weddings. Thank you kindly!"

Just then Honta Andriy, a good, quiet man, said to the groom:

"Oh, Ivan Zolotarenko! What have you done, my friend! Do you have the sense of a girl? You are thinking of the moment, but you are giving no thought to what will happen later! You have ruined the girl and all her clan! As they say: 'If you are an orphan you are free to drown!' "

And he shook his gray head.

"And why should we not have a merry time at a wedding?" replied Opanas Bobryk, with his arms akimbo. "What is spilt is spilt! Let us at least enjoy ourselves!"

"You old thoughtless fool!" said Petro. "Come to your senses! You would make merry even where good people are grieving and crying miserably!"

"But what of it, my good fellow! If one cannot help the situation by crying, one should sneeze and forget!"

"It is disrespectful to joke, Opanas, when such things are happening!" they all shouted. "Respect your gray head, if not Kozakdom!"

"All right, quieten down! You have stormed at me as you would at a fool! If you think we should not go — I will not go, but she is a Kozak's daughter, so there should be Kozak dances. However, there is, I see, no use in trying to convince you people. What a pity!"

The newlyweds stood with their heads bowed.

"May God grant you good fate and good luck! May you be healthy as water and rich as the earth! Let the good Lord give you a long life and good sense and beautiful children!" With that, the elders bowed and moved on to their homes. The newlyweds went on their way.

The young couple grew sad. They looked at each other: there was a pallor on his face and her eyes were full of tears. They fell into each other's arms.

"My love," he said in a low voice, "I think I have ruined your life!"

"My darling husband," replied Olesya, "what God will give us is what will be! Spending the rest of my life with you is all that matters!"

V

The next day they went to make their bows to the nobles. Olesya heard no word of welcome or advice, saw not a smile or cheerful look. The nobles were somehow irate, and so proud. "Be obedient," they ordered, "and be honest in your work for the estate!"

It was strange and sad for Olesya to hear this! She became frightened. By the look of things, she would be a real slave here! Her young years would all soon pass in vain! Her splendid beauty would soon be gone in daily drudgery in bondage!

They went along the street to their house. How gloomy it was in the village! Olesya remembered how it was in her village when she walked there along the street — one would greet her, another would inquire about her health, another would joke, or someone would stop and tell her about his problems; the elders would be talking and the young children muttering. As soon as the sun was up, the village would come alive with people! But here everyone you met was gloomy, untalkative, and sorrowful.

Her mother-in-law was happy about Olesya. She tried to please and comfort her, as if she were her own child; but still, she could not cheer Olesya's heart. She was too old now, and so exhausted from hard labor and deprivation that Olesya never heard any cheerful talk from her. The mother-in-law's stories were always full of sadness and misery. She was forever crying over her misfortunes, as if in this splendid, beautiful world, there was no place for goodness, beauty, or truth.

It was very difficult for Olesya to speak with her husband because he could not get away from his work even for a moment. It was doing this and that, or going here and there! He was just like a visitor in the house.

As for what came later, things only got worse. The master began to demand the house they lived in; he bought a peasant family from somewhere and needed extra accommodation.

"Go to the manor to live," he said to Zolotarenko. "You do not have a large family, and, if you want to, you can build a house of your own. You took a wealthy wife!"

They were moved to the manor and there God gave them a child, a boy. Olesya nestled the infant against her bosom and let her tears fall over him. "My son! My dear child," she cried, "you would have enjoyed life and come to love the beauty and the splendor of the world, but miserable will your fate be! While you are still in your cradle they will suppress you. You will not blossom, my dear flower, for you will be crushed while you are still in the green bud!"

VI

Four years had passed. The Lord blessed Olesya with children: three sons — like eaglets! But how she suffered, how she wept over them! It is said: "When the tip of a child's finger hurts, the mother's heart bleeds!" Whenever she went to work in the fields, she had to leave her children. As for them: one could not yet talk, one was not walking, and one did not yet know how to sit. They were so little and there was no one to look after them, because the old mother-in-law had died the same year that Olesya got married. She grieved the days away at work and in the evening, she would run home worrying: "How are my children?" She was never sure whether they were still alive and well. It had happened before that, while playing near a pond, one woman's two sons were drowned.

The children sprouted up, but then other problems came along. The master was picking on Semenko and his children were bothering Ivas, because somehow he just could not please them. The lady of the manor was scolding Tyshko for running past her and not bowing. Every day Olesya's children were beaten like drums. If a day passed without punishment, there was still uneasiness in the air and her heart was always sad, with the anticipation of sorrow and trouble for her family.

Just as the boys were beginning to mature and could then be the mother's joy and help, they were all taken away to the master's quarters. From that time on, there was not a moment of happiness or quiet relaxation for Olesya. Before her, all day and night, was the vision of her black-haired boys, tired and pale, sitting silently in a room. If they moved or talked at all among themselves, the nobles would scold them immediately: "What is the noise there! I will teach you how to sit quietly!" The little doves would become frightened and silent.

Each day Olesya would weep bitter tears: "My children! My flowers! You have wilted while still green!"

Everything that was of any value they sold and the money dwindled. And such a family needed a lot! The lady of the manor would not help; she would only say angrily: "You should have plenty of your own! You had a rich father, he had plenty of everything! If you are sorry for your children, then clothe them yourself, I have enough expense without you."

At the beginning, Olesya's husband could not stand seeing such injustice to his family. He would be sorrow-stricken! Forgetting himself, he would become enraged and would rush out of the house, his eyes flashing, his face so pale that it was terrible to look upon him then. More than once, for the sake of their children, Olesya stopped him from doing something terrible. With loving words she would calm him down and he would embrace her and the children and weep.

VII

They were living, from one day to the next, grieving and worrying, when, unexpectedly, the hardest misfortune of all befell them. The master was going on a trip, all the way to Moscow, and he was taking Ivan Zolotarenko with him. They did not even try to plead with the master not to be so hard on them. He was so cruel and unmerciful that it would be a waste of effort to implore him.

"Farewell, my children, farewell, my bright eaglets!" Ivan said. "Take care of your mother, love each other and do no one any harm ... farewell, my dear children! My beloved wife, do not remember me with scorn! Do not forsake the unfortunate one who has drowned you in an abyss and is leaving you all alone and in poverty. One day your tears will punish me!"

Olesya was past weeping. She just stood there, pale as her white kerchief, not taking her eyes off her Ivan, not letting him go from her arms. Just then the master shouted: "Quickly, quickly!" Ivan embraced Olesya for the last time and hurried off. When she came to her senses and recovered, they were already gone ... All she could see was a whirling cloud of dust and the children crying beside her.

"My children! My children!" she cried. "Now we have neither defense nor help, we are left all alone in the world!

She was right. It was much easier to bear their misfortune and sorrow when she had Ivan with her. She used to look into his loving eyes, listen to his earnest words, and embrace him. Somehow her fate was more endurable with a good soul and a sincere heart near her. But now she was left all alone, like that blade of grass in the field! Even though the village was not without good people, every one of them was preoccupied with his own misfortunes, everyone had his own troubles to look after. The only visitor she had was her old aunt. She was very, very old: all wrinkled, like an old, dried apple, but, for all that, she could still walk and enter into a conversation. She would come to Olesya and cry for a bit with her and give the children her blessing.

This was how Olesya lived, working without rest, keeping constantly at it; a year went by to her like one hour. All the time was spent doing work for the master's estate. The lady was a real slave-driver! It was work, work, and more work! Wherever her people were doing something for her, she would be there too. They would carry out a little table for her and she would sit down and play cards all by herself. It was her favorite amusement. She would sit at her game, lifting her eyes occasionally and shouting: "Do your work! Work! Don't slack up!"

Somehow or other Olesya tore herself away from her work and went to visit her old ailing aunt. That day there was a fair in the village, and Olesya had an opportunity to see her former girlfriends. What young married women they had become! How well dressed they were! How beautiful they looked — like roses in full bloom! Their husbands and their children were about them. The little ones were playing happily with their toys, and the older ones, creaking in their new boots, were gazing joyfully into everybody's eyes. Olesya stood there in an old coarse wool coat and all alone. Her husband has been taken from her; her children were worn out with hard labor, trying to please the noble breed. They had no toys, no amusements. They had no feast-day clothes. Their mother will return from the fair, bringing nothing to cheer them up, nothing to satisfy their needs. Such were the thoughts that crowded in upon Olesya. Hanna came up to her, then Motrya and Yavdokha — all were friends of hers from girlhood. They talked in a friendly way to her and asked about her children. One of them gave her some poppy-seed rolls for them, another gave her some cookies.

"Thank you! Thank you" said Olesya, overcome with tears. "May God not forget you all, as you have not forgotten me!"

VIII

Another year passed — no news came from her husband, as if he had disappeared from the face of the earth. Olesya got despondent and decided to go to the lady, because the lady often received letters.

She entered the room. The lady was busy telling fortunes from her cards and did not notice her entrance. Olesya looked around. It was the same room in which she had stood when she first came here. She was then a young newlywed, well dressed, adorned with flowers — and as fresh as a flower herself. Now! ... Dear God! Was this really herself? There stood an old, tired-out woman, grief-stricken and frightened. "Gone is my youth!" she thought.

She bowed to the lady:

"Dear kind lady! Please tell me how my husband is faring in the foreign land."

"My God!" the lady screamed. "You have spoiled my card game! Why are you creeping into my sight like that? What do you want?"

"Have you letters from the master. How is my husband Ivan?"

"Aren't you the smart one! Why should the master write about your husband? Has he nothing else to write about? How is he? What is he doing? — you ask. He is serving; that is all!"

"Did he get used to his work, gracious lady, is he well?"

The young nobles entered the room. They listened, with sneers, and the lady roared with laughter.

"What are you thinking about!" she screamed at Olesya. "The master is to write me whether your husband is well! Maybe you are drunk, or born mad. Go away! Go! Take her out!"

Both of the young nobles seized her and pushed her from the room, out the door.

"I will never see nor hear anything of Ivan any more," thought Olesya. "We met and fell in love at an unfortunate hour!"

About two or three weeks later a letter came from Ivan. "Are you alive, are you well, my dear children, my beloved wife?" he wrote. "I am always ill. I would have died long ago, if the hope of seeing you and my native Ukraine had not kept me alive. How is your life? Respect your mother, my dear sons, and love each other sincerely! May the Lord bless you all! I have nothing to send you as a gift. I have silver buttons on my uniform, but other than that I have nothing. Often, when the master goes visiting, I would be sure to starve while waiting for him, if good people did not feed me. What else is there to say! If you are born poor, you die poor."

"Your fate is no different from mine, my Ivan!" exclaimed Olesya, crying. "If I could write, I would do so every day, but now I must bow to someone and beg to get a letter written for me. Will someone do that as sincerely and as sadly as my heart feels?"

She went to ask the church deacon to write a letter.

"Very well," said the deacon, "I will write. But what will I get for this?"

She glanced at him. He was red-faced and jovial. He looked like a man who likes having a good time and drinking! There was no hope of his asking a reasonable price.

"What do you want, sir?" she asked.

"What do I want? Give me two rubles and a quart of whiskey!"

"Sir! Please be kind."

"Then go to someone else and don't bother me!"

"Write, write straight away! Let it be as you wish! He is waiting for my letter."

She began dictating the letter to him, and he wrote it down. She wept more than she spoke, poor soul! How she sorrowed! Even the deacon shook his head and finally said impatiently:

"Listen, woman! You will give me, will you not, what was promised?"

"Oh sir! Be gracious, there is more to be written. I have not told you all."

"I will write, I will write ... enough of that ... and don't give me anything! I don't need it!"

"How so, sir? What will you take?"

"Nothing!" shouted the deacon, in an irritated tone of voice, but immediately took hold of himself and said: "Let me finish, and then let us both go and drown our grief and misfortune in a glass of whiskey."

"Thank you for your kindness, sir, but I had rather not. May the Mother of God give you good fortune and good health! Thank you."

"Let me post the letter for you, woman. This is not a job for you!" he said.

"What do I have to give for this?"

"Nothing. Acquaintances of mine will do it free of charge."

IX

The deacon sent the letter to Ivan, but it was uncertain whether the poor wretch ever saw it, because soon came the news from the master that Ivan had died. The master also wrote to send for his eldest son and a boy-servant along with him. And he ordered the younger son to be sent to the capital.

Trouble began in the manor when preparations were afoot for the young lords to make the trip. They started choosing the servants to take along with them. They picked Zolotarenko's sons. Oleksandra was called in. Up to that very time no one was concerned about whether she was alive or dead; no one cared about the sort of burden the Lord had sent her to bear.

When she came in, the lady said to her, "Get your sons ready for the trip! They will go with the young lords."

She stood there, looking into the lady's eyes, as if she understood nothing. She grew as pale as a piece of chalk. The lady got angry.

"Are you deaf or dumb?" she shouted.

Oleksandra fell down in despair, unable to say anything. She raised her hands, weeping loudly and bitterly.

The lady became enraged and began to threaten her: "I will do this to you! I will do that to you! I'll show you!"

She let herself go on in this fashion, as if Oleksandra had committed a great sin by feeling sorry for her children — even God commands us to have such compassion — and she was scolded, insulted, and driven from the room! What her poor heart felt at that moment no one knew, and no one cared to ask.

She must get her sons ready for the trip. Would they be able to return to bury their old mother, or, would they like their father, die there, with no one to mourn for them! Perhaps her bright eaglets, so beautiful, good and true now, would grow slack there ... or even worse! What would happen then? Who would be there to guide them? Who would be there to teach them sound sense? At this time there was nothing to send them off with — no shirts, no decent clothes to wear. They were in terrible poverty. Anything of value they had owned she had sold or used up already for the children. There was nothing left over for herself in the event of her own death.

The children were sleeping at home for the last time, and she was so tenderly watching over them. She watched over them quietly the whole night, weeping bitterly. They were spending their last night at home! How much time would pass before she would see her beloved boys, if, indeed, she would ever see them again!

The sun had already risen ... there came the tinkling of a bell ... Suffused with tears, Oleksandra let out her children, blessing and crossing them every minute.

"My young masters!" she wailed to the young nobles, bowing low to the ground, "be kind to my boys!"

The young nobles just turned away.

"Mother of God," shrieked Oleksandra sobbing, "I am handing my children over to you! My sons, my sons!" And she fell on the ground like grass cut down by a sharp scythe.

X

The life of the unfortunate is also a long one, they say, and so it was with Oleksandra. She grieved away a few more years with little Tyshko.

There was not a bit of news about her older sons. The young nobles may have written something about the boys, but the lady did not say.

Meanwhile the lady had sold the village and moved into the town. Oleksandra and a few other people had to go with her. If only soneone knew, or cared to advise her, that, as a widow, she ought to be a free woman again! But what use now was freedom for Oleksandra!

Her health failed. She was so weak that she could not work anymore. The lady got angry: "You eat my bread for nothing!" she said. Later on she became really furious: "Off with you! Go wherever you like! Since you are too weak to work, do not ask to eat. Leave my premises and take the boy with you!"

Oleksandra left the mansion and took Tyshko with her. "A curse upon you, mansion of the lords," she said. "May no good ever come to you!"

She went searching for work. For about a week she slept alongside fences until she found work at a blacksmith's. The blacksmith carried himself like a real lord, he was so wicked and quarrelsome. He would abuse his wife and daughter and, when he got drunk, they would run for their lives, escaping through the window, because they were in for a thrashing. He would shout:

"And why should I not beat my wife or anyone else? Everyone has to be beaten, for I was beaten!"

"Is that my fault?" lamented his wife.

"So what, if this is not your fault? Each one has to answer for the other!"

That was the sort of blacksmith he was!

Had anyone chanced to see an old, miserable woman carrying pails of water uphill, with a shabby, black-haired boy jumping behind her — nobody would have recognized in her the wealthy, beautiful Kozak girl.

She had not served a month, when she fell ill and the blacksmith threw her out of the house. Where could she go now? She went back to the lady's mansion. She had just got to the gate when the lady met her and said spitefully:

"You have raised a thief for a son! Your Semenko has robbed the young master! What are you doing here? Why have you come? You are ailing, eh? Remove her out of the premises, put her out!

They led out Oleksandra from the courtyard and left her helpless and alone behind the fence with little Tyshko. The boy cried his heart out!

"O Father in Heaven! My Semenko a thief! Oh Semenko, Semenko! My good, honest child! How it feels to hear something like this about you! . . . Your father told you what not to do . . . My unfortunate son! Think of your old mother!

Tyshko, not understanding what it was all about, embraced and kept consoling her:

"Do not worry, mother, do not cry, Semenko will return. Semenko and Ivas — they will both return."

And thus comforting his mother, he fell asleep beside her.

XI

Morning came. Tyshko got up and set out begging. Oleksandra saw how her child held out his hand to the people; how one would give him a kopek,[1] or a bublyk,[2] or how another would stroke his black hair, and how still another would shove him out of the way — Oleksandra saw it all!

Then a certain man approached her and asked who she was, and why she was lying there. He asked her about numerous things. "Come to my place," he said, "while you are convalescing." And he took her with Tyshko to his house.

He lived with his mother. He was a widower and had a small daughter. They were well-to-do city people, with enough of everything. And what good-natured people they were! In a week or so Tyshko was flourishing like a red apple and tumbling about in the yard. Oleksandra could not have been happier. She recovered, regained her strength, and became younger looking.

"Work for us looking after our child," they asked her, and her soul rejoiced. She started working for them. She lived there in peace and quiet. All was well, except that her thoughts about Semenko kept nagging at her.

"Do not worry!" the master of the house said, "perhaps it is not as bad as you think. Inquire where he is serving. If he is still serving the young lord, it means he has forgiven him."

One evening Oleksandra went to the lady's mansion secretly, so that the lady would not see her, and inquired about Semenko from her servants.

"All that we heard," they said, "was that your Semenko was punished severely and that the young lord still has him."

"Well, what happened?" her master asked when she got back.

"It's good news, sir!" she said in tears, "could not be better."

"Stop crying now! The young lords will not live all their days in a foreign land; they will return and you will see your sons. Save up something for them that they will have reason to be thankful to their mother."

She sewed a little purse and bought herself a little box and began collecting her money. "This will be for my children!" she thought.

Whenever the master came from the market he would call her:

"Would you mind coming over here, dear! Here is a new ruble for you; let us trade for your old one."

Oleksandra would run and trade with him. How she would thank him! She would rejoice, like a little child! She would marvel at the shiny new money, and put it away for her children.

Then one day the master had to leave for a far-off homestead. He invited Oleksandra to go with him. If only the lady would let her go!

---

[1] kopek — penny.
[2] bublyk — a thick bread roll in the shape of a ring.

She went to the lady to ask for written permission, but she refused:

"No, I won't! I will not give you permission and I will not allow you to go, unless you pay me. How much do you earn?"

"Two rubles a month, my lady."

"Pay me two rubles a month, then, and I will let you go."

"But I have to clothe myself and the boy."

"I need more than you do. You can throw on any overcoat and it is all the same, but I need to live like people. If you will not give me two rubles, I will not let you leave!"

And she did not let her leave.

"Give her the two rubles," said Oleksandra's master, "and do not worry! We will take care of you."

But the lady now said:

"I want three rubles, and maybe even for that much I won't release you."

The master himself went to the lady and put in a good word for her.

"I will not hear a word of it! I will not let her go!"

The master went on the trip by himself.

"May no one ever know or see such people as your lady!" he said.

XII

The lady took Oleksandra into her household again and Tyshko into her rooms. Since she would not let him see his mother, the only way he could see her was by stealth.

Oleksandra became gravely ill. She was lying alone; there was no one even to give her water. She was lying, waiting for death. There was no one in the house except the nobles' old ailing steward.

"My kind friend!" she exclaimed. "Call Tyshko to me, let me bless my child! The Lord has already sent me death."

"Your Tyshko is gone, sister. I saw him drive off with the lady."

"May the Mother of God bless him!" she said weeping. "My beloved child! My children, my children! You are all scattered about somewhere and now you are not even at your mother's deathbed to close her eyes. I have raised you to be humiliated by evil people. Where are you, my doves? Where are you, my bright eaglets!"

The old steward somehow managed to bestir himself and called some people in. They entered the house.

She looked at them:

"Raise me up, good people!"

They raised her up. She took the purse from around her neck and gave it to them:

"This is for my children . . . six rubles . . . Give it to them . . . Whoever has a good soul, teach my Tyshko all that is good! . . . Do not harm a poor orphan!" she entreated them with tears. "Be kind to him! . . . Death comes to me while I am all alone . . . I reared my three sons like three gray doves . . . but there is not one of them beside me . . . My sons! My children! . . ."

So, as she lived weeping, she died weeping.

The lady was such that she would not even give her a decent burial, much less a funeral feast. The servants buried her themselves and said a requiem for the unfortunate soul.

THE CHUMAK¹

When our father died — may his soul rest in peace! — he bequeathed to us nine pair of fine cream-colored oxen! There were three of us brothers, and I, the youngest, was only a small boy then. The younger brother got married and at our mother's request gave up the chumak life. She begged him so earnestly: "Give it up, my son! Since your father's death I am left all alone and unhappy in the world; at least you will cheer me up by staying with me." I also must admit he was in poor health and was very often ill.

Well, along with my oldest brother Hryts, I got into the chumak business. Hyrts was a tall lad with dark hair and eyes — a lad like an eagle! So we began to be chumaks. Now I am old and my daughter is already looking forward to getting married in the autumn, but still as in a dream I recall the wide boundless steppe and the road stretching out endlessly; along it, travel our oxen, the wagons squeak, the moon is shining.

"Have you counted all the stars, boy?" Hyrts would call out to me like a church bell. I would start and jump up.

In order to travel from our village to Krym,² one had to pass through Kumytsi, a large Kozak village spread over two hills. The village had two brick churches and a river. Its houses were all new and every one of them was surrounded by a beautiful cherry orchard. It was a lovely village! Our aunt, a sister of our mother, was married to a man there. On our way to Krym, or back, we often visited her. She was always happy to see us. She would ply us with questions, would give us a special tidbit to eat, and chat with us. We would usually stay overnight at her place and then start off on the road. As time went on, we began staying at her place longer — for two or even three days. Sometimes my brother would wait

---

¹ chumak — a person who owned an ox-drawn cart or several of such carts for bringing salt, fish, and other goods from Crimea, to sell or trade with; a wagoner.
² Krym — Crimea Peninsula.

for a friend of his there, or his ox would be in bad shape. For me, a small boy, this was very convenient: this way I got a chance to play with the village boys or simply sit like a rooster on my aunt's fence.

II

One spring we left home early and on the evening of the third day, we stopped in Kumytsi as usual. It was warm and the cherry trees were loaded with blossom. We had not yet reached our aunt's house when Hryts stopped the oxen and said:
"Look here, Ivas, my little brother, stay right here! I will be back soon."
"Where are you going, Hryts?" I asked.
"I have to see a certain man, an acquaintance of mine. Do not leave the wagons!" And off he went. I sneaked up after him. I wondered what people of his acquaintance he was seeing.
We crossed the street and sneaked toward a new house. Hryts whistled and listened a while; then, whistled a second time, and a third time — still nothing could be heard. The soles of my feet began to itch with curiosity. What would happen next? Hryts scouted about the orchard. Right there, under an old cherry tree, which seemed to be blooming most abundantly, stood a girl, beautiful as a bright star, with her fair braided hair reaching down beneath her waist. She was standing silhouetted against the new moon. She raised her white hand and uttered these words:

> "New moon up there
> Like a flower so fair!
> Lovely sharp horns I wish for thee,
> And a bright-eyed suitor for me!"

When she began to repeat these words, Hryts whistled softly. The girl gave a start like a gray cuckoo and listened attentively. Hryts came closer.
"Hryts!" she said. "Is that you, Hryts?"
I moved a little closer to hear better, and stupidly fell right into a pit. My whole face got stung by nettles. Some rogue had dug a pit right under the fence. After that, of course, it was impossible for me to listen! I jumped out of the pit and ran back to the wagons! Probably Hryts thought that he had scared a hare.
We stayed in Kumytsi for three days. Hryts again made a pretence of waiting there for some of his acquaintances — naturally they, the so-and-so's, did not come. Meanwhile he went off each evening, returning on each occasion at dawn. During that time I learned from the village boys I played with, that the new house belonged to Danylo Moroz, a strong bewhiskered Kozak with a bad temper. He had a daughter by the name of Maryna.

III

Our trip to Krym was a happy one. Coming back, as was to be expected, we stopped at Kumytsi. Hryts excused himself hurriedly to our aunt, and ran out. Only, this evening he came back quickly and for some reason was very sad.

We sat down to breakfast in the morning and our aunt said:
"Hryts, did you know Maryna, Danylo Moroz's daughter?"
"What about her?"
"Her father married her off — unfortunate girl — forced her! How grieved the poor soul was! They took her barely alive to her father-in-law".

I looked at Hryts: he listened, gazing fixedly through the window.

"How Maryna changed after she got married!" our aunt continued. "She grew thin, became old-looking and worn out, my little darling. What a girl she was — like sunshine! She often came to visit me, chattering merrily, asking me about this thing and that."

"Whom did they marry her off to?" asked Hryts.

"To Ivan Bondar from the Dzvonari village, not far from here. Such a rich man!"

At this Hryts bowed his head and stayed that way until we reached home.

IV

Our mother kept saying:
"Get married, Hryts, get married! Why not?"
"Because," said Hryts, "I have not found the right girl yet. I do not want to marry just for the sake of marrying!"

We would sit in the house and mother would start worrying. Then, as she looked at Hryts, she would say:

"What beautiful girls we have in our village! There is probably no prettier girl in Kyiv than Katrya Barabashivna," and, with that, she would look at Hryts.

"There is not," Hryts would reply.

"Unless Motrya Yakovenko? She is a beautiful girl, very beautiful!"
"Motrya is also beautiful," Hryts would reply.
"What about Melasya?"
"She is also beautiful."

Such replies would drive our mother to tears. And thus our Hryts remained unmarried all his life. We heard from people that Maryna died soon after her marriage. They say that her husband was a very violent man. He is now married for the third time.

V

Hryts was already old and gray, but he was still making his trips to Krym. He had no desire to marry or settle down. He was a chumak. Fate served him well — he got richer and richer, but his wealth did not make him happy. He made such trips out of love for the traveling life of the chumak. At home he was so quiet! He talked very little, and avoided merrymakings. On the steppe he was a different man! He was monarch of all he surveyed. He would walk between the wagons — so lively and so bold! Or he would sing: "Oh my fate, my fate! Why are you not like the good fate of others!" His singing would resound throughout the steppe.

He sang beautifully! When he sang the song about the Kozak Nechai, it felt as if the Kozaks would appear in person any minute! The song would send shivers down one's spine. He was an honest chumak!

He put new shingles on our village church and overlaid the crosses with gold; and he helped more than one poor needy soul.

He very much respected his mother, who outlived him. She became so shriveled up, like a yellow mushroom, but, for all that, she outlived the chumak.

Three years have now gone by since his death. When the end came he was still strong and healthy. On his deathbed, he asked us to dig out from under an oak tree in the forest two treasure chests, containing money. One he asked us to give to his mother, the other to use for his burial. He wanted a high mound raised above his grave and a whole oak tree put up for a cross. So we chopped an oak tree down to the very roots, lopped off some branches, and set it up like a cross. It could be seen far, far off, on the steppe!

ODARKA

Our old deceased landlord had been a terrible man! One should not speak ill of the dead, but in his case he does not deserve to be spoken of otherwise.

Across the river from us, there was a free Kozak farm-settlement, and even the Kozaks from there were afraid of him and avoided him because he harmed them greatly. May the Lord protect any Christian soul from what we serfs had to endure from him! Any of us who met him would, without looking to left or right, run on just to get past him. The girls were particularly afraid of him. He had destroyed more than one girl's happiness. But what could one do about him? . . . There he was! Walking through the village sullen, and glancing angrily about, like a vulture.

Just the other day we were all sitting in our house talking about him in a not very complimentary way, when he himself suddenly stormed into the house. As they say: "Talk of the devil and he is sure to appear."

On entering he asked my brother: "Where is your daughter, Odarka?"

You see, my brother had a daughter. Lord, what a girl she was! She brightened the whole household like a star. She was young and gay — without a care in the world, running and laughing happily, not as yet knowing the meaning of misfortune.

When he asked about Odarka, we froze, and, just at that moment, Odarka herself came in. At sight of her his eyes glittered and he said: "Let us go to the manor, girl!"

Odarka ran to her mother and stood near her, poor child, afraid to breathe!

"She has not yet come of age. She has only turned fifteen," said her father. Her mother began to cry.

"Say just one more word, you rash fellow, and you are for it!" the master stormed at him. Then he addressed Odarka once more: "Get a move on, Odarka! Let us go!"

But she stood stock still.

"Hurry, girl!"

She stood there dumbfounded. He grabbed her and led her away.

It was as if our sun had set! It was as if the house had immediately become empty and desolate.

II

We put up with it till the evening. In the evening my brother's wife went to the manor to find out what had happened, but soon returned. "They did not let me go to Odarka," she said, "and I neither saw any sign of her nor heard her voice!" and she began to weep bitterly.

For a long while we did not see our child. They did not allow the father or mother or myself to see her. We would go and stand about at the manor gates and, without seeing her, would return home, feeling embittered against the whole world. We would inquire of the servant girls, but all the answer we got was: "We do not know, dearie! We don't know! It looks as if your child has been put under lock and key and we have no means of seeing her."

There were also others who would laugh at it all as if bereft by God of their senses, and would say: "What will happen, you ask, to your Odarka? The same as has happened to us! And why not? Is your Odarka better than we are? Were we not our fathers' children too? Have our mothers not cared for us? We were also once pure and good, and now see what has become of us! Still, our life, somehow or other, goes on."

Every day we would go and try to see her. She had already been three weeks gone from us. One Sunday evening my brother's wife returned again from the manor weeping: "I did not see her," she said, "only the servants, and they, God forgive them, laughed at me."

III

We sat in silence. The house was overshadowed by a cloud of gloom; only the sobbing of my brother's wife and the heavy sighs of my brother could be heard. Then something stirred; the door opened and our Odarka entered. We almost fainted at sight of her. She was so pale and exhausted! She greeted us and stood on the threshold like a stranger, unable to look anyone in the face.

"Well, wife," said my brother, "we are seeing our child at last. What a beauty she has become!" — and he broke into tears. That was the first time in my life that I had seen him cry — and, Mother of God, may it be the last!

We sat our Odarka on the bench and my brother's wife said:

"Oh, my daughter, my misfortunate one! So they have now released you from the manor?"

"I slipped away, mother. Guests have arrived: the young lord and his wife."

"Odarka darling, please tell us all that has happened to you there," I said to her.

"Yes, please do, let them hear about it," said my brother, and left the house as if a fire were raging inside him.

Odarka sobbed bitterly and began telling everything: how they would lock her in at night, how they would thrash and threaten her, and how she was finally brought to ruin.

"Perhaps you should have gone to the lady of the manor, perhaps she would have saved you, my poor child!"

"Mother, mother! How could the lady have helped! The master is so ferocious that everyone steers clear of him as doves steer clear of hawks. The lady will not help! She and the young misses spurn me as if it were all my fault."

So until night was upon us we worried and we wept.

"I am not well, mother. Let me stay with you at least this one night," said Odarka. "With guests in the manor they will be too busy to miss me."

IV

She spent the night at home. It seemed that she had scarcely closed her eyes, when serving lads from the manor came for her:

"Come, quickly!"

How she pleaded, and how she begged tearfully to be allowed to stay for a while in her father's house, since she was not feeling at all well!

"No," they said, "we cannot allow this. If you will not come willingly, we will, as ordered, take you by force. The lady-guest and the young ladies have been looking for you since last night."

"It looks as if some other misfortune is on the way," said my brother's wife.

"God forbid! It would have been better had she died young!" responded my brother. "Stop crying, Odarka, stop it!" he said. "Stop pleading! These lads cannot be appealed to. They are just carrying out their orders."

"It is not up to us," said the youths. They began also to feel sorry. "Oh uncle, if only it were up to us!"

We were worried about what was to happen. We did not know what to do: should we got to the manor, or await our fate at home? Just then, at noon, Odarka put in an appearance:

"Farewell, mother, farewell!"

We rushed to her:

"What is the matter? What has happened?"

"They have given me to the young master and his lady," she said. "They will take me away next week. And, aunt, they will take you as well. They said we have until Sunday to get ready."

A chill ran through my heart. I had not lived a life of luxury; I had, nevertheless, lived with my family, in my own house. Now they were giving me to strangers, sending me to strange surroundings. What had I done to deserve such treatment? I became very sad, and gave way to a flood of bitter tears. My brother's wife was thankful to God that Odarka was not going away alone.

The oldest of the young lords married a Pole, and lived in the city. For four years he did not visit his father, who was angry with him for marrying a Pole. But since God blessed them with children, the old one forgave them, and they began to visit regularly. The Polish wife somehow won the old one's favor so that he listened to her and was even giving her money, although he was such a miser!

Our lady and the daughters persuaded the Polish wife, when she arrived, to get the old one to give Odarka to her, so as to take the poor girl away from him. The Polish wife pleaded and begged until he finally gave his consent. That is why we were given until Sunday to get ready, and our new masters, went on ahead of us.

V

Sunday finally came! The family gathered to bid us farewell. Odarka said a last goodbye to her mother who hugged her, and through her tears could only say: "My child! My only child!" She was so distraught and so miserable that even a heart of stone would have broken at the sight. The girl, as if dead, shed not a single tear. She said goodbye to her father and he blessed her: "May the Mother of God protect you, my daughter!"

They took us to the manor. The horses were already harnessed to the wagons. The lady came out with the daughters and told us to serve the young nobles faithfully; then the master also came out.

"Get moving!" he ordered the coachman. "What is there here to talk about? Look out for yourselves," he said to us, "don't have masters complaining or it will be the worse for you! Get moving!"

We rode a whole day and another. I asked Odarka if she was feeling better. "Yes, aunt," she replied, "if my heart were not so heavy!" Poor girl, she never stopped thinking and grieving for a minute about her father and her mother.

On the fourth day we arrived at our new master's residence. Winking at one another, the staff eyed us up from every angle. No one talked to, or greeted us. They were all insincere and sarcastic city folk.

They took us inside. The lady of the house appeared. Perhaps you have already seen Polish women. They are all so foot-loose, happy-go-lucky, and talkative. This one was no different. When she started to talk, she did the talking for everyone, and in such a quick, zesty fashion. How impressive she wanted to make herself in our eyes! Although made up to look younger, with her shining rings, and ribbons, and curls about her temples, she was already quite old. Then the lord came out. He was handsome, portly, and very proud-looking; if he gave you a look at all, it was always down his nose. He asked if there was a letter from his father and departed. Then the children came running in to see what was going on. The lady told them in Polish: "Give these peasant women your hands to kiss!" They held out their tiny hands — there you are, kiss it!

VI

They ordered me to spin wool and Odarka to embroider. She did embroidery for the young ladies, or anything else asked of her, and would go to the lady every evening to show what she had done. The lady was sometimes not too demanding, scolding only when something failed to give satisfaction; but there were times when she became so enraged that nothing could please her ... At those times everyone was in trouble! She took a dislike to both of us, but not as much to me as to Odarka. She corroded her, like rust, iron. Once, she had her put in the middle of the room, and ordered: "Dance, Odarka, dance!" Odarka began to dance, poor thing, but her legs gave way and she fell down. They roared with laughter. "She is putting it on," they said. "She is faking!"

I saw that my Odarka was wasting away like a candle. She would sit all day long without saying a word. It did not matter what the lady did or said to her — she made no response except to cast her eyes occasionally in her direction. The nobles' children would pester her like leeches. "Oh, you are stupid!" they would say. "All of your kind are stupid! Go and dance!" They shoved, scratched, and pinched her. She would only look at them, my little darling. The lady would get angry and say: "This girl is as if she were made of stone!"

VII

Spring came. We were digging and seeding in the orchard, and Odarka never went outdoors. "For all the good that she will do," said the lady, "it is better that she stick to the embroidering."

One day when we had finished working and were leaving the orchard, the lady said:

"It is my guess that Odarka is not embroidering! Probably she is either sleeping or dozing."

"She is definitely not embroidering, mother," replied one of the young ladies. "This I know for certain."

"Quiet, everybody," said the lady. "Let us see what she is doing."

They approached the house stealthily ... and entered. Odarka was lying down, with her arms folded behind her head. She was ever so pale! Her eyes were the only bright thing about her. She lay there staring at us intently. Even the lady stopped and did not say a word. I took her into her room and laid her on the bench. She never after rose from it.

She kept on asking:

"Dear aunt! Open the door and the window; let me look in the direction of my home!"

The nobles agreed amongst themselves to send for the old woman, who was skilled in the use of herbs. She came, asked some questions, looked at Odarka, and shook her head.

"My poor child!" she said. "Evil be to those who have crushed you as they would a fragrant flower. You have not long to live!"

With that she gave the girl her blessing, began to cry, and left.

VIII

The lady thereupon ordered the girl to be taken to the hospital.

"My lady," I begged her, "let me go and look after Odarka! I will serve you sincerely in whatever you ask and will look after the girl as well."

"Oh, what a silly notion!" said she, "They will look after her there better than you ever will," and she refused to let me go.

On Sunday I managed to get away and went to see her. I entered to find that her bed was by the window and that the window was open.

"When the girl began pleading and begging to have her bed placed by the window," said the old female attendant, "I could not refuse her."

"How are you, Odarka?" I asked.

She looked at me and said:

"Dear auntie, the plum and cherry trees are blooming now at home, and it will not be long until the poppies also are in bloom. Any news of father and mother?

"No news yet, dearest," I said. "When there is, I shall let you know immediately. Do you want anything, Odarka?"

"No, auntie, I don't want anything; just don't let them move me from the window."

IX

So I visited her on Sunday, and on Thursday we heard that she had died. I ran to the hospital; she was already laid out for burial. A solitary candle burned beside her, but no one was about. She was so pretty as she lay there, like an angel of God!

The old attendant came.

"Oh," she said, "how I have cried for your child, dear! And how quiet and gentle she was! I have never in my life seen such a pure soul! I came to her yesterday; she was leaning on the window. 'Oh,' I said, 'what are you doing, girl?' "

'Let me look over there,' she said, 'let me look over there again. That is where my father and mother live.' And she cried so pitifully, like a little bird: 'Let me!' And I let her. I held her up a bit — she looked into the blue distance, and her warm tears, like pearls, poured onto my arms. The sun was setting. She noticed that the cherry tree was blooming in the orchard and asked: 'Please bring me a cherry blossom, granny!' I went and brought her one. She took it. 'Oh, how fragrant and fresh it is! Thank you, granny!' She lay down with the flower beside her. 'The sun is near to setting,' she said, and began reminiscing about her parents. She called to them and pleaded with them: 'Father! Why have you left me? Mother, take me home! Oh, you have left me, left me all alone! . . . Mother! . . . Father! . . . My dear beloved parents! . . .' May the Good Lord take her to His bosom!" said the old attendant. "I have never in all my old age cried so hard!"

On Friday they buried her. When they lowered the coffin into the grave, white doves circled above it. The sun cast its golden beams upon the ground. The morning was so bright and peaceful: no wind blew, not a cloud was to be seen. A pure soul had left this world!

THE SPELL

This story took place long ago, but it seems to have happened only yesterday. That's the young years for you! It is not without reason said that when you hear or see something in your youth, it lingers with you for the rest of your life. While spinning wool, an old woman used to tell us girls stories, conjuring up for us the odd and unusual kinds of things that used to happen long ago. We listened, grasping each word with all our hearts and souls.

Once, she related, there lived with his wife an old Kozak by the name of Zadorozhko. God gave them a son, like a falcon, to nurture and love. What a handsome Kozak he grew up to be! He was skilled with horses and weapons, and adhered to customs and chivalry. At home he was honest and good-hearted to everyone; above all he respected and honored his mother and father. The old parents were pleased and happy with him and gave God thanks.

Old Zadorozhko had lived his life and was now approaching his end. He blessed his son and wife, told them not to worry and to bury him decently, and fell asleep forever.

"You have cried enough, mother," Tymish entreated his old mother, "Please stop crying. You are angering God this way!"

"My beloved child! How can I hold back my tears if they rush forth of themselves? God gave us a happy, peaceful, and wonderful life together with your father, and now, in my old age, I have become an orphan and am left all alone! Wherever I look in this house, or outside, or in the orchard — it all reminds me of him."

"I must be off to my work, mother!" Tymish would say. "I will take you to our neighbor Hanna; so you will not be here all by yourself."

"That would be good, my fair falcon! Let us go to Hanna's, son!"

Hanna was, like her, a widow. She had an only daughter by the name of Khyma. The girl was bright-eyed and pretty, like a full blossoming flower. Khyma and Tymish grew up together like brother and sister, in true friendship through good times and bad — always good to each other, loving each other. A day would not pass that Tymish did not see the girl, and he would be uneasy if he did not; and she would cry her eyes out waiting for her dark-eyed lad. The elders took notice: "Let the young love each other," they said, "maybe God will bring them together! Let us hope that soon we will become in-laws!"

There were many young men in the village who were bewitched by Khyma's charms. Khyma had only to step outside the door and there they were! But the proud girl would not even look at any of them. There was no one else on her mind but dark-browed Tymish for whom she waited day and night. If he did not appear — the girl would become sorrowful; when she saw him — she grew happy, and the whole world looked brighter for her again.

II

The world is never without sorrow — and Khyma had her share of it too. For three evenings Tymish did not come to see her. Khyma could not sleep. She walked about the orchard, trampling the fragrant flowers she herself had planted and watered. Nothing any longer seemed to matter, for a burning sorrow entered her loyal, honest heart.

Dawn was just breaking. There went Tymish, walking happily along the street in the direction of his house.

Khyma quickly ran out and cut across his path:

"Say something to me, darling, at least one little word! Last night and the night before you did not come. Tell me honestly if you are forgetting me!"

"Oh girl," said Tymish, "how you sadden me! I must tell you the sad news: we are not going to be together anymore!"

"We are not? Have you found yourself another girl better than I am? Does she truly love you as I do? Tell me, who is she? Because of her, my young life is being ruined; let me at least see which one it is!"

"Do not be angry with her, Khyma. She is a quiet, good soul — she is an orphan."

"It is Olena Bondarivna! Is it her? So, she is the one you go to every night! I have cried my eyes out, while you are making love to her! The world went sour on me, and you are courting her and you are both happy together. Oh my grief! My unexpected sorrow! And perhaps you intend to take her for your wife?"

"I will send matchmakers to her on Sunday."

"Why are you rushing yourself so? Maybe all will not go right!"

"I wish you would not foretell such things, you wicked girl!"

"Listen, Tymish, give her up! Give her up, if you don't want to regret it forever! Regrets do not mend what is past!"

"You expect me to give her up! Out of the question! What you say will make no difference! For as long as I live, for as long as the sun shines, I will not betray my girl!"

"So you will not give her up? Think it over Tymish, and tell me for the last time whether you will give her up."

"May hot sand be poured into my eyes, if I do!"

"We shall see!"
She rushed into the house.
"Wicked girl!" muttered Tymish and lapsed into sad reflection. Soon, however, Olena, who was beautiful like a bright star, quiet and gentle as a dove, crept into his thoughts, and Tymish cried out:
"If I forsake you, my darling, let the world forsake me!"

III

He decided to send matchmakers to Olena the following Sunday. In the morning he went to consult with his mother:

"Mother," he said, "I am in love with a girl and I want to marry her — give me your blessing!"

"May God bless you! Marry then, my falcon! Whom are you going to marry? Khyma?"

"No, mother, Olena Bondarivna."

"Olena? I always hoped that you would take Khyma. She is a nice girl and respects me. But nothing can be said now! If you like Olena, take Olena. Any daughter-in-law would please me, so long as she loved you, my son."

They sent out the matchmakers, went through the customary ceremonial, and got the young couple engaged.

Old Hanna heard of this and said to her daughter:

"Maybe it was not meant for you and Tymish to be together! Yet, I was certain that this autumn your marriage would take place."

"And what is there that is certain in this world, mother?" Khyma abjectly replied.

"Do not worry, my daughter! You will find yourself someone even better. Thank God, you are young and beautiful like a ripe cherry!"

One evening Tymish went off to see his girl. He felt happy and buoyant, and the whole world seemed to him beautiful and gay. All of a sudden like a ghost Khyma appeared before him — pale of face and downcast. She asked:

"Will you give her up or not?"

He regained his composure somewhat, then answered:

"God help you, unreasonable girl! Don't you know that I am engaged already?"

"I am asking you whether you will not give her up?"

"I would rather die than have to live without her."

"For the last time, will you give her up?"

"For the last time I answer — I will not give her up!"

IV

The next day Khyma asked her mother:

"Mother, may I go to visit my aunt?"

(Her aunt lived in the next village, not far away.)

"Go, daughter, go! Maybe in this way you will comfort your heart."

And she saw her daughter off.

Khyma did not go to her aunt, but into the thick forest. She knew of another aunt there. She had never seen her, but had heard that an old sorceress lived in that forest. Poor Khyma had need of her now.

Khyma reached the outskirts of the village. There, in front of her, were two winding roads. She glanced around — not a soul was in sight, only the sound of the curly willow and the rumble of rushing water from a millstream nearby could be heard. Once more she looked around her and took the road that led to the forest. On and on she went, passing the rocky hills and the green meadows. The sun scorched her, for it was past noon; her white feet got bruised on the rocks; her long braids became entangled in the branches. She went on without as much as noticing anything in her way. While crossing a bridge over the rapid river, she happened to look into the clear water and did not recognize herself. She stopped, astonished: "Is this me? Where has my beauty gone? But why do I need it now? Let it be ruined! All I want is to get my way!"

She entered the green, thick forest. It was dark and stifling there. She looked behind her; the sun was setting, the sky, all ablaze with light, was growing red.

There she walked in the forest, listening intently. There was a rustling nearby, a birch tree swayed; a cry was heard: "Khyma! Khyma!" and its echo resounded through the dark forest.

How long she had been walking like this she could not tell. Finally she saw in front of her two very tall oaks. Between them sat an old woman. She was so very old that the moss had grown over her. Everything began to spin before Khyma's eyes. The witch asked:

"What have you come for, my beauty? Why have you so young and pretty come here?"

"I came to see you, granny. Help me!"

And she told her the sorrowful tale.

The witch then said:

"If you want, I will tell you what to do."

"Tell me!" Khyma begged.

The witch then took in her hand a knife and an enchanted feather.

"Give me your left hand, girl!"

Khyma held out her hand.

Just a flash of the sharp knife, and red blood dripped from the tip of her finger. The witch dipped the magic feather in the blood and spoke her magic words over it. "Well," she said, "you may go now! You will work anything you wish now on your enemies!"

Khyma came out of the dark forest. The sun had almost set. She felt some inhuman power within her. She turned herself into a swallow and flew away. It was getting really dark when she approached the village. The swallow struck the ground and turned into an old woman, who stood under Olena's window. She looked in — Olena was sitting among the bridesmaids, adorned with flowers, like a rose in full bloom. Everything around her, as she sat there, was so peaceful and happy, and there was such a loving expression on her face! The young bridesmaids

hovered over her like little golden bees; they sat around the table like fresh flowers, and Olena occupied the place of honor.

When Khyma saw this her heart began turning over. "Oh," she said, "I am just in time! Here they are alone for her maiden night."

She entered the house. They made her welcome and treated her, asking where she came from. But she just opened the window, spread out her arms and said:

"Fly, as a bird, young bride, and you, young bridesmaids, follow her! May you fly and sing forever!"

She uttered these bewitching words, and out of the window, one by one, they flew drumming their wings; Olena led the way.

V

What lamenting, what talk and fear arose throughout the village! The girls were gone! They had disappeared as if the earth had swallowed them up! Tymish could find no peace. He grieved deeply over such an unexpected misfortune. He wandered from street to street, as if out of his mind, and it was here that he came upon Khyma standing at her gate. He looked at her and remembered her prophecy:

"Evil girl! You predicted a misfortune for me! May you also, for the rest of your life, have no joy or happiness."

She watched his retreating figure and sorrow overcame her; yet she smiled and said:

"We shall see!"

A year passed. The old mother begged of Tymish:

"My son, my dove, get married! Why should you waste your life like this? I know it is hard for you, but grieving will not help. It will not bring her back. I am old, make me happy! Let me live in happiness for what is left of my life, and give thanks to God and to you, my child!"

"My dear old mother! It is hard for me to marry! I will never find another like the one whom I once had!"

"Take Khyma, my son! She is a good girl, and how she respects me! May God give her happiness and good fortune! She loves you truly as well."

"Do you want me to marry Khyma, mother? She is my foremost enemy! She wished this disaster on me!"

"Oh my beloved son! Why do you remind yourself of that! Everything is God's will! Whatever the girl said in sorrow was not what brought on the disaster. Such is your fate!"

She begged him, first with tears and then with tender words, and finally persuaded him to take Khyma. They say that water wears the rock away! And so it was in this case. By constantly nagging him with: "Marry her! Marry her! Have pity on your mother, whose health was spent in bringing you up," she got her way. The young Kozak agreed — he sent the matchmakers to Khyma, and he married her.

At last the old mother got a daughter-in-law. It made her very happy. Khyma served her mother-in-law, comforted her, and pleased her, as if she had been her own child. As for Tymish: she loved him very much, clung to him, would not let him for a moment out of her sight, even though he was always downcast and never tender to her. She did not pay too much attention to his behavior but nestled up to him, comforting and pleasing him as she would her beloved child! If Tymish ever smiled — good Lord! It was as if the sun had shone on her: her eyes would light up and there would be a blush upon her cheeks!

VI

One day Tymish and his wife were sitting silently in the orchard. Her eyes were fastened on him. He sat with his head bent. He was sad. All of a sudden they heard a noisy chirping sound. It grew very loud. They looked — above them were birds flying in circles. One bird was below the others, and hovered over Tymish. He could feel the closeness of its wings.

Khyma grabbed him by the hand:

"Shoot this bird, Tymish!" she said, and turned very pale.

"Why should I? I have no cause to shoot this harmless chatterer!"

"Shoot it, Tymish! Shoot it, my love!" she begged, tightening her grip upon his hand.

"I will not shoot! It is shameful even to speak of it!"

"You will not? It does not matter to you when your wife begs you! It is because you do not love your wife."

As she spoke these words her tears fell onto his hand, burning him like fire.

"Oh wife!" he said, "how like fire your tears are!"

"That is because they are bitter, Tymish! And I have cried many tears!"

Again she began begging him to shoot the bird. He paid no heed to her.

"Go!" he said, "go, you wicked person!"

She got up and ran out of the garden.

And the bird flew down lower and lower over him. Tymish looked and it seemed that the bird was so dear to him that he could not take his eyes off it. He could have listened forever to its gentle and lovable chirping! Suddenly great sorrow overwhelmed him and tears streamed from his eyes. He sank forward on to the ground and watered it with his tears.

Then he heard a loud noise high above him. It was a black raven. It fought its way through the other birds and now it was after the most beautiful of them all. The latter sped like a bullet, but soon the raven enfolded it with its wings, as with a cloud.

Tymish jumped up and ran to get his rifle. He shot the raven and it hit the ground beside him. He looked and, behold, it was no raven: it was his young wife. From under her left hand black blood flowed, and with her right hand she was holding Olena, his first beloved — dead. His young bride looked exactly as she was on her maiden night, adorned with flowers and beautifully dressed. There she lay before his eyes, like a lovely, magnificent flower!

They buried Olena beside the church, under a cherry tree. When they put up the cross, little birds flew overhead and perched on it from top to bottom, warbling mournfully. Every spring they fly over and chirp above Olena's grave. Those were her bridesmaids who, on her maiden night, sang at her side.

Tymish did not have long to wander about the earth. Sorrow consumed him. His house fell into ruin, weeds grew in his yard, the trees in the orchard dried up, and the deep well caved in. The place became completely overgrown with moss and slowly crumbled away.

THE DREAM

My father had three of us, all daughters. I was the eldest. Our father was so very strict! Only once in a while would he allow us to go out and have fun with the other girls.

"The female tribe is good for nothing," he used to say. "All they can think about is having a merry time! They spend all their time frolicking and chattering like magpies."

"Did you not have a good time when you were young?" mother would say.

"I never played the fool, thank God!"

Even though father was stern, he loved us very much. If he happened to go to Kyiv, he would bring us back lovely presents: an ochipok[1] embroidered with silk or maybe a red plakhta for mother; a most beautiful necklace or ribbons or a red belt of the best quality for me; for my little sisters necklaces or earrings. But again, if he happened to get home early he would not give out the presents until the second or third day after his return. We would keep looking into his eyes, walking around him, but nothing doing! First of all, he would relate how he quarreled there with a market woman or something like that. And, when he finally took out all the presents and began distributing them amongst us, our joy would know no bounds!

"Father dear! Oh, our beloved Father!"

"Well, well! Enough! Enough of this commotion! Why are you all bustling about like stirred-up bees? Perhaps you think I bought all this stuff? Well, my clever little ones, just listen to this: I sold my wheat and, with what was left over, I made a deal with a merchant who came along and insisted on an exchange of goods. I agreed just to get rid of him. That's how I got you the presents."

And so he would make up stories, never admitting that he remembered us and bought the presents for us. No, he never would! That is how my father was, may he rest in peace!

---

[1] ochipok — the oldest form of head covering; a married woman's cap.

Ours was a lovely house with a large orchard and garden. In the orchard grew cherries, apples, chestnuts, pears, and a guelder-rosebush. Our yard was large and the gates were new. It was a pleasure to look inside the house. There were benches and tables made from the wood of linden trees, and beautiful Kyivan ikons by famous masters. The ikons were all draped with flower embroidered towels. There were flowers and all kinds of fragrant herbs everywhere.

II

My sixteenth year had passed and my seventeenth had begun. We had just finished celebrating Pentecost, when one night I had a strange dream. I was standing in green rye that reached above my waist. Around me the wheat wore its tassels and the poppies were in bloom — and before me there were two bright moons, one brighter than the other. They were coming straight toward me. The brighter moon moved ahead of the other and finally fell right into my hands, while the other disappeared behind a cloud. When I awoke, I related my strange dream.

"That certainly was a queer dream" said mother, with a smile.

"There is nothing these foolish girls would not dream!" remarked my father. "See, she caught the moon with her hand as one would catch an ox by the horns! If one sleeps, one dreams! Dream is illusion, but God is reality. It is in God, and not in dreams, that one should trust."

III

On Sunday I somehow persuaded father to allow me to go for a walk with the other girls. We walked past the village until we got up to a mound; we sang and romped about. Suddenly we were startled by someone shouting: "Hey! Hey!" The echo sounded and resounded through the hills. We looked about us. It was the chumaks making their way down the hill. Their oxen, all of a gray color and with huge horns, wore heavy, carved yokes. The chumaks were all young and handsome.

"You naughty vagabonds!" said the girls. "You frightened us!"

"Listen, let us greet the chumaks," said hazel-eyed Motrya Chemeriwna, who was fleet of foot and agile.

With that she began to sing, "Oh chumak, chumak . . ." And we all joined in. The chumaks were eyeing us, then they began to chase us! We made a run for it, scattering in all directions. The chumaks pursued and finally encircled us like a cloud.

"Let us pass, dear chumaks," begged Motrya. "Please do!"

"Oh!" called out one chumak. He was standing there tall as an oak without moving a muscle. He had his hands out to catch us. A pipe clenched in his teeth. "Oh, my girl, but you don't know the ways of the chumaks!"

And with that he became silent.

The others began to joke with the girls. I hid behind Motrya until one of the chumaks, very dark and handsome, with the piercing eyes of a young eagle, moved in our direction.

He stepped up to me, with his arms akimbo, and said:

"My beautiful doves! What a bright star there is among you! If she were to swim like a fish in the dark blue sea, I would catch her with a silk net; if she were to fly like a bird, I would tempt her with grains of gold; but now I must ask you, who is the father of this girl?"

All the girls answered in unison: "She is the daughter of Ivan Samus! Ivan Samus's daughter!"

Then he took me by the hand and said:

"My girl-charmer, will you permit me to send matchmakers to you?"

Things went hazy before my eyes. . . .

IV

We were all late in getting home that day. The chumaks went on their way.

I could not sleep. There was a humming noise like a windmill in my head and my heart uttered the chumak's loving words. From that time it seemed as if the world centered on him. He was all I thought of, all I was concerned about. Mother had noticed, and was worried.

"My daughter! What has happened to you? You have grown thin, my child!" she said.

And father, although he said nothing, looked at me quizzically.

I would go among the girls and they would gather round me and ask:

"Why are you so sad? What is on your mind? You are so quiet as if you had a mouthful of water! Maybe you have been bewitched? You behave as though you were engaged to someone you are not in love with. Tell us the whole truth, Domasya dear!"

And I tried to keep quiet, fearing that I might let the truth out.

"You see, you do not consider us trustworthy!" they said angrily.

"What am I to tell you, my sisters?" I would answer. "I just don't feel well."

"All right then, let us play!"

They would join hands and, dragging me along, would romp about laughing and stamping enough to make the earth shake.

"Eh, girls!" said Motrya. "Domasya does not have our merrymaking on her mind. I know well what longing has come into her heart."

The girls began to question her: "Tell us, Motrya! Tell us!"

"Our Domasya has fallen in love with a young, handsome chumak!"

"So she has! With that dark, tall one! The one with the squeaky boots?

Oh, he is charming! So facetious and talkative! A real golden-lipped type!"

I felt as if I was covered with hot ashes. "Shame on you, Motrya," I said to her.

"But I am telling the honest truth," she answered. "You don't think so! If not, say so! You see! You see, your lips don't even open! Just listen to me, all of you! I have something to tell you, but give me room to breathe. Why are you hemming me in. Sit down in a circle and pay attention."

We sat down in a circle and listened. My heart was pounding within me, ready to leap out.

"I have found out where these chumaks come from."

I let out a cry, "O! from where?"

"They are all from Mazowyshche."

"Where did you get this information?"

"From the bottom of the ocean."

(This Motrya was actually the type who could have got things from the bottom of the ocean if she had wanted to.)

"The one who was sweet on Domasya is Danylo Donchuk, and the one whom I like best is Kyrylo Savtyr."

"And which one is this Kyrylo?" asked Olena Yakovenko. "The fair-haired, merry one?"

"I never inquired about your fair-haired one. The Lord has sent that one for you. My Kyrylo — he is the one with the dark, high-set eyebrows, who smoked the pipe all the time. He is the one who was so serious, as if contemplating an attack upon the Turks, and so motionless as if formed out of gold! All that time he hardly spoke a word. He did not take up with any one of the girls and glanced at me only twice, as if by accident. Good Heavens! Everybody was joking and laughing and he was standing there like a crane-bird, raising his eyebrows. Still, he is the one I liked. Well, there is nothing to do now but wait until they come back from Krym."

"And then?" I asked.

"Then they will send the matchmakers," she said. "I am sure of that! Come girls, let us extol Domasya." And she began:

> "The stars were shining! The stars were shining!
> With whom did you stand, Domasya?
> It was with you, Danylko, with you I stood.
> Under a green willow tree,
> With you, chumak Danylo!
> Under your embroidered sleeve."

"Tell me Motrya, my sweet, how do you happen to know all this? Who told you?"

"I sent the white-sided magpie and she brought back two reports under her right wing: one about Danylko, and the other about Kyrylo."

So, joking and laughing she answered, but never speaking the truth.

V

Autumn was on the horizon. The field work was completed. The harvest festivities had gone by. The matchmakers began to be seen on the streets; everyone could hear young girls boasting:

"I am engaged to my Mykhailo!"

"My father gave Pavlo and me his blessings!"

Grief and sorrow overcame me as though I had been in the midst of a black cloud. The only happiness I had was in meeting Motrya and talking to her. I begged her:

"Tell me, darling Motrya, was what you told me true, or was it one of your jokes? Who told you that they will send the matchmakers?"

"Did I not tell you that I sent a white-sided magpie as a messenger?" At that she began to giggle. "I will put your heart at ease with a good thought: Do not ask about things you are not supposed to ask about. Here, however, is something for both of us to think about: what married life would be for us amongst strangers and how we would exist there! Dear God, let us hope that it would be a happy existence! We would visit our fathers and our mothers and be their guests. We would come — I magnificent and beautiful, and you, still more beautiful, in our thin namitkas.[2] We would come with our loving husbands in wagons drawn by gray oxen (for there are gray oxen in Mazowyshche!). Let our enemies envy us then!"

When she began making up these stories and daydreams, I would become fascinated listening to her.

One day I was working in my orchard, when my younger sister ran up to me:

"Domasya! Domasya! The matchmakers are coming! They are close at hand!"

What a calamity! Oh dear Lord!

I ran into the house and halted in the hallway. I heard them talking outside with my father, telling him that sir Ihnat sent them. Father opened the door. I fell at his feet, weeping and entreating him:

"Father, dear father, do not ruin your child!"

"Who would want to ruin you?" said father. "Stop! Stop crying!"

"We will not force you, my child," said mother. "What is there to cry about?"

Overjoyed, I thanked them:

"Thank you, mother, for understanding me and for not giving me away to someone I don't love!" Father extended his hospitality to the matchmakers, thanking them for their kindness.

"Our child," he said, "is still young. Let us still love her ourselves and guide her onto the right road."

"My daugther," said mother when the matchmakers had left, "this is your moon that disappeared behind the cloud."

---

[2]namitka — a married woman's headdress, worn over her ochipok.

VI

When I got rid of my misfortune it seemed as if I became happier. I waited for Danylo from Krym and daydreamed of what a homecoming it would be, and how I would greet him! Only, at the thought of some mishap befalling him on the road, my heart grew cold. I would go out and sit somewhere in the orchard and become lost in thought — one thought getting the better of the other. I had no desire to do any work. I would spend the whole day like this.

One morning I was very depressed when my mother called:

"Domasya, come to the house! The Lord has sent us good guests."

"Who are they, mother?" I asked, with a tremor.

"Mr. Korniy Donchuk wants you to marry his son Danylo."

Oh my God! I cannot remember my mother leading me into the house, and giving me the marriage blessing! The procedure of accepting the marriage offer was gone through. So we were betrothed.

The elders went into consultation with the matchmakers and Danylo bent down, close to me.

"My girl," said Danylo, "do you love me as I love you — so very much?"

I kept silent. It was such a joy to hear his voice!

From then on he would come to me every evening in the orchard, and I never realized how quickly the time could pass.

My mother said then:

"This, my little daughter, is the moon that rolled down into your hands."

VII

Motrya got engaged to Kyrylo Savtyr. We were both married on the same day. It was after this that Motrya confessed.

"I sent," she said, "old Bulbykha to Mazowyshche to find everything out. She even saw Kyrylo and Danylo and brought me all the news."

After the wedding my father asked Kyrylo:

"How is it, Kyrylo, that you got married? If I had not seen it with my own eyes, I would never have believed that such a wanderer would marry."

"I got married, sir, as you can see," said Kyrylo. "She caught my fancy like a little singing bird. Let her now sing in my house."

My father-in-law was so good! He pampered me just like my father used to do. My mother-in-law was kind and jocular. Things had turned out luckily for me, thank God! Only in spring, when I saw my Danylo preparing for the road, did I realize why people sorrow and weep. Such indescribable grief enveloped me when I accompanied him out of the village. After seeing him off, I stopped and looked. There was nothing around me but the boundless, green steppes.

My mother-in-law, in tears herself, tried to cheer me:

"My dear daughter, you must accept what the Lord has sent you. Look at me: I have lived my life in luxury and married my love; my sons are like eagles. But, for all that, I have wept bitter tears. First I used to part with my husband and now I must part with my son. I do not even know if I will live to see him again, for I have lived long, and the Lord might call me to him any day. But you! You are young! You will see him again. Why worry? You will grow thin and this will sadden him."

Motrya would come over to visit.

"What is this, Domasya?" she would ask. "What are you crying for? I also saw my Kyrylo off to Krym! Mother of God, how thin you have become! If your husband were smart he would not even look at you. And this is what he should do! When my beloved returns, he will cuddle and kiss me because I will meet him, looking like a poppy in full bloom."

And so she could cheer me up.

By sheer determination I held out till autumn. Every hour I would run out the gates to see if anyone was coming. At night I could not get to sleep: I would dream that I heard the gates squeaking, or my husband's voice, so I would leap up and run out — no, there was no one, all was still, and the gates were closed.

Before the Sunday of the Feast of St. Peter I dreamt that a full moon rose so very red over our house. Framed in the moon, a white rooster fluttered his wings and crowed so that it resounded through the entire village.

"That is a good dream that you have dreamt," said my mother-in-law. "You will see, your Danylo will return soon. If a young girl dreams about the moon, she will marry; but if a married woman dreams about it, her husband will return, or a son will be born to her. Be on the look-out for Danylo. He will be home in no time."

And so it happened, that on the second day in the evening, he returned, my gray dove. How we talked! I told him my dream about the full moon.

"And all I dreamt about was a little, bright star," he said, caressing me.

HORPYNA

Old Yakymenko had married off his son — and what a daughter-in-law he got himself! As lively as a hare, fair-complexioned, beautiful and gay! She worked briskly both inside the house and out, cleaning and organizing, singing and laughing. Her voice was heard far off like the tinkling of a bell. She was always up with the dawn like an early bird, putting everything in place and running about doing her daily chores and seeing to the comfort of her father-in-law, as well as of her husband. The couple lived happily and harmoniously; the old father saw it and gave God thanks.

One thing only worried them — God had not given them any children! Whenever the daughter-in-law came across a child belonging to someone else, she would caress and cuddle it and heave a heavy sigh.

Then at last — a girl was born to them. How Horpyna loved and fondled her first born! She did not let the little one out of her arms. If the child woke up or stirred suddenly, she was instantly at the cradle, blessing and kissing her, rocking and singing to her. When she was summoned to go to work in the field for the landlord, she took her child with her. She worked, but always with an eye on her child.

Sometimes the women folk would joke:

"How is your daughter, Horpyna?"

She would begin to tell them:

"She is already smiling, my dear sisters, stretching out her tiny hands to me! She already knows me and doesn't go to anyone but me. My father-in-law may show her a poppy-seed roll, but she will not go to him! She is already clapping her little hands! If I leave the house, then steal back and peep in, she will be searching for me with her little eyes!"

"She has grown to be very intelligent, very intelligent indeed!" they would say. "You might as well hurry up and get the dowry ready because the boys will soon be asking for her hand in marriage!"

The little girl was really like a tiny flower opening in bloom. What a beautiful child she was, as gay and healthy as could be!

II

Just then our old landlord died and the young one began managing the estate. The old one was terrible, but the young one, God help us, was absolutely awful! He drove us serfs harder than oxen. We worked three days on his estate and on the fourth day we had still another task assigned by him. On Friday and Saturday, we were again put to some other job. So it went day after day, week after week! We had hoped that the young master would treat us better — and look at what we ended up with! He was not very rich, but he wanted to live like the rich! What concern was it of his if the people were collapsing in the field? He would get the best horses for his stables, would buy a new carriage, or go into town and throw his money about. The lesser landowners of the neighborhood would come to talk to us (they often do this — talk to other landowners' serfs while, at the same time, mistreating their own, just as the big landowners do). They would say: "It looks as if you've got yourselves a very good owner now! Just hear him speak about the simple folk — the peasants must be educated, sympathized with, and all the rest of it! He seems to have a proper grounding in the subject!"

It was true. At the beginning he did speak of building us new houses, with three windows! Look at what came of that! The houses we are now living in are practically in ruins! Perhaps his grounding in the subject was for the better, but who can change a landowner's nature!

Sorrow and unhappiness overshadowed the whole village. Everyone was so sad that it was pitiful to behold. Only Horpyna was the least bit gay. She found pleasure in her little daughter and forgot about the misery of those around her. Misery, however, did not pass her by! Her little daughter became ill. She screamed and cried. Horpyna cried along with her, but there was nothing she could do to help her. The old father-in-law ran to the village mid-wife but she was not at home. There were not even any women about to help! They were all in the field. Soon Horpyna had to go to the field as well.

"Why don't you go?" they sent to ask her.

"My child is ill," she said, in tears.

"You must work for the master. He could not care less about your child," was the reply.

She had to go. She took her daughter, bundled her up and off she went. The poor little one screamed all the time. When they reached the field, the master met her himself. He was so angry, Mother of God have mercy on us! He began to give her a tongue-lashing. The child in her arms screamed and kicked. The master became angrier than ever.

"Away with that child! Out with it!" he shouted. "You have to work and not fuss with the child!"

He ordered the section foreman to take the child home.

"O dear master, at least let me take her home myself," begged Horpyna tearfully. "My dear master! Be merciful! This is my only child!"

"Take it, take it," he said to the foreman, "and you," he said to Horpyna, "will do your work, if you don't want to be punished."

They took the child across the field. For a long time Horpyna heard its cry, pitiful and pained. Then it grew fainter and fainter and finally died away.

III

Heaven knows how she got through that day's work! She got home breathless in the evening.

"Oh, my child! My little girl!" she lamented. "Have you taken care of her, dear father? Tell me — how is she?"

"Stop worrying, my daughter," said the old father-in-law. "Thank God she has quietened down a bit."

But not for long. During the night the child woke up and started to cry again in even greater pain, burning with fever. Horpyna sought advice from the other women but, alas, it was to no avail! Morning came, and she had to go to work in the field. She recalled having once heard that if a child does not sleep, one should soak poppy seeds in milk and give the child the mixture. That is what she did. "At least let her rest and get relief from pain," she thought. As soon as she gave it to her, the little one became silent and fell very soundly asleep — in fact, so soundly that she did not wake when the section foreman shouted: "Get to work!"

Horpyna laid her daughter in the cradle, blessed her, and went off crying.

How she was scolded that day! How she was shouted at! She paid no heed. Her only thought was — let it be evening soon! At last her suffering was ended. The sun had already set behind the blue mountains. Dusk came. She ran home as fast as her legs would carry her and dashed into the house. All was quiet and in darkness. She rushed to the cradle for the child. The child lay there cold, neither moving nor breathing.

IV

"Father!" screamed Horpyna.

"Why do you frighten me, daughter? I dozed off. The little one is still sleeping."

Horpyna stood transfixed, clasping her little daughter in her arms. The old man had dozed off again.

"Lights! Put on the lights! Lights, father!" she screamed.

The old man struck a light. "What has happened to her?" he thought. When he lit the lamp and looked he was dumbstruck with fear. There, in the middle of the room, stood Horpyna, her face darkly overcast. She was terrible to behold! In her arms lay the dead child.

"Daughter," uttered the old man, "daughter!"

"You see what good it has done! My child has grown silent, she does not cry!" was her reply.

Horpyna wept and lamented. Where did her tears come from! They flowed like a stream, like a ceaselessly flowing fountain.

The people heard and came running. They attempted to comfort her. She acted as if she had lost her powers of understanding. They could not tear the child away from her. Her husband paced about as if out of his mind with grief. Her father-in-law became ill.

They began to prepare for the funeral. They had brought a small, new coffin and lined it with fragrant flowers and herbs.

"Horpyna," they said, "give us the child."

She would not. She washed it and laid it in the coffin with her own hands. It was time to carry it to the cemetery grounds, but she just stood there and stared. The people talked to her — she did not hear and did not listen.

Somehow they persuaded her to move away from the coffin, and carried it out. Then, for the first time, she looked about her, crossed herself, and joined the others. Step by step she followed the people, without speaking a word. In the church, too, she stood quietly. But when the burial began — Dear God! She threw herself into the grave after the child. They rescued her with difficulty and brought her home, as if she was dead.

She was gravely ill for about three weeks. Somehow God had mercy on her and helped her regain her strength, but not her mind! It came to be that she seemed not to have complete command of her senses. She would walk about silently all day and pick the garden poppies. If someone asked why she was doing that, she would answer: "This is for my child."

During the winter she kept wailing: "There are no poppies! How can I save my little girl?"

When the first poppy blossom peeped forth, she spotted it, picked it right away, and took great delight in it. Before that, she pottered about the house, but as soon as the poppies began to bloom she would leave the house and stay all day among them. As you go past the gardens you will see her sitting there, beautifully dressed in a white blouse and beads. She is still young — only as pale as a sheet. She is playing with the poppies smiling like a child. And the poppies bloom abundantly with blossoms white, and gray, and red. . . .

REDEMPTION

I will tell you about Yakiv Kharchenko, of what sadness befell him in the village of Khmelyntsi, while he was wooing Kokhanivna.

One Sunday at sunset we approached that village together. My lad, I saw, was beginning to lag. I kept observing him silently — he had slowed his pace, and changed completely. All the way along the road he was so talkative and merry, clattering like the town bell, but now he suddenly became silent as if his mouth had been full of water. He drew his brows together and hung his head.

"Why are you pouting, Yakiv, like a snipe in the wind?" I said.

"What sort of snipe have you dreamed up, uncle?"[1] he grumbled.

"Perhaps you are tired, boy?"

"No," he snapped back, and continued walking in silence again.

"What is this, Yakiv," said I. "At first you hurried like the wind, but now you begin to procrastinate?"

Just then we reached the brow of a small hill, and from there the village of Khmelyntsi lay spread out before our eyes, as if on the palm of a hand.

"Let us recover our breath," I said.

We sat down. My Yakiv kept on looking at the village, his eyes darting about. I kept on looking too. Every part of it was familiar — the houses, the orchards. It was a fine village, if only you could see it! The church stool tall. Some old colonel built it. The cemetery was overgrown with cherry saplings and herbs that were almost waist-high. The little houses were hidden in the cherry orchards. It was lovely!

We sat and looked on. People were talking in the village and later they separated one by one. Two women were chatting; they parted and met again, waving their arms about all the while as if they were thrashing pea pods. If one of their husbands had not stepped outside and broken it up, they would not have separated till dawn. The village grew quiet, except

---

[1] Uncle — no relationship in this case, implied — customary mode of address from a younger to an older person.

where a window rattled occasionally and the agile youth darted past a gate.

"Come on, let us go!" said my Yakiv as if someone had pricked him with a needle. "It is late already!" And he grew pale.

"What a calamity!" I said.

"What calamity, uncle?"

"The calamity that has befallen you, Yakiv! You left home healthy, happy, singing, talking, but now you are as if you had been scalded with boiling water. You did not lose your money, did you?"

He reached up for his cap.

"I have my money," he said.

"You have your money and your girlfriend is waiting for you, but you act as if you were going to have a yoke put on your neck!"

No sound came from his lips.

"Come, we will spend the night together at old Kokhan's place," I said.

"Very well, if they would do us that favor, uncle," he said.

That made my anger boil up.

"You had better talk sense, Yakiv! Why are you mincing your words like a priest's daughter at a banquet? If you will not explain your behavior immediately, I will not consent to being your best-man!"

He then began to speak.

"What good is my money to me? Will it buy me my freedom?"

"Why have you spun such a tale of woe? Why should it not buy your freedom? As long as there is money, you will get your freedom."

"But suppose the lady does not consent to let me go?"

"And why should she not consent to let you go? Have you ever come across any landlords who don't have a liking for money? I have never come across any of that sort," I said.

"Oh uncle! Perhaps she counts her money by the basketful!"

"It does not matter," I said, "whether she counts her money by the basketful. Like all the landlords, she is as fond of money as a gypsy is fond of bacon, brother. They will always have too little, till the day of judgment! Don't worry! I will go to her myself. We have seen them all before, some even worse. You will make your bows to your girlfriend's father."

"He has already told me: 'I will not give my daughter away to a serf. Better for her that she should enter a monastery.' And Kokhan's say-so is final — even a child knows that."

"Well," I said, "we shall see how it works out. We are almost there. See, there is his house!"

II

We were proceeding along the street and already from a distance saw that there was a light inside the house. We went up to the door and I knocked. A pup barked nearby; someone opened a window but probably saw nothing, because the sky was overcast with clouds and it was completely dark outside. A latch rattled; out came Marta Kokhanivna.

Good Lord! What a girl she had grown to be! So young and pretty, like a poppy in bloom! She was adorned with flowers, and wore a red coral necklace, an embroidered blouse, and tiny shoes. What a girl! Like a little star!

She ran out with the night-light and saw Yakiv and me.

"Oh, it is you, uncle!" she said.

"Yes, but here is Yakiv," said I.

He almost knocked the night-light from her hands.

"Marta, my dearest!" he whispered.

By then old Kokhan was looking out and behind him was his wife. They greeted and welcomed us.

"Eh, daughter," said the old one, "such dear guests should be asked to come into the house, and here you are fluttering about! Come, my little swallow!" And he let her pass through the door.

We also entered, bowed and sat down. The old man invited us to have supper. The mother and daughter bustled about the table and the stove, while we cast glances at one another trying to start a conversation.

Kokhan — you probably have not heard of or seen him before in your life. Everyone respected this man from his youth up. When he was a young man, all he had to do was twitch an eyebrow and the girls would pine and go crazy about him, and now, when he had grown older, he had only to twitch his gray moustache — and the whole community would take notice. The foremost citizen in the village was Kokhan. If you could only have seen him! What are those city lords compared to him? Like scalded sparrows! When Kokhan put in an appearance he was a sight to see. He was tall, gray, and moustached. He wore a black coarse woolen cloak, a red belt, and a gray fur cap. He had the genuine bearing of a Kozak, one of the old-time sort. Even if you were an enemy of his, you could not help taking your cap off to him. There are lots of old men going about the village. You might bow to one or you might not notice another, but this one you noticed immediately, as you would a hetman.[2] He would raise his fur cap even to a small child and pass on. He married Oksana — old Yakovenko's daughter, also of good Kozak stock. She was round-faced, so neat and black-browed, a true Kozak type!

We sat for a while, looking at one another.

"That is how it goes, brother," said Kokhan.

"That is how it goes, brother," I also said to him.

Kokhan's wife set the evening meal on the table and we were offered whiskey.

"Do have one more glass!" they entreated. "You are probably exhausted," said Kokhan's wife. "Such a long road, and a cold wind blowing."

---

[2]hetman — commander-in-chief elected by the Kozaks; head of the Ukrainian Kozak State; here, the highest official.

"Ah, dear hostess," I said, "but it is never a long road that leads to a loved one," and drank another glass.

Then the old man broached the lad, asking him how his earnings stood.

You see, Yakiv was working in Kyiv. It was possible for us serfs to do so, provided we could give the landowner part of our earnings. Yakiv had earned a lot this year. He tried as hard as he could, realizing what he needed the money for.

"No problem, thank God, where my earnings are concerned!" said Yakiv.

He took money from his cap and put it on the table before the old man's eyes. He stood up, bowed, and looked on.

The old one just twitched his gray moustache. "Money!" he said.

Yakiv bowed again.

"I have placed all my hope in your generosity and your goodheartedness, father!"

Marta, I observed, halted, stretched her head forward like a quail, and listened breathlessly. Her mother, too, cast a side-long glance at us.

"Tomorrow we go, God be with us, to the lady," I said, "and then to Your Honor for the marriage blessing."

"Go, and God be with you," said the old one then, "try your luck. Buy yourself off, Yakiv, and you will be my son-in-law, and if not, so be it! I will not give my daughter to a serf. It is as I said earlier and I will hold to that until my dying day. I will not change my mind. She is from a great Kozak breed! Is it like me, with my gray hair, to disrespect such an honest and noble race? That would be like letting the Kozak breed die out like the foul Jewish faith! There is no race in the world greater than the Kozaks!"

And saying that, he stood straight up, almost supporting the ceiling. His eyes shone, his voice was resonant. It was as if he had grown young again, and was advancing against the Turks.

"Yes, there is no one greater than the Kozaks! No one! What more need be said!" quietly affirmed his wife, nodding her head.

My young lad went as white as a sheet, and a change came over the girl. She stood there, her bright eyes downcast, like one dead.

"In what respect is he not a Kozak?" I asked both of them. "Look at him, good people, is he not a Kozak? Let Marta say what she thinks!" I said.

Marta said nothing. She hid her face with one of her embroidered sleeves and left the room.

"How will it be, brother?" I asked.

"It will be as I have said. Go to the lady and ask for his freedom."

"But suppose she wants a lot of money?"

"If it is only money, don't worry. I will give you money."

"Well, thank you, brother!" I said. "You are, I see, an honest Kozak!" And I poked my young lad so that he would take notice.

Things brightened up a bit for us. We each drank one more glass and began to consider how we should approach the lady, how we should bargain, and what we should say and do. Kokhan's wife followed her daughter out of the house. They probably sat down somewhere in the orchard, worrying together. We saw no more of them that evening.

III

The old man took us to the barn for the night, and we lay down to sleep. I listened. For some reason my young lad could not get to sleep. He was turning about restlessly in the hay, sighing. A little later he went out.

"Should I go after him? Perhaps I shall be needed to keep an eye on things," I reflected.

I lay there trying to think, but sleep enfolded me. The hay was fresh and fragrant. I heard a sound. "Well," I thought, "a good thing that I did not go after him. Here he is . . ." He stood about a while, then dashed off again. "Oh no, just a minute," I thought and this time went after him. I saw him approach one of the windows of the house. He pressed close to it and rubbed himself against it like a pigeon. He knocked on it gently as if with a blade of grass, but the window did not open. Was the young Kozak girl asleep, or was the father still awake? Who could tell? But we departed from the window as we had come — with nothing.

"Don't worry," I said to soothe him, "some day the sun will shine for us as well!"

He just waved his hand and buried himself in the hay.

"Yakiv! O Yakiv!" I called.

He was silent as if he did not hear me, as if he were sleeping.

Then I, too, turned on my side and fell asleep.

We were up before the sun. The old man saw us out of the village (Khmelyntsi was a Kozak village and we had still about half a mile to go to the lord's village). He doffed his cap and said: "God be with you!" We, too, bade him farewell. As we were proceeding on our way, Marta appeared from somewhere. She wanted to say something, but was too shy and blushed brightly.

"What is this, Marta," I said to her, "you have also come to bid us farewell?"

I had to start up a conversation, because all my young lad could do was make eyes at the girl. He was moving round behind me to get to her.

"I was at Halya's place," she said, "and I am going home now. God be with you, uncle!" And took off into the willows.

IV

We entered the lord's estate. The sun was already high in the sky. We made inquiries and were told that the gentry were still asleep. We sat down by a decorated porch and looked at what met our eyes. Immediately in front of us there was an orchard. Paths covered with yellow sand ran here and there, flowers were blooming in small round clumps, and the benches were all green. It was all so clean and orderly.

"What a fine garden, Yakiv!" I said.

"It is indeed, Uncle!" he replied.

We sat worrying and waiting for quite some time. At last came the announcement: "The lady is up!" We were called inside. Our eyes were bedazzled — green, red, white, blue . . . what wasn't there! Have you ever been inside a Jewish store? Here, as there, were a great many things. It was impossible to distinguish at first glance what was good, or, please forgive me, what should have been thrown out on the rubbish heap, since apparently it was there only to fool folk. Things gleamed in corners and shone on walls. What a display of flashy gimmicks! Some young ladies ran out, short and swift like magpies. They turned round in front of us and disappeared through the door! About mid-day the lady herself rolled in as if on wheels. She was so bloated as if she had been full of rising yeast. She had rings on and was attired in satin. She went straight to the mirror, turned about twice before it, and the rustling like dry leaves, made by her clothing, filled the room. She plopped down into a chair, bounced back up, and started on to us.

"What do you want?" she asked.

"To see Your Grace," I said and bowed low, explaining what we had come for.

She began to look at us more intently, and said that to her knowledge everything now was more expensive and that she had heard of other young men who had had to pay half a thousand to a certain landlord for their freedom.

"What certain landlord, my good lady?" I asked and bowed low again.

"Why do you have to know that?" she exlained irritably. "What business is it of yours?"

"Why, none," I said. "May God give that certain landlord good health for having such rich people that they could pay him so much!"

"How much are you thinking of paying to be bought off?"

"Well, your ladyship, we were thinking, if we could afford it . . . But with our money . . . What is the use! The good Lord did not intend that this should befall us!"

"What price were you thinking of?"

"There is no point in troubling Your Grace any further! Farewell, your ladyship!"

And I went to the door.

Yakiv grabbed me by the sleeve:

"Uncle!" he said.

I winked at him, as if to say: "Keep out!"

"Listen you," shouted the lady, "wait!"

She called me back and asked again:

"How much are you prepared to pay?"

But I was still not telling her.

"There is no point in bothering with us, gracious lady!" I said.

I noticed then that her face had begun to get as red as the heart of a fire.

"I, gracious lady, thought of two hundred rubles."

"You must have been born mad!" she shouted.

I simply bowed silently as if she had said something meaningful. She finished speaking her mind and rose.

"If you want to buy him off, then do so quickly for three hundred, because later on you will not be able to do it for even a thousand."

My Yakiv was overjoyed and like a fool went down on his knees before her! He was thanking her, you see, for serving up his own bacon to him.

"Well, have you brought the money?"

And at that precise moment she looked as if she would have jumped right down our throats.

"No," I said, "gracious lady, not all of it with us, just a little."

"I need the money now!" she shouted, "I need it this instant! I will be going to town today; you, too, must be there, and there we will wind up the business. Go and get the money!"

She grabbed a little bell and its ringing resounded through every room. Young lads and servant girls came running up to her.

"The carriage!" she said, "and don't be long about it!"

She herself meantime was barging about like one demented, selecting papers from behind the mirror, opening and closing drawers. Two girls, like frightened foals, were at her back assisting her.

V

While they were getting themselves ready, we ran quickly to Khmelyntsi and created such a hubbub with our laughing and rejoicing, then returned to the noble's mansion. The lady ordered a little wagon for us, seated herself in the high carriage, and we made off.

Ours was a small town. My father said that there had been a time when it was occupied mostly by colonels and lieutenants, so that wherever one looked, there would be a great variety of military uniforms, like red poppies. Now Jews have settled there like locusts. Nobles, however, live there as well. At fair-time common folk can also be seen, mostly at the market.

Our lady arrived at the home of old Moshko, the Jew. The rooms were all high and beautiful, but what a musty smell!

They sent immediately for some office-clerk called Zakharevych and told us to wait by the door until he came. He soon arrived. He was wretched-looking, pock-marked like a seive. He was wearing wide blue trousers and a sort of short cloak. Round his neck he had a green kerchief, and under his right arm he carried a fur cap. He entered and crouched-down as if trying to make himself inconspicuous. His steps were stealthy and his big boots were quite muddy.

The lady called him to her immediately. Whenever she was talking to you, it was a habit with her to sit bolt upright, like a good cabbage stalk in the garden, and observe what sort of brows, what kind of moustache, what sort of clothes, you had. You would have had to be a general, perhaps, for her to tilt her head slightly to one side, or look pleasantly into your eyes.

We waited a little longer until the lady had conferred with Zakharevych. He came out, gave us a wink, and said: "Come with me!" And the mistress followed up with: "Go with him!"

So we went.

He was a jolly man, that office-clerk Zakharevych! As soon as we left he began to laugh, talk, do everything but dance. Later he patted me on the shoulder with great gusto and said:

"So! You want to be free? That's good!"

"So far as we are concerned, it's the best!" I said.

"The only unfortunate thing is," he said, "that it is hard to put the deal through. I don't know how it will go."

"What is the matter?" I asked, and Yakiv grew pale.

"I must now write down your personal descriptions for identification, and that is difficult! I would outline them, but what would Mr. Bykarch say? He has to read them."

"If you wrote them well, the man would not have anything to say, except thank you."

"Perhaps you should give him a present? And I will take it to him. This I can do. What do you say to that?"

Yakiv could not hold his tongue:

"What kind of present is needed? Tell me, sir!"

"Money, possibly. A hundred rubles even would do it. He will take it. He is a good man!" said the clerk, roaring with laughter.

"No, sir, you tell us exactly what needs to be done." I told him. "What do we have to give money for? Or else we shall ask our lady?"

"This is not absolutely necessary. We can do what you like but think about what is best for you. It can be done without money."

And when he told us this he was not laughing. He sat down at the edge of the table. It was crooked. Somehow his whole house was crooked. There were holes filled with dirt in the corners of the room. He wrote something and said:

"There is nothing more that I can do here. You can tell that to your lady. There is nothing to write about!"

"Why nothing? For other people you can write something, sir! Why not for us?"

"I write personal descriptions, for identification purposes, you artful old dodger," said Zakharevych, swearing at us. "What personal description has he? The same that everybody else has."

"Thank God for that!" I replied.

"Yes and no! If there are no personal descriptions, there is nothing to write!"

We were tortured like this until we had to give him two rubles or so. After that he immediately found some personal descriptions and quickly sketched them out on paper. He became very jolly again, just as he had been before, and saw us out the door, saying:

"Don't worry! All will be as it should be. That is what brains and friendship are for! Even a small present was required. As they say: 'A penny from everyone makes a poor man rich."

"The trouble is," I told him, "that there are too many poor men like you holding their hands out."

VI

As Zakharevych promised, it all worked out well in the end. We bowed to the lady and, wasting no time, went to Khmelyntsi. In Khmelyntsi everything was ready for the wedding. They were all waiting for us. So the wedding took place.

Both old and young had a good time. The news of our wedding spread through the whole village; the music played and the drums rolled — it was a jolly, magnificent affair.

It is true, as people say, that a pretty girl makes a pretty young married woman. And what a young married woman our Marta turned out to be! When she was a girl she ran about, all laughter and chatter; but now she has grown somewhat wiser. Now she walks with dignity and looks at you respectfully. Her ochipok is red, her namitka white and long — she is, in short, a wife fit for a hetman!

They are still living together with old Kokhan and love each other sincerely. A boy was born to them as dark-browed and dark-haired as his father. He is growing up and, God be praised, he is healthy.

THE MOTHER-IN-LAW

Once there lived in our village a widow named Orlykha. I was then a little girl and recall only what my late mother — may her soul rest in peace! — told me about her. She was a close neighbor of Orlykha. As for myself, I recollect her dimly — tall, wearing a red ochipok, and her dark eyebrows always drawn together in a frown.

Her husband had died long ago and her elder son had been killed in Turkey. Her younger son, the handsomest young man in the village, was filling the role of master of the household. He was lively, cheerful, and hard working. He respected his mother very much and she was deeply devoted to him.

One day Orlykha decided to get him married, so she set out to look for a suitable match. She went looking in places where girls played or got together most. She would listen to, and observe them closely.

"Don't take a rich bride, my son; we are not rich ourselves. Look for one that will be good and obedient," she said.

"Very well, mother, find me the sort of girl you want and I will marry her."

While the mother was searching, he found one on his own. He found her in Vyshenky at the fair, and, from that time on, he began to visit her every evening. The mother noticed this sooner than anyone else and found out that Vasyl was courting Hanna Korolivna.

"My son," she said, "do not choose her, for she is a rich girl. She will be overbearing, for she is her father's daughter, hard to please, particular and proud — break it off with her!"

Vasyl begged and pleaded, and finally got his way. The matchmakers were sent out; a marriage arrangement was made; the wedding took place; and the bride was brought to the mother-in-law.

God! Worlds above! What a dowry she had! There were nine wagon-loads of it and four gray oxen pulling each of the wagons: silk aprons, scarlet sashes, sheepskin coats embroidered with silk. . . .

The bride had on a golden ochipok; her namitka was sheer as vapor; red corals fell to her waist — everyone gazed on her with admiration. She truly looked like a rose in full bloom! Only old Orlykha, as she greeted the newlyweds with bread and salt, looked rather joylessly into her daughter-in-law's eyes.

II

A year passed. They had built a shared house, the newlyweds living in one part of it and Orlykha in the other. At first the young Orlykha would get out and about. She would strike up a conversation or laugh, making even the old folk merrier. After a while she went out very rarely; she seemed to be spending most of her time indoors.

If anyone asked old Orlykha:

"How are your children! Is your daughter-in-law a good girl?"

"As good as her father's daughter could be," she would answer, or would not answer at all, as if she did not hear the question.

One day my mother was doing her housework and in walked Hanna. Mother noticed that Hanna was very sad. She sat down beside her and said:

"Why are your eyes sunken, my little Halya? Why do you look so troubled?"

Hanna clapped her hands and the tears, like pearls, came rolling down her cheeks.

"My mother-in-law does not love me!" she said. "She gossips about me and is constantly bickering about my being my father's daughter! . . . O, my dear father, if you only knew. If only you had foreseen my fate which holds so much misfortune, you would have drowned me in the deepest well while I was still in my swaddling clothes!"

Then my mother asked what the trouble was, and what they were quarreling about.

"She disliked me from the beginning," said Hanna. "She ruined my most beautiful silk aprons — they seemed to decompose at a touch of my hand. Well do I know, she was the one who did it! She filled my clothes-chest with some sort of powder and, at that, even my golden ochipkas lost their sheen and my red sashes became discolored. . . . She will ruin all my possessions! She kept saying to Vasyl: 'Sell, sell those oxen!' (which were given to me by my father). Vasyl did not sell them after all, but she came at me for that: 'Oh, you bastard! You have bereft me of my son! My Vasyl wants nothing more to do with me! Just wait! You wait! . . . Some day I will make you pay for this!' "

"Let her have her way, Hanna," said my mother, "there is nothing else you can do!"

"Why must I let her have her way?" shouted Hanna. "I will not! 'What you mete out to others will be meted out to you!' "

III

One night my mother could not sleep. As she opened her window she heard a whisper coming from the neighbor's orchard:

"Halya, my sweetheart!" said Vasyl, "have you been crying again?"

"Vasyl, do not leave me alone! I don't know how I have lived this one day without you! It was so sad and oppressive here for me!"

"What is it, my little darling! Is it mother, perhaps? Before I left I asked her not to sadden you."

"She did not say a single word to me all day, Vasyl, and did not even give me as much as a glance. It was so very depressing in the house."

"What is that Orlykha up to?" reflected my mother. "Yet, she seems a sensible sort."

IV

Harvest had come, and every ear of Vasyl's wheat had ripened beautifully. The field that Hanna and Vasyl owned was close to ours, so my mother used to go into the field with Hanna. One morning she waited and waited for Hanna, but she did not show up, so she left without her. Hanna arrived later, sometime after lunch, looking very pale and unsteady on her feet. My mother became frightened and asked her what had happened.

"I seem to have a pain that burns like a fire near my heart," Hanna replied. "I cannot keep my feet! I barely reached the field."

"And how is your mother-in-law?" asked my mother.

"Oh, dear aunt! This night I saw her in our storehouse. I woke up and there she was, so pale and bedraggled, standing in the moonlight. I cried out and she scurried off."

"You must be imagining this, my child! Why would she come there at night?"

"No, no, I saw her very well."

"Did Vasyl also see her?"

"Vasyl did not sleep at home last night. He was away. . . . And he, too, does not believe me. . . . I do not think I can stook a single sheaf today. I feel so weak; I can scarcely lift my hands. I will wait for Vasyl here. He said he could come for me in the evening, so he will help me to get home then."

V

My mother went back to the harvesting. In the evening she looked about for Hanna, wondering if she had gone home. She asked the other women if they had seen her passing by. She called her, but there was no answer. She went to the place where Hanna was supposed to be harvesting, and she was not there. It was very unusual! Finally, as she was walking along between the stooks, she found her. . . . There she lay, as if asleep, beautiful and fresh like a flower.

Under her head she had a sheaf of wheat, her hands were crossed. The evening was so very clear and calm. She was lying there in the wheat just as if alive; the heads of wheat were bent over her as if in sorrow. . . .

My mother ran to Vasyl. He was nearby, scything the wheat. She met him while he was on his way to her; he was as happy as could be. When he saw his Halya dead, he lifted the scythe so quickly that it was impossible to stop him, and in one fleeting second cut his throat with it. There, by her side, he fell to the ground.

VI

My mother ran to old Orlykha. She met my mother, standing in front of her gate, as if she was expecting her.

"Your daughter-in-law is dead!" said my mother.

Orlykha clenched her teeth and clutched at her sides.

"Such was her fate!" she said.

She did not shed a tear, just stood there, every bit as white as her kerchief.

My mother became frightened and did not know how to tell her about her son. At that very moment they were both being carried towards them.

"Here they are! Both of them!" my mother said.

"Why both of them?" she cried out.

"Granny, your Vasyl is also dead!"

How she rushed up to them! She almost knocked her dead son from the hands of those who carried him. She took his head in her hands, lamenting over him. How terrible she looked! There she was, without a kerchief on her head, her clothes in disarray and herself covered with blood, her dishevelled hair hanging down on her shoulders. She kept pacing distractedly about her dead son, wailing and acting as if the dear Lord had taken away her sanity.

The young couple were prepared for burial and placed one beside the other on a table. Some of the people who attended went home, others stayed overnight. They looked around and noticed that old Orlykha had disappeared just as if the ground had opened up and swallowed her! It was not until the next day that she was found dead in a ditch, as blue as an elderberry.

They buried the young couple together, and the old mother at a distance from them. The house they lived in was abandoned and fell apart; no one wanted to buy it, because, so the story went, whenever the moon rose, young Orlykha would appear and wander about the courtyard. On nights of deepest gloom she would sit facing the moon, with her white hands folded, lying in wait for her mother-in-law, and thus she would rebuke her: "You robbed me of my earthly life while I was still young, old Orlykha!"

FATHER ANDRIY

As it goes in the song, "Love conquers all!"
In our village there was a man, Petro Samiylenko, a distant relative of mine, a very good and honest man. He never offended a soul in his whole life. And what a happy man he was! Whenever people gathered at Petro's home on feast days, he would start the conversation by telling them funny stories, such as: how the Jew went off to war, or how a certain captain counted the stars, or stories about Poles. Petro despised Poles. He would never look a Pole straight in the eyes. Instead, he would wrinkle up his face, or else, he would keep coughing or sneezing.

Once the factor of our landlord's estate, who was a Pole, asked him: "What's wrong with you, Samiylenko?" And he replied: "Well, sir, that is my nature! If I see a noble like you, I immediately start to sneeze. Maybe, while I was still a young lad, some mean witch cast a spell on me."

If late in the evening in the village you should happen to see a group of people passing by roaring with laughter, do not ask them where they are coming from — they are coming from Samiylenko's.

Samiylenko had a good and hard-working wife. As for children — God gave them only one child, a daughter, Oksana, who, being the only child, grew up well cared for and very much loved. If her mother went to the garden or to the neighbors perhaps, Oksana would follow her like a rolling ball of yarn. Whenever her father had to go to the field, she liked to trot along behind him. And what a great chatterer she was! Frolicsome as a minnow, she was, yet a bright, obedient, little child.

II

Oksana's twelfth birthday arrived! Old Samiylenko passed away, may he dwell in the kingdom of God! His passing caused great grief to his wife. Even though they were prosperous and had a nice house and some cattle, with him gone, they became like orphans.

One day I went to visit them. The daughter was in the orchard and her mother was looking in a worried way over the property.

"My dearest!" she said to me, "great is my sorrow! It is as if the whole world has fallen apart! I am so sad and solitary. My sorrow is hard to bear!"

"It is God's will, my dear," I replied. "Tears don't mend misfortunes. Think about your daughter, she needs you."

Then she said:

"Just before Petro died, he told me that under an old cherry tree in the orchard he had buried some silver coins. 'Let the money,' he said, 'be for our Oksana. Do not dig up the coins, but, if you do, beware of the mean Poles; give the money to Father Andriy for safekeeping.'"

We went immediately to dig up the money. Just as Petro had told her, it was there — a tall pitcher full of silver rubles. We counted them and took them to Father Andriy.

III

Soon after that, my husband also passed away. I went to work in the city, where I became a servant for four years in a rich household. It was good for me there until the young master got married. He married a young, beautiful girl, but what a character she had! After the marriage she lost no time in changing things to her liking in the house. Nothing would please her! She might say to me: "You do not speak properly! That is an awful kerchief you have on! Change into a dress! What a get-up you are wearing!" And I wore in those days much the same clothing as I wear now — plakhta and zapaska.[1] The young bride did not miss anyone. In the morning she would start to discipline her old mother-in-law. "Where is your bonnet, mother?" she would say. "Why have you come out without it? Who ever saw such a thing? Without it you look like a peasant woman!" The old one would come to me, or take refuge in the orchard, and cry her eyes out!

I left them and went back to my own village.

When I saw Oksana now, I was dumbfounded. Before me stood a tall, shapely girl. She was so beautiful with her long braids reaching to her waist, so friendly, courteous and affable!

And the boys! They went wild over her! Even though she was still very young, many suitors had set their minds on marrying her. All of them were good, rich people! She did not want to marry yet.

She fell in love with a certain young fellow, not a landlord's man, Tymish Kryazh. He was in love with her too. Wherever the one went, the other followed. At merrymakings, on the street — they were always together, like two love doves. They were waiting to get married in the autumn. The periwinkle for the bridal wreath was ready; the ceremonial towels were prepared. How happy and gay they were! How wonderful it was to see such love; the sight of it made folk like me feel young again.

---

[1] zapaska — parts of the Ukrainian traditional garb (wrap-around skirts).

IV

However, like a bolt out of the blue misfortune fell upon them. The factor noticed our Oksana and was soon hankering after her. He waylaid the poor girl at every turn, attempting to allure her! Then he gave orders to have her brought to his place.

A dark cloud seemed to overshadow the village and a great stir arose among the folk. The whole community assembled in deep gloom and sorrow. Women shouted and wept, and Oksana's mother walked as if bereft of life. The people took counsel together all that morning and decided to free Oksana from the Pole that very evening.

Tymish gathered the young men. "My brothers, my good friends!" he pleaded. "Help me!" That evening they all laid ambush to the landlord's buildings, hiding behind a nearby mound. When it got darker they crept up under the windows and looked in. There they saw Oksana standing with her hands hanging down in despair, her face as pale as a white kerchief, and the factor, with his hands on his hips, laughing and trying to get her to give in to him. Then he pulled her by the hand. She grabbed a small table standing nearby and raised it over his head. She gave him a long, sad look. So sadly did she look at him that the hearts of the boys outside froze.

The factor shouted for a while and walked out, locking Oksana in again. Our boys stormed in like wildfire causing the glass in the windows to rattle. They forced their way into the room, grabbed Oksana, and took off for Father Andriy's place.

V

I was a servant then with Father Andriy, who was a widower. He was a very, very old man with a long beard as white as milk. When the boys burst in with Oksana he was sitting in his room reading the Holy Book by the light of a candle. He got up and said: "Good Lord! Merciful God! Where is Your justice? My dear children," he said to Oksana and Tymish, "I will marry you; go to the church!"

He took them to the church and married them immediately. He blessed them and told them to have no fear. "I hold myself responsible," he said.

After the marriage ceremony, young boys, in typically carefree way, gathered together musicians from somewhere and led the newlyweds about the village cheering and singing, having a jolly time. They danced all night, without leaving the married couple's side. They guarded them like an army. In the morning they led them to Tymish's father's place, and went to work for the landlord as if nothing had happened.

VI

Immediately after Oksana had been rescued by the boys, the factor went into a rage. He was yelling and hitting out all over the place. He was afraid, however, to pass beyond his courtyard gate. He even ordered the gate to be barred and bolted and posted a guard to keep watch.

When he found out that Oksana had already married, he chased his servants for their lives and in his mounting rage tore out one side of his moustache. He handed out abuse right and left to the serfs and ran to Father Andriy like a wild animal run loose. He knocked and kicked and hammered on the door, pretending to be brave.

Father Andriy came out to him. The factor kept on shouting.

Father Andriy lifted his hand and said:

"Violence is not proper in my house. I am an old man and serve the Lord. Calm down!"

The factor calmed down immediately.

"You wanted to ruin a poor girl. Did you never have a mother or a sister of your own? Come to your senses! God prevented that great sin from being committed, and now you are rushing in to harm an old man! Woe betide you! Do not harm the poor! I will not allow this as long as I live. I will have the law on you! Go and God be with you!"

The factor left in disgrace, as if he had been tarred and feathered. Ever since then he has avoided Father Andriy's dwelling.

MAKSYM HRYMACH

This happened long ago at the time when Poland and Moscow were ruling our Ukraine. Moscow ruled Ukraine on this side of the River Dnipro. Although there were toll-houses, they were few and far between. The guards did not keep such close watch as they do today along the River Zbruch or elsewhere. Because of that many things were smuggled in duty-free along the Dnipro: silks, velvet, gold brocade, costly oils, and other valuable items such as real gold and silver by the barrel load.

As it happened, Maksym Hrymach had his homestead near Cherkasy just below Domontov close to the Dnipro. For a long time he had been taking part in these smuggling activities. What a rich man he was, going about dressed in silk and velvet! He was handsome too: full-faced, dark-browed, and black-moustached. He was always happy and jocular. People liked him very much! When he went out on Sundays they would gather round him to talk.

"Well, brother Maksym," someone would say, "you are dressed like a lord!"

"Yes, brother, I am. Dress yourselves, too, good people. Lords live well, the hangman does not get them! I am done with sticking out my neck for you! Enough! I will eat and drink and dress well — exactly as befits a real magnate."

But this is the way he really was: he would help anyone from our village who needed assistance or was in trouble, even at the risk of losing his own life. Any stranger bothering someone from the village would be courting disaster; Maksym would descend on him like a tornado, demolishing him completely. Once a certain Polish nobleman took a Kozak's land, so Maksym burnt his house, scattered the ashes, and set him packing over the Dnipro. If that fellow is still alive he will remember what kinds of wire whips were made on Master Maksym Hrymach's homestead.

Maksym was a widower with two daughters. One, named Katrya, already a grown girl, gorgeously beautiful, like a princess; the other — Tetyana — who was still in her teens, was petite and lively. She flitted about in the courtyard or in the house like a bumblebee. They lived with their father in luxury.

At midnight, smugglers would sail down the Dnipro and dock under the old willow tree. Maksym would take them to his house and receive the goods he needed. I have forgotten the name of the man who was sending all the merchandise by boat to Maksym. Apart from a few loyal Kozaks, though, I was the only one who knew that he lived somewhere in a rock-cave in the hills near the Dnipro.

II

A young Kozak named Semen, handsome, slender as a reed and brave as a falcon, came most often to Maksym's homestead and our proud Katrya fell in love with him.

Rich people from good families were seeking to marry her — not one, not two, or three, but many! Her answer was always: "I am not interested. I will not marry them."

"Listen daughter," said Maksym, "you are too haughty, my darling! The best people in the village are trying to marry you; the boys are all young and handsome! Why do you reject them?"

"It does not matter to me if they are young and handsome. My heart is not drawn to them."

"To whom, then, is your heart drawn, my little daughter? Listen here, my child, I am not going to force you on someone you don't love, but neither will I let you marry some landless vagabond, even if he were to snatch the moon out of the sky for you. I will not give my consent! It will be as I say. I never go back on my word, and you know it."

"I do know that, father. So what sort of son-in-law would you like to have?"

"A free Kozak, daughter, so that he would be his own master and no man's slave. That is the sort of son-in-law I would like to have!"

"And what if he will be his own master?" she asked.

"Then you have my blessing, and the blessing of God."

"Well, then I will wait."

"Wait then, my sweetheart, I will not stand in your way. I think I have already guessed what's in the wind. Right? Who is he?"

"Why do you have to know who he is, father? First, let him gain his freedom, then you will know."

"Very well, my dear child, so be it!"

When Semen heard this he said:

"What should we do, Katrya my love? We must wait! This is my third and last year with my master. If the luck holds out — this year a rich booty can be expected. My headman will not let me down. He is an honorable fellow. I will thank him for his bread and salt, and then I shall find a nice little homestead for us. That done, I will ask your father for permission to marry you — only love me truly, my sweetheart!"

So our young doves wait. Now Semen sails with the speed of lightning along the Dnipro; his boat barely breaks the surface of the blue water.

Once again the Kozaks were setting out for more booty, and Semen along with them.

"My falcon, my Kozak!" said Katrya, clinging to him. "When will you return? Soon?"

"Soon, my little darling, soon! When the first cherry tree blossoms in your orchard, and the gray cuckoo begins to call — I will sail back to you. I will return, Katrya, not as a bondman, but as a free Kozak!"

The Kozaks left in the autumn; they said to expect them in the spring.

III

There sits our Katrya in the parlor, embroidering sleeves and towels with silk thread, and looking constantly out of the window to see if a blizzard is raging, if the snow has started to melt yet, and how soon the spring winds will blow.

The ice broke and drifted away at last. The Dnipro roared on its way, now gray, now black, lashing against its shores. The willows burst forth and the rushes became green. Our Katrya is happy; she walks about, just gazing at it all.

The cherries began to blossom, the gray cuckoo gave voice. It was beautiful in the orchard! The periwinkle spread out and blossomed with blue flowers, the sweet pea sent out its tendrils; the star flower was reddening, the poppies — gray, red and white — were in full bloom. A carpet of blue duckweed covered the ground, green rue was dotted about. Among these flowers walked Katrya, herself the fairest flower of all! She kept her bright eyes fixed on the blue Dnipro. As soon as the moon appeared and shed its rays over the dark water, Katrya would wait under the old willow on the shore, watching anxiously for the skiff, to see whether her loving Kozak might be at the oars.

Week after week passed. One night she sat waiting beneath the willow tree. The night was still and full of stars; only the notes of a nightingale and the Dnipro's roar broke the silence. Suddenly in the distance something flashed, like a gray seagull. . . . It came closer, and still closer. It was a boat! It flew as though on the wings of the wind. She stretched out her arms toward it. What Kozak was that steering the boat? It was not Semen. Next thing, a boatman was right by the shore. He leaned on his oar and whistled once or twice. Her father came out and met him. Behind the willow, Katrya strained to hear. Old Hrymach asked the boatman:

"What news?"

"Disaster, Master Maksym," the Kozak said. "Disaster!"

"What is the matter?"

"The day before yesterday, just before the storm, in the middle of the night, a poplar tree was set on fire (the Kozaks, to bring news of their return from a smuggling exploit, usually set fire on the Dnipro shore to a poplar or some other kind of tree); on catching sight of the fire we set out to meet them yesterday. No one turned up. There was only the Dnipro with smashed boats borne on its waves."

"Was it a big storm?"

"I have never seen the like of it in my life. Huge oaks were torn up by the roots; the reeds were levelled by the rain as by a sword; the Dnipro threw sand up from its bottom. The night was very dark; all that could be seen was the flashing of the lightning. When the thunder roared it seemed to shake the hills round the Dnipro."

"And no message?"

"No message, Master Maksym. We have all come to the conclusion that the Dnipro has swallowed our boys up."

"They were lively boys, brother! Oh, lively boys they were! Well, let us go into the house."

"Father, my betrothed Kozak is free at last! You got yourself a free man for a son-in-law!"

The old man gave a quick look. There was his Katrya, so very pale, standing silhouetted against the moonlight.

"God be with you, my daughter!' he exclaimed, catching one of her cold hands.

She looked into his eyes, drew her hand away, and departed without saying a word.

IV

He took the Kozak into the house, treated him hospitably, sent him on his way and went back to his daughter.

She was sitting in the orchard braiding a wreath of red and white poppies and intertwining it with periwinkle. The sun was already rising above the slopes of the Dnipro.

"Katrya, my child!" said the old man, taking his seat beside her, "God has given you a heavy load to bear. Raise your head, my daughter, and look at your old father!"

She raised her head and looked at him.

"Oh, my daughter, how old you have suddenly become!"

"No, father, I am still young." Once again she busied herself with her wreath, and sighed.

How he cheered her up, how he pleaded with her! But she just kept on braiding her wreath without saying a word to him.

The old man went and called the younger daughter:

"Tetyanka, my little darling, go to your sister! She is in deep sorrow — try to cheer her up."

"What is the matter? Where is she?"

She came running into the orchard:

"My sister Katrusya! Heart of mine! Why are you so sad? Summer is already here!" She threw her little arms about her.

"My dear little sister! My foolish little chatterer!" said Katrya, her heart going out to her.

"Oh, what a lovely wreath you have there, sister! How very beautiful! Dearest sister, when will you wear it?"

"I will wear it tonight."

She hung the wreath over the water and strolled about the orchard holding her little sister by the hand; the little one kept on chattering.

Their father called them to supper. Katrya came and sat at the end of the table. With her white hands she poured mead for her father and joined in the conversation; she avoided every attempt he made to lead up to talking about her.

In the evening she went to her father and kissed his hand. The old man clasped her head in his hands:

"Katrya, my unfortunate daughter, may the Mother of God have mercy on you!"

She went to her little sister and held her to her heart, then went out again to the orchard. How prettily she was dressed! She had on a thin blouse with a silk plakhta, a silver-embroidered belt, and high-heeled shoes. Her fair hair was done up in fine braids and a gold ring shone on her right hand.

She came to the edge of the river and took the wreath she had made in the morning: "You did not wither, my poppy wreath!" she said, and placed it on her head. The willow tree on the river bank had sent its branches away out over the water. She sat down at the foot of the willow and bowed her head on her white hand, completely lost in thought. There, under the curly willow, the moonlight shone on her, beautiful and sad, with the poppy wreath on her head.

When the moon sparkled on the water, she said: "The bright moon has risen!" (It was always when the moon rose that Semen came sailing to her). She stepped her way along one of the branches of the willow tree. She stepped on it as on a shaky gangplank, looked in all directions, and threw herself into the river's depths.

V

In the morning there was the sound of panic in the household. Tetyanka was crying, old Hrymach was walking around without his cap and with his clothes in disarray, asking constantly:

"Where is my Katrya? Where is my loving child?"

They rushed to the water — only the poppy wreath floated and whirled about.

Old Hrymach shut himself off from the world. For five whole years he did not pass beyond his gate. He was done with the smugglers' headman and with profiteering. He became old and gray like a pigeon.

God granted him strength to see his second daughter grown to girlhood. She was tall, dark-browed, and shapely. She made a good match — a handsome young Kozak lieutenant from a good family. They put on a flashy wedding. From her house to the church the road was laid with red carpet and the guests drank from silver goblets. Many came to the wedding! There were people in the house, and outside, at the gates, they filled the entire street. The feasting went on all week.

After the wedding the father blessed the newlyweds and saw them off to their homestead.

It grew lonely for Maksym in the house all by himself. He looked then at the Dnipro — remembered his older daughter, and the tears rolled down his gray moustache.

"Katrya! Katrya! My beloved daughter! I ruined your young life!"

DANYLO HOURCH

The Kozak village of Hlybove was located by the Dnipro shore, surrounded by steep hills. The road to the village wound through a thick forest with only the open sky visible overhead. The forest full of fragrant mists and the sound of muffled noises in the distance, were all the company the traveler had. The feel of a fresh moist breath of wind, the first glimpse of the blue glittering of old Dnipro among the green reeds, the red osiers and the steep gray hills would announce that the village, with its white houses and flourishing gardens, was at hand. The ancient church with its high steeple, its brick wall overgrown with moss, and its grass-grown cobbled cemetery, would be next to come to view.

Just behind the church there used to stand a fine house, with an orchard and a lovely garden. At one time Okhrim Polishchuk lived there with his wife whom he brought from somewhere far away. She was a dark-browed beauty, majestical, and proud! She would walk about with her eyes cast to the ground, never once looking up, pretty as a picture. Heavens! How elegant she was!

At first they were very rich. Ivha on all occasions used to dress herself in the best — necklaces, head-coverings, and the like. They had so much wealth that it was impossible to tell how much there was of it. But they did not live long in luxury. Okhrim was such a good man that, whenever he saw anyone in trouble, he would give a helping hand, in spite of the cost to himself. He lent his money right and left. In addition to that he liked to live in style! Before he quite realized it, his wealth was exhausted. The riches disappeared from his courtyard and his chests, once full of goods, became empty.

Ivha grieved so deeply about it that her beauty faded and she aged rapidly. She went about downcast, and even her only child could not cheer her up. What a lovely little daughter she had! "You have been born, my child, into grief and misfortune!" she would say. "You will waste your life in poverty, my daughter, and take your poverty with you to your grave." She would grieve like this, and the child, not understanding, would look lovingly and happily into her mother's eyes, clapping her little hands.

II

Time does not stand still. A good many years went by and although Ivha got somewhat used to her poverty, she was never the same again! Her girl Natalya was coming on, like a poppy in full bloom, fresh as the woodland berry, and blythe as a singing bird! What an honest and earnest soul she was! No one ever hard her speak an ill word of anyone. It was just not in her nature to quarrel like other people! At evenings-out, at dances, or at home, she was a darling — cheerful and friendly to everyone.

Mykhailo Bruy was seeking Natalya's hand in marriage. He was a fine young man and of good family. It was evident to everyone that he loved her dearly. People admired them when they were seen together at a wedding or a dance. They were both so young and good-looking, like flowers at the height of their beauty. "Such a good match! It would be splendid if the good Lord united them!" the village-folk would say.

Mykhailo sent the matchmakers. Girls were already getting ready to be bridesmaids and wondered what Natalya's wedding would be like. Just then the matchmakers were turned down. Natalya's parents refused to give their consent to the marriage! The father was not so much against it, but the mother would not hear of it — the young man was poor. Mykhailo was overcome with grief and Natalya cried her eyes out, but nothing could be done about it! The young people parted, and Mykhailo became a chumak. His idea was to work, earn some money, and marry Natalya some day, no matter what.

III

In the meantime, while Mykhailo was on the road, there came another suitor, a rich man — Danylo Hourch by name. He was of the Kozak breed, and lived like a lord on independent means. He owned a farmstead, pasturelands, and wheatfields. For all that, he never wore anything else than a gray sheepskin cap and peasant clothing. Once tradesmen, who came to make certain purchases from him, said:

"Brother Danylo! You would be a far more presentable person in every way if you were to throw out those peasant rags of yours and wear the caftan as we do, instead."

"You will wait a long time before that happens, you impertinent scoundrels!" he shouted at them. "Ridicule my clothes, and you can get out of my courtyard!"

The poor souls were glad to get clear of him.

God preserve us, what a temperamental type he was! When he got angry, his eyes would flash fire and his face would become as white as chalk. Still, what a handsome man he was, with his high hetman forehead and his expressive brows! His bright hazel eyes shone like stars, and his smile, which was at once tender, proud and sad, made one's heart flutter.

He had been an orphan from childhood. His mother died young and his father was killed in the war. The old people used to relate that he also had a sister, a pretty girl by the name of Katrya, who happened to fall in love with a Pole, without Danylo knowing anything about it. The elderly woman, who lived with them, and brought both of them up, was the only one who knew of the affair. No matter how she warned Katrya against the Pole, she refused to listen, and, when the brother was not at home, she eloped with her lover to Poland.

On his return, he asked the old woman:

"Where is my sister? Why doesn't she come to greet me?"

He loved his sister as if she had been his own child. His thoughts were always centered on how to cheer and comfort her.

In answer to his questions the old woman said tearfully:

"There is no one but me to greet you now, my dear boy!"

"What is going on? What has happened? Where is my sister?"

The old one reported to him now, ignoring her pleas and warnings, Katrya had fallen in love with a Pole.

"Yesterday," said the old woman, "a horseman arrived in the evening. She went out to him and I ran out after her. As you can realize, she, being younger, kept ahead of me. He caught her in his arms and rode away with her. That was the last I saw of her!"

"Is this not the Pole who lived on Maksymchyn's farmstead?"

"The very same, my dear! No matter where we went, he would always be turning up."

Danylo made no response. His face was as white as a sheet. He gazed at the ground, deep in thought.

"Goodbye, old one!" he said eventually.

"Where are you off to, my eagle, leaving me here all alone in grief and sorrow? Will you be back soon?"

"I will be," he replied.

He leaped on his horse and sped away. He was gone for about two months. With tears of longing the old one awaited his return. "I brought them up, I cared for them, and now they have both left me!" she would say in tears. Then one evening she heard someone in the courtyard. The old woman ran out, and there was Danylo fastening his horse.

"Oh, my son! My blossom! Where have you been all this time? Have you heard anything of your sister? Where is she, my little bird? Whatever has become of her?"

His lips were sealed.

She accompanied him into the house, and the look on his face frightened her. What a change had come over him!

"Danylo, my dearest! How morose you have become! Have you, perhaps, been ill, or are you tired out from your journey?"

"I am tired," he said. "I want to rest."

He was so downcast and unhappy.

The old woman hovered about him for a while, but he remained silent, and she let him be.

So, the two of them went on living their lives. Danylo never again mentioned his sister; it was as if she had never existed. The old woman missed her greatly. One day she said, sighing heavily:

"Where is my beloved Katrya now? If only I could see her, the dear, dear child! What kind of life does she have in a foreign land?"

Danylo acted as if he had not even heard her.

"My dearest Danylo! Surely you are not turning your back upon your sister? Is it possible that you feel so little for the poor girl that you never mention her name? Whenever I speak of her you always leave the room. How many times have I begged you to find out where she is. That Pole may have left her and perhaps the poor soul is now wandering about, afraid to come back home. Are you going to leave a member of your own family in disgrace?"

"Do not worry, old woman, your Katrya will not be disgraced!"

"Where is she? Where is she? Have you seen her?"

"Pray for the peace of her soul!"

"My God! You have done away with your sister, haven't you? O my poor, unfortunate Katrusya! Your life is spent like a poppy blossom! Danylo, you have a great sin to answer for!"

"Come now, granny," he said, "stop crying; it will not do any good!"

"And where is the man she went off with?"

"Ask the black raven that scatters his bones."

IV

Such was Danylo Hourch, the suitor, who now came seeking Natalya's hand in marriage. Ivha, however, thought of nothing else but of having a rich man for a son-in-law.

As for Natalya, it was as if the poor girl had been struck by lightning. The news unbalanced her completely.

"Mother," she wept, "don't ruin my life, don't drown me by giving me to Hourch. I would rather be dead than married to him!"

Ivha did not listen to her daughter's plea and forced her into marriage. The wedding took place and the couple were given a send-off to their home. The old one greeted Natalya with the customary bread and salt.

"My young mistress! May the Lord bless you with good fortune and health! May you be as healthy as water, rich as the earth, and as beautiful as a rose! You will bring cheer to this house and make old me feel younger!" said the old woman, between laughter and tears, to the young bride.

Danylo became quite a different person when he got married. His black brows were no longer drawn together and a pleasant smile was on his lips. He came to love his young wife dearly. She, however, was timorous, like a little bird chased out of its nest. He would talk to her — she would not raise her eyes to him. He would take her by the hand — she would grow pale and the hand he held would shake.

They had lived in this way together for half a year and the young wife had still not got used to her surroundings. Once more Danylo's black brows were knit into a frown and he often looked at his young wife with a fixed, angry stare.

The old woman passed away and the house became gloomier than ever. While the old one was alive, she would strike up a conversation, or ask questions, or crack a joke — she loved Natalya very much. But now the young couple would sit all day without saying a word. While Natalya busied herself he would lean his curly head on his arm, watching her all the time, and staring at her so intently and so coldly that it sent a chill through her heart.

One day, she asked if she could go to visit her mother because she had not seen her for a long time. Danylo said nothing. She raised her head and glanced at him. He was so very pale. There was a strange brightness in his eyes; they seemed to burn through her. She started back in fear. He smiled.

"Have the chumaks got back, then?" he said stiffly. His voice sounded as if not his own.

Natalya could barely keep her balance. She wanted to say something but could not utter a word. He rose and left the house.

V

The chumaks had indeed returned and Mykhailo along with them. Natalya, however, neither knew nor heard anything about it. God only knows where and how Danylo discovered that she had once been in love with Mykhailo.

From that time on he watched Natalya carefully so that she could not take a step out of the house. Whenever she was working in the garden or making an effort to cheer herself up by singing softly, or doing something indoors, he would appear upon the scene and keep staring at her. It frightened and saddened her.

One day he was getting ready to go to town. Natalya saw him off. She stood before him pale and sad, and even he shuddered to see her like that. He embraced her with earnest affection.

"You are my heartache, Natalya! You do not love me! I have ruined both of us!"

She wanted to say something, but only wept. Danylo leaped on to his horse and rode off, never once looking back.

Left alone, Natalya completed her usual chores and went out into the woods. It was quiet and deserted there with the road running through it. The leaves rustled, the birds chirped, flitting to and fro, and in the grass, the lizards scurried about. Everything was so green and fresh and fragrant! New shoots had sprouted from the stump of a linden tree; a birch reared its lofty head; an aspen fluttered its delicate leaves. From behind a dark oak peeped a branch of the guelder-rose, its clusters of red berries glowing like fire. The prickly wild rose was showing its tiny leaves and fragrant blossoms; the conifers looked straight as arrows, and the mountain ash, laden with red-gold berries, spread its green canopy. All sorts of herbs and flowers grew round about — clusters of ferns, fragrant bindweed near a decaying stump — such a variety of reds and blues was there, that it dazzled one's very eyes! The warm rays of the sun poured down piercing through the coolness of the dark thicket.

Natalya looked around; grief got the better of her. "Oh, the bright and beautiful world!" she exclaimed, like a refrain, "and what a miserable fate is mine!"

She leaned her head on her white hand, and wept, remembering how it had been before she got married. How merry and carefree it was then! She remembered bright-eyed Mykhailo. How tender and affectionate he was.

"At least I will go and visit my mother," she thought. "Danylo will be back tomorrow — he will not know. It may be the last chance I have to see her and say goodbye. I will see my village and walk along the street. If I am late getting back my mother will see me home."

VI

She started to run along the road. The darkness was descending and the dew was already on the grass. Natalya never stopped running — her heart pounded so furiously that it felt as if it would take leave of her. The moon rose. The night was warm and still. There, ahead of her, was the Dnipro with is blue waves, the boats dotted along the shore, and the ferry. It would take less than an hour to cover the distance — it was not far now.

Just then there fell on Natalya's ear the sound of someone hurrying after her. She looked back — there was Danylo hard upon her heels. He was gaining on her every minute. Panic-stricken, Natalya threw herself into the water and struck out strongly.

Danylo came running up. "You will not get away! You will not!" he shouted. He launched a boat into the water and went after her; there were not oars — he rowed with his sharp sword. The boat fairly flew but still could not overtake her. She was by this time well ahead! The rapids carried her red kerchief away; her long braids streamed free on the water. Danylo caught her by her silken hair — a quick swing of his sword, and warm, red blood coloured the gray waves of the Dnipro.

So Danylo did away with his wife. He also met his end — either by his own hand, or by an act of God. They were both found by fishermen in the morning. She looked tired and sad; he looked demented and enraged. His strong hand held her long braids in eternal grasp. Thus, joined together, they were found.

Think what a man of such strength of character might have achieved! He was genuinely honest and sincere — never intended offending anyone — yet he ruined his own life.

INSTYTUTKA[1]
Dedicated To T. H. Shevchenko

People marvel at my being always happy. They seem to think that I have known neither sorrow nor misfortune. But I have been like this all my life, born, as one might say, with a good disposition. There were times when I was beaten (it would be better not to mention it at all) and could not keep from crying, so I cried, but only for a moment — after reconsidering a bit, I would laugh and become happy once again. There is no joy without alloy! So it was with me. If I had cried at every misfortune that befell me, I would have cried my eyes out by now. I never knew my father or mother and grew up an orphan in strange surroundings, among strangers. Even though there was no hard work for me to do, I being still a child, many a time no one ever cared whether I was hungry or cold, whether I was alive or dead.

When I reached the age of ten, I was taken into the manorhouse. The lady of the manor was, you might say, sedate — actually she was enfeebled by old age. She could scarcely drag her feet after her and spoke in such a whisper that at first one couldn't make her out. And as for whippings! That was not to be thought of! She spent her entire day on the porch, and at night would sigh and moan. In her youth, they say, she, too, was not without her whims, but there is a season for everything and one has to give up sometime.

During the period of my stay there, however, all was peaceful; the only unfortunate thing was that no one was allowed to venture outside the house, except perhaps on a big feast-day when we begged leave to go to church — but on Sundays, never! "You will slack," the old one would say angrily. "I won't let you go! There will be time enough for you to worship God — you are still a long way from death's door."

Day after day we sat toiling in the girls' quarters. And it was as quiet round about as if a spell had been cast over everything. All you could

---
[1] a graduate of the college for daughters of the nobility.

hear was the lady moaning, or one girl whispering something to another, or an occasional sigh of boredom. It was tedious work — so tedious, it tortured you. And what could one do about it? One had to be grateful that at least we didn't get whipped ten times a day as others had been, so we heard!

Sometimes we would get jolly for no reason at all. We would be oh, so overwhelmed with joy. Our hearts would go pit-pat! If we had been free, we would have sung then so, as to let our song resound through all the village. But we didn't dare! At such times just looking at each other made us laugh. First, one would give a wink, then another would follow suit; another would be tied to the footstool by her braids; still another would jump up and begin to dance a little jig, turning, whirling, in such a way that the old lady would not hear. The things we wouldn't do!

The old lady did not have any relatives, except a granddaughter in Kyiv, who was studying in a — let's see if I can pronounce it — in-sti-tute of some sort. She often sent letters to the old one, and the old one used to read them every day, crying and laughing over them. Finally the granddaughter wrote, asking to come and take her home. Mother of God! The whole household was in a turmoil — painting, washing, cleaning up! We were expecting the young lady! The young lady would be arriving soon!

The old lady seemed to have pepped up. She traipsed from room to room, looking out along the road from every window and sending us to the outskirts of the village to see if the young lady was on her way. That was just what we needed. It could be said that during the week we awaited her arrival, we really had the time of our lives. They sent us out and we ran like the wind. It was good to see the steppe and the lovely fields! The green steppe seemed to recede before our eyes into the very horizon. It was lovely to breathe in freedom!

We would pick flowers and make wreaths, adorning ourselves with them like brides, and would show off with them until we reached the manor house; only on entering would we take them off and throw them away. How sorry we were to throw those wreaths away!

II

At long last the young lady arrived. What a pretty face she had! Where did she get those good looks from? No artist, it seemed, could have depicted such a beauty! When the old one finally got her arms around her granddaughter, she could not let go of her: she kissed, caressed, and admired her, escorting her round the house, showing and explaining everything. The young lady just kept turning from side to side, surveying everything with a curious eye.

The old one set her down at the table, coaxing her: "Perhaps you would like this to eat? Or perhaps that to drink?" Having had all kinds of food and drink brought to the table, she herself sat down and fixed her admiring gaze on her granddaughter. The young lady for her part pecked at her food, like a sparrow, making a clean, quick job of it. We were peeping from behind the door at them and listening to what the young lady had to say that might throw light on her thoughts, her character, and her habits.

"How did it go, dearest, living alone?" asked the old one. "You are not telling me anything."

"Oh, dearest grandma! What is there to tell? It was so boring!"

"Did they teach you much? What did they teach you, my dearest?"

"Oh, that's what you want to know! It was fine for you, grandma, living here in freedom; and what I went through in that course of study! Do not remind me of it, ever!"

"My darling! It is understandable — you were among strangers. They insulted and offended you. But why did you not write me about this immediately?"

"How could I, granny? How could I do that? They would have found out about it instantly."

"My poor darling! Tell me all about what they did to you there?"

"Oh, granny! They tired us out and aggravated us with all sorts of stupid things. Learn this, that, and the other. Stuff it, stuff it into your heads! Why should I know how the stars wander about the heavens, or how people live across the seas, or whether they like it there or not? All I need to know is how to put on my best face in other people's company."

"But, my treasure, there must be a reason for people studying! Even our local young ladies, though they are poor, squeak in French."

"Oh, granny!" prattled the young lady, "I also applied myself to the French language and to music and dancing as well. What is necessary is necessary. They're things everyone pays attention to and praises; as for the rest — it is just a perfect nuisance! Learn and forget! It is boring for those who teach, and misery for those who study. A lot of time wasted for nothing!"

"How can this be? Was it poor teaching?"

"I am telling you, it was boring, a waste of effort, and unprofitable. All they thought of was how to get their fees, and all we thought of was how quickly we could get out of there. Come, come, now grandma, what are you thinking about?"

"That is precisely what I am thinking about, dearest — they took good money from you, and taught you badly. What is going to happen when you have forgotten it all?"

"Bless you, granny! How could I forget? When one is among guests or at a party, how can one possibly forget music, dancing, or even French? But where that overseas trash is concerned. . . . Well — it went in one ear and out the other. In fact, I really don't know anything about it. Away with it!"

"But what would happen if someone asked you how those stars move about the heavens or the like? People right away would react critically: 'She has studied but doesn't know anything!'"

"What is all this granny? I have admitted this only to you. As for other people, they will never suspect, even if they kept on questioning me all day long. I can wriggle my way out of anything and I can certainly outsmart them — and that's how it is, granny! Would you like me to sing for you? Listen then."

And at that she burst into song; her voice had a beautiful silvery tone.

The old one started kissing her: "My sweet! Joy of my heart!" And the young lady fawned on her:

"Buy me nice clothes, granny, the ones in the latest fashion!"

"My child, do not worry about that. You will have everything. You will be queen among noble young ladies!"

We servants exchanged glances: some training our young lady had received! What she had learned best, it seemed, was how to fool people!

III

"Let us go, dearest," said the old lady. "I would like you to pick out a servant-girl for yourself."

And she brought her to us. We ran from the door into a corner and huddled together.

"This is your young mistress," the old one said to us. "Kiss her hand!"

Without giving us as much as a glance, the young lady held out two fingers to be kissed.

The old one pointed all of us out to her: "This is Hanna, this is Varka, and this is Domakha. . . ."

"Heaven help us!" the young lady cried with a clap of her hands. "Is there any of you who knows how to braid my hair and dress me?"

She stood with her arms folded, looking at us.

"Of course they know how to, dearest," said the old one, "and if they don't, we will teach them."

"What is your name?" the young lady asked me, and without waiting for my reply, turned to the old lady and said: "This one will be mine!"

"Very well then, let this be the one. Any one you want, dear! See that you are a good servant, Ustyna — the young mistress will be good to you."

"Enough of that, granny! Let us go!" the young lady broke in, making a wry face. She leaned to one side, shutting her eyes and itching to be off — just like a cat when someone puffs smoke into his whiskers.

"We have to teach her common sense, my dearest," the old one said. "They are all empty-headed. I will teach her one thing, you will teach her another, and this way we will turn her into a human being."

"What a pity, granny, that they have not been taught already! You should have sent one of them to the city; it would have saved us trouble now."

And they prattled on as if they had been talking about horses or some such thing.

"Oh, Ustyna!" said the girls, concernedly, "how is it going to be for you, working for her, and her so unfriendly?"

"Oh well, girls," I said, "what's meant for you won't miss you! There is no escape from one's fate. We shall see how it will be."

And that set me thinking.

IV

In the evening, they called me: "Go to the young mistress — help her to get undressed."

I entered her room. She was standing before the mirror, already tearing off everything she had on.

"Where have you been running off to? Hurry up and undress me! I want to get to sleep!"

As I was undressing her, she kept shouting at me:

"Faster, faster!"

She threw herself on the bed:

"Take off my shoes! Do you know how to set hair?" she asked.

"No, I don't."

"Good Lord! Good grief! How stupid she is. Get out!"

The girls were already waiting for me.

"How did it go, Ustyna? What happened? What is she like, dear?"

What could I tell them?

"I am stupid, girls," I said, "because I don't know how to set hair!"

V

The next day our young lady got up quite early. She washed, dressed, and inspected all the buildings, all the grounds, and even the orchard. She was so happy.

"I am home!" she said, "I am home! I am free to do anything I want!"

And she kissed the old lady and asked over and over again:

"How soon do we go visiting, granny? When are we going to have guests?"

"Well, let me enjoy you for a start, dearest. First let me see all I can of you!"

"But how long must I wait, granny? I thought that when I came home it would be very jolly for me, lots of people, music, dancing. Granny, my dearest, my loveliest, do tell me!"

"Very well, my little bird! Let us make some preparations and then invite the guests."

The preparations began. The old one rolled the trunks containing velvet and other delicate materials out of storage and took the young lady's measurements. The young one was jumping for joy, becoming flushed and happy with excitement. She hopped from mirror to mirror looking at herself; got a glass of water and, while holding it, admired her beauty; did up and undid her hair, or tied it with ribbons or adorned herself with flowers.

"Oh, dear grandma," she would say, "when will I wear the satin dress?"

"When you are betrothed, my child," replied the old one. "I will give you away to a prince or to a count, to the richest man on earth!"

And the young lady would give herself airs and acts as if she were already a real princess.

They did nothing but chatter endlessly about princes and men of nobility. They would talk of weddings, with black horses saddled and bridled, and build all sorts of castles in the air. They would ramble on in this fashion until the young lady sighed:

"But granny! It is all talk. We have not yet had anyone to visit us!"

"Just wait a little, they will be here — so many that there won't be room enough for them."

VI

Guests indeed did come. One group would be leaving just as another was arriving. We servants got neither sleep nor rest. From morning till night we were kept busy with running and serving. Sometimes such a crowd would come, that we wondered at so much variety! All that mob would be roaring with laughter, dancing, eating, drinking, all of them bearing the marks of luxury, and all of them so coddled! Some of the ladies could hardly squeeze through the door — and, as for young men — so many of them came! They swarmed about our young mistress, buzzing like bumblebees. She moved among them all with a word here, a lift of her eyebrows there, inquiring about this one's health, or lamenting to another about her being lonely without him; still another she would place beside her as if he had been one of the family. The poor souls got all worked up and made complete fools of themselves. Day after day they came, each trying to go one better than the next, staring coldly at each other. Did she really appeal that much to them, or did they simply have nowhere else to go to amuse themselves — who knows? They settled on us like insects. You see, how else can the idle rich spend their time except in dining sumptuously, drinking their fill, and showing off their finery! What else is left for them to do?

VII

Little by little the young mistress had the household just as she wanted it.

"Please stop weaving, grandmother! Is there no one to do that for you? Whenever anybody comes visiting, you always have a piece of knitting in your hands, as if you were a servant."

"But it is boring without work, child," replied the old one.

"Get hold of a book and read it."

"What can I read? I can't see to read."

"Well, then, take a stroll; only, dearest grandmother, stop knitting! I would rather have my eyes plucked out with that needle, than see you using it!"

"All right, all right, calm down!"

The old one gave up her weaving and got bored. The young mistress dressed her up in a bonnet adorned with polka dot ribbons and placed her in a chair in the middle of the room. Should guests arrive, she would be ready to receive them.

The old one was bored stiff, but the young one was delighted:

"How grand it all is, grandma! What pomp and splendor in our home!"

VIII

She put all us girls to embroidering, teaching us herself, and making sure that we kept at it. When we had time off for lunch, she frowned and scolded. She got progressively more cross, now swearing at us, stealthily pinching or pushing us and becoming, in consequence, red in the face with embarrassment. This was how it was until she became accustomed to us. Then, after she mastered the situation, we really discovered where misery lives in this world.

Whenever I had to dress her up, what derision I had to endure! I plait her braids — wrong! I unplait and replait them — wrong again! The whole morning would be taken up with doing that. She would pinch me and poke me with her comb and bobby pins, or she would pour water over me. You have no idea what she would not do to poor me!

On one occasion, we were expecting some regimental officers from the city. Everything inside and out was spick and span, as though we had been preparing for Easter. The young mistress sat down to comb her hair. Good grief! It would have been better if I had taken a red hot coal in my hand rather than get mixed up with her fair tresses. It was: come here, you good for nothing slut! Go there! Leave me alone! Come back here again! She pushed and shouted at me, so that I got frightened! Then she screamed, shrieked, stamped her feet, and ended up by bursting into tears! I ran out the door into the orchard and she ran after me: "I will tear you to pieces! I will choke the life out of you, you snake!" I glanced back at her — she became so terrifying that my legs gave way under me. She grabbed me by the neck with both her hands. Her hands were as clammy as snakes. I wanted to scream, but something stopped my breath and I collapsed near an apple tree, regaining consciousness later with cold water being splashed over me. I saw all the girls, white as chalk, crowded round me, and the young lady stretched out on a bench, crying. The old one was standing over me in a black fury, swearing at me for all she was worth.

"What have you done, you slacker! How dare you anger the young mistress? I will send you to Siberia! I will chase you off the face of the earth!"

And she comforted the young lady.

"Don't cry, don't cry, my little angel. She is not worth your tears! You might make yourself ill, which God forbid! See how cold your little hands are! Stop crying, dearest. Why do you take so much on yourself? If there is anything that displeases you, come to me."

"As for you," she began laying into me again, "you will get what is coming to you!"

I don't know how I had the luck to escape a beating. Perhaps it was because of how weak I felt at the moment — so all the old one did was jab me with her foot and order the girls to take me into the cottage.

The girls picked me up and carried me inside where they knelt beside me, crying: "Ustyna, dearest! What an awful thing to happen to you! Mother of God! For what reason is this misfortune sent on us?"

IX

All spring they fed me warm milk, until I got better. I would lie all alone and the others would be working in the field. As I lay there by myself I thought: "Lord, to think that one so young could be so heartless!"

It was quiet and cool in the cottage where I lay. Silence reigned within its white walls and there I was by my solitary self. A light gust of wind would cause a branch of fragrant lilac to dip in front of my window. At midday the sun's rays would sent a hot, trembling streak of light through the cottage, suffusing me with warmth. It would be sultry and sleepy, but I would not be able to sleep. All the time I was left like that with my thoughts, wondering what was to become of me. I would be overjoyed at times — when the orchard rustled, when the sky became overcast, and when the rain rattled on the ground. I would hear the patter of feet, laughter and noise, and a throng of children would pour into my room. Happy and rosy-cheeked, they would greet me and sprinkle me with the raindrops that had fallen on them. They would scramble to the window, impatiently waiting for the rain to cease, singing at the top of their voices:

> Let the sun shine out again,
> Let it shine on our priest's grain;
> On our grandma's herbs let is shine,
> On your courtyard, and on mine.

As soon as the sun peeped from behind a cloud, they would disappear quickly from the cottage. For a long time after, I would still hear the echo of their laughter in one corner or another, as if someone were ringing silver bells.

At dusk, the people returned from their labors on the estate, tired from the hot sun and hard work. They would all be silent, except for someone sighing heavily or singing sadly and quietly.

From time to time one of the girls would dash across from the manor-house to see how I was:

"Ustyna, dearest!"

"What is happening over there, dear?" I would ask her.

"It would be better that you did not ask, Ustyna. Terrible things are happening! Hanna was beaten today, yesterday it was Paraska, and it may be my turn tomorrow. Mother of mine," she would cry out, "what if they look for me now and I am not there! Oh, Ustyna, what is to become of us?"

"Are they saying anything about me?"

"What aren't they saying! They are raising the roof. 'Why doesn't she go to work! Why is she being pampered like a lady of noble birth?' That's what they are saying, if you want to know. Well, I have been here long enough. I must fly! Goodbye, Ustyna!"

X

One morning, while I was still convalescing, Katrya ran in.

"Come, Ustyna, come quickly!"

"Come where?"

"To the young mistress and the old one! And hurry! They have sent for you to come immediately. The young mistress has complained to the old one that you have completely recovered, but don't want to work. Come along, let us go!"

"How can I go, Katrya, when I cannot even put a foot down!"

"I will help you, dearest! Use all your strength, so that you won't get the worst of it. Let us go! Let us go!"

I managed somehow to drag myself to the manor-house. The young lady met us at the door.

"Why are you taking your leisure? Why don't you come to work? You are a slacker! Just you wait? I will think up a punishment for you the like of which you have never seen or heard of!"

My God! How she went on shouting till she was out of breath. She began pushing, pulling me by the sleeve. What a black hour for me! How furious she got, what a terrifying look her lovely face took on!

Her screaming brought the old mistress just in time to join in the shouting. She, too, began to scream and promised me a beating. And we, the Lord be praised, had never experienced anything like that from her, before the young mistress arrived.

From then on it was punishment as well as sweeping every day for us. If someone laughed (and that was a rare occurrence!) the young lady would run to the old one: "Granny," she would say, "they do not respect me!" Or, if someone started to cry: "Granny, they are not going about their duties, they are crying!" Our executioner, she was all day long on the lookout for some fault or other to find in us; and the old one would get furious, and, renewing her youth, hand out the punishment as she used to!

XI

The only time we breathed freely was when we had young noblemen as guests; then, the young lady would forget about us for a while. She would receive them so genially and cordially, twittering like a bird. What a change! You couldn't have told that she was the same person. As for the young men, they were crazy about her. One would show himself off in front of her, another from a corner would size her up with gleaming eyes, another would traipse after her, and still another would give her a lingering, sidelong glance. She moved among them like a pea-hen.

"Which one of them will fall into her trap?" the girls would say. "Poor soul! He is in for a tough, miserable time!"

At first the old lady was highly delighted with those guests, but later, when quarrels broke out among them over the young mistress, she began to be unhappy at the whole business, and was at her wit's end to know what to do about it. Each of them had one and the same thing on his mind — to win the young mistress's favor. They abused one another, argued and bickered among themselves. The old lady began to call them dogs behind their backs. Suddenly, toward autumn, out of a clear sky, things took quite a different turn and our young lady's fate was sealed. The young noblemen bolted from her in all directions, embarrassed and ashamed of themselves.

XII

The local regimental doctor became acquainted with our young mistress and started to visit her daily. He was a quiet, ordinary man, polite to everyone, and without the remotest resemblance to a noble! How did he happen to meet her? For a long time she had been hearing from the local young ladies who visited her, about a certain regimental doctor: tall and handsome, black-browed and rosy-lipped — so indescribably good looking! There was one thing about him, however — he happened to be a very proud man. He could not even look at, or talk to, girls, no matter how they tried to make up to him.

Hearing this, the young mistress would often say to the old one: "I wish you would invite that doctor to our house, granny. I would love to see what he looks like!"

And the old one would reply:

"My child, what you have heard is just the chatter of those magpies. What is so special about that! A regimental doctor! Poor as a church mouse! Why should you even rub shoulders with such people?"

"Well, just to see him, that's all, grandma; to find out if he is all he is praised to be!"

"Away with him! He might force himself on you! You are already quite a storm-center, and yet not one is getting serious. All they do is get in one another's way and quarrel. A plague of rabies on them all!"

The old mistress was so opposed to it! But the granddaughter kept at it: "Let us have the doctor, let us have him!" As a result, at the next party, the old one announced that she was inviting the doctor to the house. This was well received by the guests, who agreed to bring him along next time.

"And when will that be?" asked the young lady, turning right and left, and gazing into their eyes like the little fox she was. "Will it be soon?"

"Since you are so gracious, we shall make it the day after tomorrow," said the guests delightedly.

And they left feeling happy, the stupid fools that they were!

XIII

How prettily the young mistress dressed that day! The old one scowled and grumbled:

"What use have we for that penniless character?"

The young lady pretended not to hear what was being said, and the old one was taking it out on us.

The regimental guests came, but without the doctor. "He thanks you for the favor," they said, "but does not have a minute to spare. He has too many patients to attend to."

"Don't force him," said the old one. "Let him attend to his patients, and God help him!"

The young lady blushed and bit her lip.

We servants got our medicine after the guests left! We had to take the whole brunt of it!

The same week the young lady took ill. She was moaning, groaning, and screaming. The old one got alarmed; she wept and called for a doctor. The regimental doctor was said to be the most knowledgeable, and he was closest at hand — let him be called in!

Meanwhile the young lady dressed herself up in her best and arranged herself in bed, like something out of a picture — waiting.

He came, examined her and asked some questions. She talked to him softly in a sing-song tone of voice. He stayed an hour or so, and took his leave. "I will look in tomorrow," he said.

The old one quizzed her granddaughter about the visit, but she, wrapped up in her thoughts, only nodded her head. When the old one asked: "What do you make of the doctor, then? What is he like?" — the young lady awoke from her reverie: "Proud," she said, "like a high and mighty lord. And who does he think he is?"

The poor deluded soul! He devoted so much time to curing her that in the end he fell head over heels in love with her. The young lady also fell in love with him. The other suitors got the message immediately and cleared out.

The old one tried everything she could think of to put a stop to it, but it was like beating one's head against a brick wall.

"If you stand in my way, granny," said the young lady, "I will die! Hold your peace! Don't talk me out of it! Have pity!"

The old one gave in, but kept on moaning.

XIV

On the manor grounds it became very silent and deserted: the tramping of horses' feet, the rumbling of carriage wheels were no longer heard. The young lady also quietened down: no more cursing, no more beatings, no more complaining about us to her grandmother. She spent all her time deep in thought.

As soon as the sun rose, the doctor would roll up in his carriage-and-pair. The young lady would already be waiting for him by the window, prettily dressed and blushing like a red poppy. He would come rushing in. If one of us happened to run into him he would say, "How are you, my girl? How is your young mistress?"

He would stay all day, sitting near to the young lady, never for a moment letting her out of his sight. The old mistress would dart from the one door to the other, eavesdropping — wondering what the two of them were saying to each other. It bothered her no end that they were together, and that she could not separate them: she, too, was afraid of her granddaughter.

The time came when he asked for the young lady's hand in marriage. The old one wept and lamented:

"I expected to give you away to a prince or a noble of high degree!"

"Oh my God!" the young lady cried in tears. "If he had been rich and famous there would not have been a thing for me to worry about! I would have been married to him long ago. But what can I do? Such is my luck! Such is my bitter fate!"

"But aren't there any better than him?" asked the old one, just for the sake of asking, for she had no more courage left to contradict her.

"There is no one better in the world for me — there isn't now, nor will there ever be!"

The young lady became very sad. She lost weight and grew pale. The old one got thoroughly worked up about the whole thing and she no longer knew which side to take or what decision to abide by. One moment she would say: "Don't marry him!"; the next, when the granddaughter got angry and wept bitterly at her saying so, she would console her to cheer her up: "Don't worry, you will get married soon!"

The granddaughter was cursing her bad luck:

"The Lord has sent this misfortune on me," she said, "I don't know what can be done about it!"

The bridegroom began to take notice and became concerned:

"What is the matter? Why are you so sad?"

"But I am not sad."

"Tell me all about it, do tell me!" he pleaded, kissing her hand.

"So, we get married," she said, "but how will we live? In poverty!"

"Oh, so this is what is bothering you, sweetheart. Why do we need all these riches, when our life together will be beautiful, and our lot a joyful one?"

"You see!" she retorted. "You are not thinking of me at all! It will be pleasant, will it not, when someone comes to visit us, and mocks us saying, 'How poor they are!'"

And at that she began to cry.

"My dearest, what can I, a poor man, do about it? Where can I get it all? Riches were never of any concern to me, but now I crave for all the luxuries to please you. But how am I to acquire them? There is nothing I would not gladly do for you," he said. "I would bend the sky for you if I could, but it cannot be bent!"

And they would both worry about it.

XV

She loved him, but in a strange sort of way, not as other people love. Occasionally some of the young ladies of the neighborhood would visit and quiz her:

"Is it true that the proud fellow has fallen in love with you? That he has proposed? Is he jealous? What present is he giving you? Do you respect him? Does he listen to you?"

"Judge for yourselves," said the young lady, smiling.

And she would begin to belittle him in front of them.

"Listen," she would say to him. "Go to the city and buy me this and that and be quick about it! Hurry up, don't let me get angry!"

He would go right away, and buy what she had told him to.

"Heaven help us, what is this you have bought? I do not want this! Go, get it changed! I have no need for it! It is worthless. Wherever did you get it?"

Again he would go and have it changed.

Or it was this way. He would want a drink of water and she would say:

"Don't drink, don't drink!"

"Why not?"

"I do not want you to! Stop doing it!"

"And what if I want to? I am thirsty!"

"But I don't want you to! Do you hear? I don't want you to!"

And she would look at him or smile in such a way that he would listen. Sometimes she would get angry at him. She would not look at him or talk to him. Almost in tears, he would beg her forgiveness.

The young ladies who were visiting were astonished: "Who could ever expect such love from someone like him! What did you do to win it? How did you get God to help you?"

Our young lady would just smile.

They asked what presents he gave her. She would spread out in front of them the satins and velvets which the old lady had once presented to her, and boast: "This is what he gave me!"

How strange is nobles' love!

The bridegroom very much disliked those neighbor ladies, probably wishing that every trace of them might be obliterated.

While talking to him now and then about this and that, the old mistress discovered that he owned an estate.

"My child!" she said to her granddaughter. "He owns an estate!"

"Really?" exclaimed the young lady, springing up, "Where? Who told you that?"

"It is not very far from town. They say he inherited it recently from some aunt of his. The aunt was childless and he was raised by her."

"For God's sake! Why did he never tell me about it? Probably because it is only a small estate — nothing to boast about. But it is an estate for all that! It is still landed property."

That day she received him joyfully, and greeted him graciously. He was delighted, little knowing that the greeting was not for him but for his estate!

XVI

After Christmas they were engaged. What a crowd of guests attended! The young lady was so happy, so talkative, her eyes all aglow, as she walked hand in hand with the bridegroom. He could not take his eyes off her — so much so that he stumbled as he walked. The merrymaking continued until dawn.

As soon as the guests and her intended departed the young lady burst into tears. She wept and bemoaned her fate:

"Look what I have done! Look what I have started! What a poor life lies ahead of me! Why was I born into the world! Woe is me! Such is my fate as an orphan!"

The old one was not happy with the engagement either, and tried to cheer up her granddaughter, pleading with her:

"What have you to cry for? Come now, stop it!"

"Why didn't the Lord make him a wealthy aristocrat!" cried out the young lady, her face covered with tears, as she paced quickly about the room, wringing her hands.

"My child! My dearest heart! Do not cry! You will not be the richest one, but you will not be poor either. All that I have is yours."

At that the young lady threw herself on the old one, embracing and kissing her:

"My granny, my dearest mama! I thank you with all my heart and soul! Suddenly everything has brightened up for me! You have given me a new lease on life, mother of mine!"

"Come, come, before you know it I will be bursting into tears too! That's enough now!" said the old one, crying and laughing herself.

"Granny dearest, my dove! Will you live with us?"

"There is nothing I would like better, but it cannot be. This, I think, is what I shall do: I shall stay on in Dubtsi and look after your estate. Could there be a better way? If one or the other place is vacated it will become rundown and you will have no peace of mind. As the wise saying goes: 'It is the landlord's eye that makes his cattle grow fat.' "

"Well, splendid, grandma! Let it be this way! Oh, granny," she said, "you have given a completely new beginning to my life!"

"Then be happy, and don't cry."

"I won't cry, granny, I won't!"

As soon as the bridegroom appeared in the doorway, the young lady informed him:

"Grandmother is giving us her village Dubtsi! Granny is giving us Dubtsi!"

He smiled softly and said calmly:

"You are happy, and I am happy that you are. I myself like Dubtsi. It was here we met and here we fell in love. Remember, how this orchard was, all green and blossomy, and how we walked through it together talking?"

And she replied:

"The orchard indeed was green and blossomy, but, dearest, don't forget what a good investment Dubtsi is!"

A tremor ran through him: He looked at her, and astonishment and fear together clutched at his heart.

"What is the matter?" asked the young lady, "Why do you look at me so? Have I said something one should not say? You do wish to farm the estate with me, don't you?"

And she took him by the hand, smiling affectionately. He smiled back at her:

"My beloved homemaker!" said he.

XVII

The young lady cheered up, occupying herself with her trousseau, giving orders and making arrangements, seeing to everything herself. They brought in from the city shoemakers, dressmakers, tailors, and merchants. She was running about, pushing the bridegroom around — buying, laying out patterns, getting things together. The house got like a pot on the boil! It was the most difficult time for us servants, for this is how it goes — no matter whether the lords have a good time or a bad one, it is always the same for servants — hard work! As they say: "For some folk, a wedding — for a chicken, death!"

Many lords and ladies came to the wedding. Indoors it was like a beehive! The inquisitive young ladies feasted their eyes on the dowry exclaiming: "Oh, how pretty that is! Oh, this is grand! Look at this! And this — it is probably very expensive!" Another would notice a particular scarf or dress and it would so touch her heart that she would close her eyes in admiration. They clung about it all, as flies cling to honey! It was a hard job getting them out of the house.

XVIII

With all the goings on I could not spare a moment to bid my friends farewell. It was only when the horses were harnessed and ready to go that I found time to run indoors. Words failed me; all I could do was embrace the young and the old folk.

The bridegroom came for his bride with a carriage drawn by four raven-black, spirited horses. It was driven by a broad-shouldered coachman with a moustache and a high cap. The lords were saying goodbye; there were sounds of talking and weeping, but the coachman, who was trained to meet aristocratic requirements, sat on the driver's seat as if made of steel — neither turning round nor looking at anyone.

The nobles took their seats inside the coach and I occupied the place provided at the back for the postillion.

"Godspeed, Nazar!" shouted the lord happily.

It was a calm, bright, and bitterly cold morning when we left. The willows were all bedecked in hoarfrost, their hoary branches glistening in the sunlight. The girls poured out onto the street, bowing me farewell. The horses kept up a lively pace and everything went past me in a flash. Soon the village faded from sight. Ahead was nothing but the road and still more road — the desolate, lonely path, the path into the unknown.

XIX

We reached the city in next to no time and plunged in as if into the middle of an ants' nest. People going about on foot and in conveyances, selling and buying: common people, nobles, Muscovites, and market women. Wherever one looked there were Jews in their long coats chaffering like May bugs.

The lord ordered the horses to be stopped at a wayhouse and led his young bride into it. He gave the coachman money to buy some lunch, but never a thought of me.

I sat alone and looked about me. Everything was strange, unlike what I was used to! Then someone shouted: "Hey, Beautiful!" I started. It was the coachman calling to me. I gave him a close look: Heavens! How swarthy he was, like a raven! He smiled and his smile revealed a mouthful of teeth as white as sour cream.

"Whom do you want?" I asked him.

"Why, you! . . . What is your name? . . . Ustyna, is it not? . . . Come with me, come with Nazar, to lunch."

I'm very cold, but how can I go? I thought. The young mistress might kick up a row!

"No, thank you," I replied, "I am not hungry."

The coachman smiled: "As you wish, my girl!" and he took off.

XX

I sat there a good hour, until the lords came out. Just then the lord glanced at me.

"Are you still sitting here, Ustyna?" he asked, "did you have lunch?"

"Hey you," he shouted to the bearded innkeeper who, on the porch, was loudly counting money into his palm, "give the girl something to eat!"

The innkeeper put the money into his pocket and went off to get me something.

"What is this, what is this?" exclaimed the lady. "Are we to wait for her?"

"What else, dearest heart!" said the lord. "She is very hungry and cold!"

"What of it? They are used to it. We will be late on the road and I'll be afraid."

"Run, girl, be quick," the lord told me. "Hurry, so that we won't have to wait for you."

The lady went red to the roots of her hair with annoyance.

"It is time to go!"

"But she is hungry, sweetheart. Look, how cold she is!"

"I am cold, I am the one that is cold — I!" she said, with such emphasis on the 'I'.

"Take your seat!" she shouted at me and jumped into the coach herself.

The lord was bewildered. He did not know what to think or say — he just stood there stockstill.

"Well, what is it now?" asked the lady. "Hurry up!"

The poor fellow got in beside her.

"So you are not ordering any lunch for the girl?" the bearded innkeeper asked.

The newlyweds talked together for quite some time, but for a still longer time after they were silent.

XXI

By dusk, we arrived at the estate. Here and there were houses lighted up. We proceeded along the street and stopped before our future home. People were standing on the porch with lighted candles and bread. They were bowing and welcoming the young couple, according to tradition.

"Thank you, thank you," said the lord taking the bread in his hands. "I have brought you a young mistress. Is she to your liking?"

He was laughing happily: for who would not find such a good looker to his liking!

The lady flared up and darted a glance at him. Her eyes threw off sparks, and her face changed color. The people came still closer — to greet her in their own way. She, however, merely grabbed a candle from one of them and bolted off indoors! The people drew back from the door in astonishment without having had a chance to answer the lord's question.

Ill at ease and saddened, the lord went with bowed head into the house.

I, too, went in and looked around. The rooms were not big, but they were beautiful and clean. The chairs, the tables — everything was new and shiny. I heard the couple talking. I listened closely — my mistress was sobbing, and the lord was pleading with and consoling her!

"Don't cry, don't cry, my life, my dearest heart! If I knew it would offend you, I never would have said it!"

"You have probably got all the peasant folk used to taking you for an equal! How nice! The way they inspected me, smiled at me — almost took to embracing me! Oh, how miserable I am! How could they!" she finally shouted, bursting into tears.

"Sweetheart! They are good, simple folk. . . ."

"I do not wish to know, hear, or see anything about it!" the lady said in a rush of words. "Do you wish to drive me mad or what?" she shouted through her tears.

"Come, come dearest! You might make yourself ill. . . . Oh, don't cry, don't cry! From now on I'll do everything the way you want it. Fogive me just this once."

"You do not love me, you have no sympathy for me. . . . God forgive you!"

"It is a sin to talk so! How can you say I don't love you? . . . You yourself know that it is not true!"

Then I heard them kissing.

"Look," said the lady, "if you don't do things my way, I'll die!"

"I will do them your way, I will, dearest heart!"

XXII

I went from room to room; nobody was there. "Have they all run away and left us?" I thought. I went out on the porch — it was a moonlit, starry night. I was standing there looking about me, when — like the plucking of a string behind me, I heard: "How do you do, little girl?" I shuddered. Standing there before me was a tall, handsome young lad looking smilingly at me. I was abashed and frightened. I stood there dumbstruck, as if made of stone, just staring into his eyes.

The young lad spoke again: "You are standing here all alone, perhaps you don't know where to go?"

"If I did not know, I would ask you," I replied, regaining my composure. "Goodbye!"

And I quickly stepped indoors.

"Goodbye, sweetheart!" he called after me.

XXIII

The lords were still walking about the rooms. The young bride was peering into every corner to find out what was what. Behind the icons she saw some herbs:

"What is this?"

"The old peasant woman, my housekeeper, has adorned the icons."

"What? So, she is the one who says how things are to be around here! Throw those herbs out, dearest! This is utterly peasant-like."

"All right, dearest," he said.

And she kissed him: "My darling!" she said.

They walked and talked for a long time.

"Why is there no one about," said he, "where has the old woman, my housekeeper, gone?"

"You see," jabbered the lady, "you see how you have spoiled them! She felt like going and she went."

"She can't be far away! I'll call her."

And he began to call out just like an obedient little boy:

"Old woman! Where are you, old woman!"

"She will be here in next to no time, dearest," he said consolingly.

"And where is she?"

"Probably she is doing something, my love. She is the only servant I have here."

"And where is my Ustyna? Has she also learned already to run off without asking permission? Ustyna! Ustyna!"

I presented myself instantly.

"Where were you?"

"Here, in the next room."

Once again I placed myself behind the door, listening and looking about me.

XXIV

An old woman entered — so old that she was almost bent double. She was all shrunken and wrinkled — shining dark eyes were the only things that were still alive about her. She came in with a light step, bowed to the lady and asked the lord:

"What is it that you want, sir?"

The lady bridled at the old one's being so forward with the master.

"Where have you been, woman? I had to call for you," said the lord.

"I was at the stove, sir, helping Hanna, so that your supper would be a good one."

The lord saw that his wife was upset, but still, he did not have the heart to scold the old granny. He blinked, coughed, and paced to and fro, not knowing what to do. The lady kept turning away from him. The old granny stood in the doorway.

"Well, is the supper ready?" asked the lord, this time with a rather frowning look.

"It is, sir," answered the old one, quietly and composedly.

"Sweetheart," said the lord (turning to the lady), "perhaps we should have supper?"

"I do not want any supper!" retorted the lady, running out and slamming the door after her.

"Then I won't have any supper either, granny," the lord said sadly.

"I'll go, then. Goodnight to you sir!"

"Off you go, but watch out, woman, that you don't have me running after you!" he said, raising his voice just for a moment. He composed himself immediately, however, when in her simple way the old one replied: "Very well, sir!"

She bowed and went out.

XXV

The lord paced for a while about the room. Through the wall he heard the lady weeping. "My God!" he said to himself in a quiet, sad tone of voice. "Why is she weeping?"

He could not bear it. He went to her and consoled her with his kisses. It was a good hour before she quietened down.

"I still don't want any supper," she said, "I can't even stand the sight of your servants! They behave towards you as if you were a brother of theirs or some other relative!"

XXVI

I sat alone in the maidservants' quarters. All around it was so sad and so quiet. This was how my life was going to be! Just delightful in every way! "Now," I thought, "the girls will have a jolly time without my mistress to bother them! It is cheerful and pleasant for them, all together. But, for me — a place among strangers, without knowing a single living soul!"

Suddenly someone knocked on the window! Knock! Knock! I blushed and got flustered, half guessing who it was. I kept sitting as if I had heard nothing.

There was a pause and then the knocking began again. I leapt up and shut all the doors, so that the lords would not hear.

"Who is there?" I asked.

"It is I, turtle-dove!"

"Perhaps," I said, "you have made a mistake. You are at the wrong window!"

"It looks like it, doesn't it? Why are there eyes in one's head when one cannot see what is what!"

"Why come to this window! Imagine starting a conversation through double glass! Go away! The lords might hear us!"

And I moved back from the window.

He persisted:

"Girl! Girl!"

"What are you doing prowling around the window, Prokip?" someone said softly. "Supper was ready long ago and none of you was there!"

XXVII

Someone stepped into the hall. I opened the door; it was the old granny.

"How are you, my girl?" she said to me. "Supper is ready, my dear!"

"Thank you, granny."

"Let us go, then."

"I must ask the lady first."

"Ask what, dearest? It is supper-time!"

"If she will permit me to go."

Granny was silent for a moment, then she said:

"Go then, my child, and I'll wait for you here."

The lord and lady were sitting together, happy in their love, talking.

"Why are you barging in like this?" said the lady when I entered.

"Permission requested to go to supper, my lady," I said.

"Go, then, and have your supper!"

XXVIII

I went with granny across the courtyard into the servants' cottage.

"I have brought you a girl," said she, showing me in.

There at the table sat the dark-browed Nazar with his young, pretty wife. The flames which shot up like a foundry from the stove illumined the white walls, and the icons-corner, adorned with embroidered towels, dried flowers and herbs. On the shelves green, red, and yellow bowls, platters and saucers glowed like precious stones. Everything was so gay, clean, and bright in that cottage: the distaff of soft flax on the loom, the black sheepskin coat on the hook, and the basket-work cradle with the child in it.

"Please come in and join us," they said, and greeted me.

"Such a beauty could sit beside me, perhaps?" said Nazar.

"Are you the pick of the bunch, uncle, that I should?" I asked. I looked round and noticed that the lad who came to my window was there already. He was sitting in a corner, watching me. I became hot all over.

"To be sure, I am!" said Nazar. "Just give me a good look over. Ain't I handsome! Ain't I worth looking at!"

"Perhaps in the dark!" said his young wife jocularly.

What a charming woman Nazar's wife was! They called her Katrya. She had a fair complexion, a slightly turned-up nose, clear, bright blue eyes, and was round and fresh like an apple. She was wearing a red ochipok and a green baize skirt. Risible and slightly haughty, she was brimming over with energy! She talked, flitted about and rocked the baby in his cradle — all at the same time. Her embroidered sleeves and the rings on her fingers were to be seen at the stove the one minute, at the table the next.

"Well, well," Nazar said to her, "if it were not for these here dumplings, I would take you up on that!"

At that precise moment Katrya had set a bowl of dumplings before him.

"There is no sin in having a good supper if you haven't had your lunch!" said Nazar, giving me a wink.

XXIX

Even though Katrya talked and joked, she seemed somewhat sad and ill at ease. Granny was sitting quietly at the table pondering her thoughts. Nazar was the only one joking and laughing, his teeth flashing in the wick light; and his teeth, I tell you, were as white as sour cream! As for that young lad, well — I did not look at him at all.

"Well, dearie," granny asked, "have you been long in service with the young mistress?"

"How pretty she is!" Katrya butted in.

"A lot of good that will do, when she gives looks that can turn milk sour!" exclaimed Nazar.

"Enough of that, Nazar, enough!" said granny and sighed havily.

"Our lord is so good-natured," said Katrya. "He has probably never harmed anyone in his life."

"So, then, let's hope that God gave him a wife like that too!" granny said.

"How is it going to be for us now?" Katrya said sadly. She sighed and reflected. "How is it going to be?" she repeated softly, looking at me as if asking with her eyes.

I said nothing.

"It will," said granny, "be the way the Lord wills, dearest."

"What will be, will be — we'll get through it all!" bellowed Nazar. "For the present we have the dumplings to attend to. And you, Prokip, why don't you join the company, or has the young mistress caught your eye? Or this beauty here perhaps?"

And he winked at me.

"God forbid my even dreaming about that mistress!" replied the lad as he sat down in front of me. "How could one possibly be born so unfriendly!"

Then Nazar's wife turned to me and said:

"My dearest girl! Tell us the honest to goodness truth."

She paused. Everyone looked at me attentively. And the lad never once took his eyes off me. If he hadn't been there, everything would have been fine, but with him around I felt so very self-conscious; I blushed and came pretty close to crying.

"Tell us, girl! Is our young mistress bad?" asked Katrya.

"She is no good!" I replied.

"Lord have mercy on us! I felt it in my heart from the beginning! My dearest child!" she cried rushing to the cradle and bending over the baby. "Could I have foreseen that things would work out like this for me, when I, a free person, was marrying a serf! She has almost devoured us with her eyes already!"

And she began weeping so bitterly — the tears streamed down her cheeks.

"The devil isn't as black as he's painted!" said Nazar. "Why get all keyed up? One should, for a start, take stock of the situation."

But Katrya was crying and sobbing as if the young mistress with her evil eyes had already devoured her child.

"Come, my darling!" granny begged Katrya. "Why should we despair? Don't we have the merciful Lord watching over us?"

The lad kept silent; only, wherever I looked, I would meet his eyes staring at me.

XXX

Having had supper and crossed myself, I was running back to the big house when I heard behind me:

"Goodnight, girl!"

"Goodnight to you!" I answered and dived into the hallway. I entered the maidservants' quarters — my heart was all a-flutter! I kept thinking.

... How he stared at me! And the thought of my lady also came back to me: here she was, barely over the threshold, and already she had cast a gloom over everyone. And why does that lad bother me? How handsome he is! The moon shone full before me ... reminding me of the song:

> Oh lovely moon above
> Shine only for my love!

The words of the song really touched me. I could not be sure within myself whether I truly wished that lad to appear again at my window or not.

XXXI

A day, a week, a month, a half-year passed, like a river rushing by. It seemed quiet and peaceful in the little village with its blossoms and its greenery. If only one could see what was really going on behind the scenes! People woke up crying and went to bed crying and cursing their lot. The young mistress had twisted everything to her own liking. She handed out the hard work and a tough time to everybody, forcing everyone to put a shoulder to the wheel — the handicapped and little children not excluded. The children tidied her orchard, and tended her turkeys; crippled folk sat in the orchard scaring off the sparrows and other birds. The mistress always found reason to pour words of scorn on everything, so that it made you feel that the work you were doing was slave labor. She saw all that went on as if she had had a hundred eyes. She glided back and forth about the village like a lizard, and God only knows what it was in her: she had only to look at you and it would be as if she was crushing your heart in her hand.

The neighboring landowners, however, had nothing but praise for her: "There is a mistress for you! She is the wise and thrifty one! Even though she is so young, we all have a lot to learn from her!"

At first the people pinned their hopes on the young lord, but after a while they sort of gave up hoping. He had a good heart and was kind, but he was absolutely useless. He tried at first to reason with his wife, but she was not the kind to be reasoned with. Latterly he was even afraid to mention anything and pretended neither to see nor to hear a thing. He had neither the spirit nor the energy. It is said that a good master does not beat or scold his people, but he cares nothing about them either. When the lady would begin to swoon and moan as if in pain, or shout, he would kiss her hands and feet, weeping and cursing folk himself: "Destroying the one who is most dear to me! How could you! How dare you!"

"Don't expect anything from him," said Nazar. "I saw the sort of spineless character he was, when he gave Ustyna the money for her dinner. If I had a wife like that I would push her into an ant-hill and let her take what's coming to her!"

At that, he roared with laughter, and the sound of it echoed through all the cottage. That is the kind of man that Nazar was: everything the world over was amusing to him. He gave you the impression that, even if he had been roasted at the stake, he would still have cracked a joke.

Katrya shed many a tear! Heaven knows where all those tears were coming from. She would take her child in her arms and cry and cry! Then she would begin lamenting loudly.

Prokip, too, was very worried. He was always deep in thought and would not even joke with me.

"How very sad you are!" I told him on one occasion (this was in the evening). "Why are you so downcast?"

He took me by the hand — embraced and kissed me. By the time I got over it, he was gone.

XXXII

All the village folk were washed out and weary, only the granny was always her usual self — hale and hearty. No matter how much the lady scolded or shouted at her, she got neither frightened nor disturbed. She moved about quietly, talking calmly and looking steadily at everything with her bright eyes. Without giving it a thought, you would cling to her, weeping, as a child clings to its mother.

"Don't cry, my child, don't cry!" she would say in a soft, soothing voice. "Let the evil folk do the crying. Don't lose courage, see it through! Surely you can put up with it for a while?"

O Lord! What a miserable, sad life we lived! Neither the sound of laughter, nor the chatter of voices could be heard. Not a living soul from the outside world would visit us — unless on business — and even when we had such a visitor, he would glance about so fearfully, and be in such haste, as if desperate to escape from a mad animal in the wilderness.

Once for some reason I was late with my supper and was on my way back at a quick run. "Why didn't Prokip at least come to supper?" I was thinking. Just at that moment, there he was right in front of me, barring the way!

"Ustyna, dearest, tell me the truth: do you love me?"

I would have run from him, but for some reason I stood there rooted to the spot, hot all over.

He grasped me by the hand, embraced me and repeated his question over and over again: "Do you love me?"

He was so strange!

We sat down. We talked and caressed each other for a while — and all our misery was forgotten. My heart was full of joy and the world was a delight to me at that moment. Everything around me was wonderful and lovely! Even the lady noticed: "What is the matter with you?" she said. "Why are you looking so flushed, as if somebody had slapped you? Or perhaps you have stolen something!"

XXXIII

Heavens! How I would wait for darkness to come down! The lady would let me off to go to supper — Prokip would be waiting for me. He would step in front of me and we would stand for a while talking and sharing our sorrows — in the daytime, even if we chanced to meet, we could only exchange glances and go about our business without saying a word.

"A fine time, indeed, for you to fall in love!" Katrya would say.

"You are the smart one and no mistake, my darling Katrya," joked Nazar. "But I bet you would not miss the chance of falling in love with me a second time! I bet you would lick your lips over that! Wouldn't you?"

"What are you getting at? Love! Who is talking about love? That's the furthest thing from my thoughts now! My heart breaks at the thought of what the future holds for these two."

"Why do you pester and frighten the girl so?" granny would butt in. "She has fallen in love, let her love. Such is her fate."

XXXIV

The lady was becoming more angry and ferocious. If I were the least bit late or detained: "Where were you?" she would ask challengingly, and here I was right in the soup again.

At first that really got me down, but I got used to it all as time went on. As they say: "One may as well be hung for a sheep as for a lamb!" While she was going on at me, I would give way to tears, but it wasn't long until I wiped my tears away and was happy and in a merry mood again! Everything about me was just right — my hair would be nicely braided and my blouse spotless — I kept my troubles to myself. What help could anyone give me anyway? It would only remind them of their own misfortunes! Prokip, however, went about like a dark night and at such times he neither ate nor drank, nor talked to anyone.

God have mercy! I thought — here am I with my misfortunes and other people with theirs as well. What was one to do about it? Where was one to begin? Katrya's child became ill, and yet she had to cook lunch and supper for the landlords, dig and plant the garden with the lady storming at her all the time as well: "You don't do a hand's turn, you slacker! You don't earn the bread you eat! I will show you how to work!"

Katrya would be up all night tending her child. By daybreak she had to be off to work. Granny would then look after the child. She would console Katrya, would take the child to her or come by herself and say: "The little one is quiet!" or "The baby is asleep!" In this way she was a constant help, like a guardian angel sent from heaven.

"Why do you keep on so, Katrya, without rest?" I asked her.

"I shall go on working as long as I have strength," she said (her eyes sunken with fever). "Perhaps I shall manage some day to please her ladyship, and earn her mercy!"

But she neither pleased her ladyship nor earned her mercy. She worked without a wink of sleep until one day sleep overcame her as she sat beside the cradle. She woke up with a start, but the child was already near to death. The unfortunate woman had time only to look at the infant, pick it up, and clasp it to her breat, when it expired.

Katrya was heartbroken, but at the same time she was happy for the child:

"My child has gone to be God's angel, and is set free from sorrow!" And at that she wailed: "Who will stretch out those little hands to me? Who in this world will cheer me up? My child! My daughter, you have left me!"

Nazar, pretending that the child's death had not upset him all that much, comforted his wife, trying to calm her down by reminding her that she was still young. But one could see how strained his voice had become, how sorrowful he was within himself.

After that blow fell, Katrya was prostrate with grief. Not only could she no longer work, she could hardly even walk. The lady, nevertheless, never let up on her:

"Why are you slacking? I will let you have it! I will show you!"

"I am no longer afraid of you!" replied Katrya. "You may eat me alive now, if you wish!"

The lady paid her back for that!

"Prokip," I said, "what is going to happen to us now?"

"Ustyna, dearest heart! You have my hands tied!"

XXXV

The lady sent Katrya from the house into the fields, in spite of the fact that her husband was the coachman.

The lord gave her a ruble on the sly so that the mistress would not see, but Katrya refused to take it; he put it on her shoulder, but she brushed it off as if it had been a loathsome frog. The ruble fell on the lawn where it lay till it grew black — no one touched it. Finally, while taking a leisurely stroll in the courtyard, the lady caught sight of it and picked it up.

"You are probably the one flashing the money about?" she said to the Lord. "O, my God! What next!"

The lord went the color of beetroot, but made no reply.

Katrya had no desire to go on living. Something came over her after the shock she had experienced. She ran about the woods and marshes looking for her child and then one day the poor soul was drowned.

The lord became very concerned, but the lady paid no heed:

"Why are you worrying when there is nothing to worry about? Didn't you notice that for a long time she was crazy? Her eyes had a rather frightening look and what she said never made sense.

"That's true," said the lord, taking comfort from her words. "When you come to think of it, she did behave like one demented!"

So they made her out to be demented! What an inspired thought! And with that they put their minds at ease.

XXXVI

They hired a Muscovite of some sort from the city to be their cook. How queer he was! When his cooking chores were over, and he had eaten his fill, he would lie on a bench and would whistle on and on; then, all of a sudden, he would burst loudly into song! It resembled the tinkling of a bell or, more exactly, the crowing of a rooster. He was indifferent to our miseries; he would only ask: "Were you beaten today?" and would add, "It can't be otherwise! That is service for you!"

A change came over Nazar. He sort of drooped, although he kept on joking: "I wish someone were in service to me just for one day; I would be grateful for it all my life!"

The lady praised the cook for being so good and for showing so much respect to her! He would stand before her at attention, straight as an arrow, with his hands at his sides, his eyes fastened upon her: "I was hunting the spotted piglet; the spotted piglet escaped into the weeds, then I went after the black piglet. I caught the black piglet; I scalded the black piglet; I roasted the black piglet." So he would mumble it all, blinking stupidly as he waited to hear what the lady would answer.

"Good! Good! Everything is just fine! Only don't slacken in your work like the rest of that pack of wolves," the lady would reply.

"I will never dare do that, your highness!"

He would bow low to her, clicking his heels right and left, and go out to the bench to whistle again.

"When will you ever stop that whistling!" I told him on one occasion. "All around you is nothing but grief and misery, and what do you do?"

"Don't grieve! Don't grieve, girl! This is what being on service means; what else? See, how many teeth I have left. I lost these on service! We once had a captain. . . . Ouch!" he shouted, and that was all.

"And what do you think? What do you figure out living in the world is? What is service about? How do you reckon one advances? They beat you up, they tear you apart, they deceive and discredit you, and you must put up with it all without even as much as batting an eyelid! All I can say is — God forbid!"

Having said that, he resumed his whistling. Prokip was so annoyed, as he listened to his philosophizing, that he hurled his pipe to the ground in anger.

"Even oxen in the yoke bellow, so why should a Christian soul suffer all kinds of reproach and injustice and not retaliate!" stormed Prokip, so that the Muscovite even stopped his whistling and looked at him as a goat would look at a new gate. "I am not made that way," said Prokip, "it is do or die with me!"

"And I am all for showing a clean pair of heels!" guffawed Nazar. "Run away! That's the way of it with me."

"They will catch you!" shouted the Muscovite, jumping up. "They will catch you, and you are done for!"

Whatever inner feelings any of us may have had at the time — we all laughed.

"It is not every captain who is a fast runner," said Nazar. "Some may trip up. You had better tell us where to run to? It is an out of the frying pan right into the fire situation. And he burst out singing like the clanging of a bell:

> "Everywhere there are dukes,
> Everywhere there are lords . . ."

XXXVII

The old dowager, our lady's grandmother, died in a year. How she did not want to die! She prayed, read holy scriptures, and attended litanies all the time; candles were kept burning continually before the icons. Once one of the girls carelessly allowed a candle to got out — she ordered the girl to be whipped: "You are a sinner," she said, "and you wanted to spoil my chances of salvation too!"

XXXVIII

Our mistress grieved and wept bitterly over the dowager.

"Now I am left all alone in the world! They will fleece me now like a linden tree of everything I have! I cannot keep an eye on the whole property by myself. As for you," she said to the lord, "what can I expect from you? You will never add to our property, you will likely scatter what we do have to the four winds! You do not seem to realize that we are soon to have a child. For the child that is coming, then, if not for me, my friend, take a tumble to yourself! Be the master, take charge of things and, most important of all, don't spoil the servants."

"God preserve you, dearest, what is this now! There you go again, getting upset about things! I will see that everything is attended to the way you want it!"

This is how he would reassure her.

On one occasion, wanting to cheer her up, he said:

"Come, dearest, give your mind a rest. Just listen to what I have to say. I already have a godfather picked out for us."

"Whom did you ask?" broke in the lady.

"A friend of mine. A charming good fellow."

"My God! I guessed who it would be right off! He has invited some poor wretch! . . . I won't have it! I won't! I do not want to hear anything about it! It will not be!"

And she burst into bitter tears.

"Sweetheart, don't cry!" pleaded the lord, "sweetheart you will make yourself ill! . . . We won't have that godfather, then. I will make my excuses to him and that will be the end of it. Just tell me whom you want and I will ask him."

"The colonel is the one to ask — that's who!"

"The colonel? All right, then. The colonel let it be! I will go to him tomorrow. Forgive me, dearest heart, for making you sad!"

"And so you do! You do make me sad, you never give me sympathy, you are always grieving me!"

"My dearest," the lord said quietly, "give me also a little sympathy. You are always snapping, angry, quarreling, and I was looking forward to. . . ."

And, at that, he began to weep bitterly!

"Why are you crying, what's wrong?" she burst out.

She tried to take hold of his hands, but he covered his face with them and kept on sobbing bitterly! With her kisses and embraces she got him finally quietened down.

"Tell me," she said afterwards, "why you were crying? Please do tell me!"

"I do not know myself, my love," replied the lord, making an effort to smile. "I cannot tell the reason why . . . I do not feel too well. Don't think any more about it, just laugh at me for crying like a baby." And he heaved a sigh.

"Perhaps you think that I do not love you any more?" said the lady.

"No, I know you love me."

"I love you, how much I love you! But we cannot stay together all the time. We have our responsibilities to attend to, my dearest!"

And she kissed him.

In the morning he left to ask the colonel to stand as godfather.

XXXIX

A son was born to them. What a crowd of guests arrived for the baptismal celebration! A magnificent dinner was arranged. The colonel-godfather rolled through the gates in a carriage drawn by gray horses, with a jingling and jangling of bells. He was a stout gentleman with a round red face, and his shoulders thrust back. He was continually curling his moustache with his right hand, while resting his left hand on his sword.

I was happy that I was a little freer than usual. I ran out to Prokip and stood talking with him near the porch. Just then the lord came on the scene looking as happy as he was when he was courting the mistress.

"Why are you two standing here? What are you talking about?" He was laughing.

And Prokip burst out:

"My lord, give me permission to marry this girl!"

"That's all right with me; take her, Prokip! I am not standing in your way. Get married and live happily!"

"What about the mistress?" said Prokip.

The lord sighed, reflected briefly, and said:

"Come with me! Take her by the hand, Prokip!"

He went into the house and Prokip, squeezing my hand, led me in after him.

"Dearest heart," said the lord, "I have brought you the bride and groom! Are they to your liking?"

The room was full of noble guests! Among them the colonel was strutting about like a prize turkey.

Our mistress occupied a chair. She gave us a quick glance and turned her head away. The smile faded from her face; she gave the lord an angry look and asked:

"What is the meaning of this?"

Prokip bowed, beseechingly.

"I have already given them my consent," the lord said, "give yours as well, my love. The Lord blessed us with happiness; let them be happy too!"

The lady bit her lip and still said nothing. At that moment the colonel trumpeted:

"Pair them up, pair them up, damn good-looking they are, I would say! We have to get them hitched, dear relative of mine! Do you want to get married, girl?" he asked me, making an effort to give me a wink and closing his eyes instead: it was too big an effort for him — he had had too much to drink.

All the lords joined in with him:

"Marry them off, marry them off! You heard what the colonel, your godfather, said: they make a good pair."

So the lady finally said:

"Very well, let them!"

When her words reached us, we were out of the room like a shot. We got married right away, for fear the lady might come between us.

When the party was over she vented her anger on the lord:

"You have deceived me," she stormed. "I cannot forgive you for the way you have pulled the wool over my eyes!"

"And as for you," she shouted at me, "you will get what is coming to you!"

"So be it!" I thought. "We are married anyway!"

It made me very happy that I could now talk to and look at Prokip openly, because he was mine!

XL

I remained in the lady's service as previously. She was worse than ever, keeping my nose to the grindstone, quizzing me continually: "Well, how are you finding married life? Are things any better for you?"

If my husband had not talked to, and comforted me, life would have been unbearable. When I was with him all was merry and bright; all my troubles were forgotten. He, however, got more and more morose. Seeing him like that made my heart ache.

"Don't you love me any more, Prokip?"

He would put his arm about me and look into my eyes so lovingly that I felt as if I were growing wings.

"But why are you so sad, Prokip? We are together now for life."

"O my dear heart! It was hard without you, and with you it is even harder. . . . Not a moment passes without trouble and humiliation for you here . . . and I do not have the power to defend you. . . . It is hard to live so, Ustyna!"

"We will overcome our troubles somehow. Two, in my opinion, will do better than one!"

"Perhaps you are right, dearest!"

And he would smile and caress me.

My heart rejoiced whenever I was able to cheer him up and talk him out of it!

XLI

So we lived — in poverty and anxiety till autumn. Then something happened.

One day we were picking apples. My husband was shaking them off, and from time to time he glanced at me playfully through the branches, Granny soon got tired and sat down to rest.

"Well, the beautiful summer is gone," she said. "The sun still shines but gives no warmth."

So saying she looked about her.

"Ustyna, dearest! Could those be children peeping through the foliage?" she asked me.

I looked, and indeed there was a group of children gathered near the fence.

"What is it, children? granny asked. "Why are you here, my little dears?"

The little ones said nothing. Their eyes were full of the baskets of apples.

"Come a little closer, you boys. I will give you each a little apple!" granny told them.

The children streamed into the orchard. They surrounded granny, like sparrows round an ashberry tree and she kept handing out apples to each of them. A lot of noise and chatter got up, as one would usually expect from children. All of a sudden the lady's shrill voice was heard:

"What is this?"

The children became frightened. Some were crying, some took to their heels; only the drumming of their feet told that they had been there. My heart began to pound.

Granny calmly explained the situation to the lady.

"I gave each of the children an apple," she said.

"You did, did you? You dared to do that!" shrieked the lady (she was shaking). "You country bumpkin, stealing my property like that! Thief that you are!"

"Me — a thief!?" said granny. She turned as white as a kerchief, and her eyes glistened with tears.

"You won't steal any more!" shouted the lady. "I have been watching you for a long time and now you are caught red-handed. . . . Giving away the master's apples!"

"I have never stolen in my whole life, mistress," granny replied. She was calm now, except for a tremble in her voice. "The master never forbade it; he often gave apples to the children himself. God has provided enough of them for everyone. See, surely there are plenty left for you!"

"Shut up!" shrieked the lady with a threatening gesture.

The branches creaked and my husband stuck his head out from among the green leaves. How stern was his look! My eyes pleaded with him.

"Thief! Thief!" the lady went on shouting. She thrust her nails into granny's shoulder, pushing and shoving her about.

"There's no truth in what you say, lady! I am not a thief! I have lived uprightly all my life!"

"So, you dare to argue with me?"

At that, as if with an axe, she struck the old one across the face.

Granny reeled, and I rushed to her. The lady sprang at me; and my husband sprang at the lady.

"Thank you, my child," granny said to me. "Don't worry about me, and don't anger the lady."

By this time the lady had me by the hair.

"That will do, lady! Enough of it!" stormed my husband, grasping her by the hands. "You have gone far enough! Stop!"

The lady was furious and utterly astonished. She kept shouting:

"What is this? What is the meaning of it? Eh? What?"

When she had collected her senses a little, she sprang again at Prokip. He, however, kept on as before:

"No. Enough of it!"

She then began to scream. A crowd collected and stared. The lord came running up.

"What is this?" he asked.

My husband then let go of the lady's hands.

"There are your fine folk for you!" said the lady, hardly able to speak. "Thank you! Why do you not say something!" she yelled still more loudly. "They almost broke my arms and you have nothing to say!"

"What happened?" he asked, looking around in bewilderment.

Then the lady began: the old one had robbed her; everyone there was after her. What a story she made of it! She sobbed and shouted and cursed so much that the lord got mad as well.

"Cutthroat! Murderer!" he stormed at my husband.

"Keep your distance, master, don't come any closer," my husband responded sullenly.

"Aha, so this place now cannot hold you," said the lord. "Just you wait; you can indulge your rioting to your heart's content when I put you to the soldiering!"

The lady shrieked:

"To the soldiering with him! Off with him to the soldiering! It is the right time too — they are recruiting in the city. Pack him off at once!"

"Take him!" shouted the lord to the people. "Tie his hands!"

Prokip did not resist, he held out his hands and even smiled.

Just then Nazar called to me:

"What are you afraid of? Why are you crying? It won't be any worse than here! Whether it will be any better — I do not know."

XLII

They led Prokip into the house, and a guard was posted at the door. Out in front the horses were being harnessed to the lord's carriage and the wagon was getting ready for Prokip.

"Ustyna, sit beside me!" said my husband after reflecting for a while.

"What have you done, my love? What have you done?" I said to him.

"What have I done? You will be free, that's what! You will be free, Ustyna!"

"Freedom! What is freedom without you?" I said and sorrow overcame me.

"Freedom!" he shouted. "Yes, freedom! With freedom any hardship can be endured! In freedom I can move mountains! But in bondage even the bright moments for serfs are overcast by misery!"

At that instant the rattling of the wagon could be heard. They led Prokip out, and, just as I was, I jumped into the wagon with him. Granny gave both of us her blessing: "May the Mother of God protect you, my children!" and tears flowed quietly from her gentle eyes.

They hurried us off. It was lucky for me that the lady had not yet come completely to her senses, so she did not notice me. If she had not been so busy giving orders to the master she would not have let me go!

We sat in silence, holding hands. I did not cry or grieve, but my heart thudded and palpitated.

Now we were approaching the city. The lord in his carriage overtook us and pulled ahead. We entered the city, quickly passing from street to street, and stopped near a tall building.

Prokip let go of my hand:

"Don't worry, Ustyna."

They took him to the recruiting depot. For me, as I waited on the porch, it was like being in a graveyard.

"Don't let it get you down," said Nazar. "One sorrow gives way to another, and there are always plenty more to come. ... So don't worry!"

But he himself had begun to give up the struggle and gray was already showing in his hair. He was cheering me up, but it was evident that nobody would be able to cheer him up any more.

At that moment my husband was led out. Good Lord! My heart missed a beat; but for him it was like Easter Sunday. He was happy and elated.

XLIII

I had one hour in town with Prokip. It passed as quickly as a flash of lightning, but I will never forget it as long as I live!

They handed him over right away for military training to a Muscovite — a tall man with dark eyes and bristling hair and moustache. He walked like a ramrod, spoke in a loud voice, and carried himself very proudly.

We both bowed to him, but he said nothing and just stared at Prokip with a glum look on his face. Prokip gave him some money:

"Forgive me, sir, for there being so little; a serf cannot come by much."

The man coughed and spat.

"After me," he said.

"Let us go downtown, wife, let us have a good time!" Prokip said.

So off we went.

We were strolling along the street and avenues, enjoying ourselves, when Prokip asked:

"Well, Ustyna, do you feel you are a free soul now?"

And, smiling, he looked into my eyes.

Even though I was still uneasy, and my heart was heavy, I smiled back, as if I had something to be happy about.

I came upon a house that was for rent, but we had no money, and no means of getting any. We had nothing to sell. I had left the village without taking a stitch with me, and, even if I had taken what there was, it was not much — a few shirts, two skirts or so and a sheepskin jacket. The day I left I did not have time to think of this and later the mistress refused to return my things to me. I then had an idea: "I will get myself a job by the day!" So Prokip and I agreed on it and we went to the woman who was renting the house. We explained what our problem was, and asked if it would be all right with her if we paid for the house by the day.

"Fine," she said, "If you have the money, pay me by the day and, if you don't, I'll wait."

We then moved into the house.

XLIV

Our landlady was an elderly widow, friendly and kind-hearted. What a talker she was! She would go on and on, and always about her troubles. She told us how her kinsfolk were gone and she was left all alone in the world like a blade of grass in a field. She would sigh repeatedly and cry quite often, at times, even over what had befallen us. Occasionally when I would be sitting talking with my husband she would start lamenting tearfully that here we were — fine, young people, who should be enjoying life and its pleasures and were not. She wept and wailed. We begged her not to do that! But she would only stop when the Muscovite arrived and shouted: "The old dame is going sour again!"

She was very much afraid of him. His disposition was such that no one could talk to, or ask him anything.

"What a man!" the landlady would say. "How unfriendly and how ferocious! Heaven protect us! Has such a fellow ever had flesh and blood connections? Who can tell why he's like that?"

I got up every day at the crack of dawn and hurried to my work, returning late, but happily clutching in my hand the money I had earned.

My husband would meet me on the way home, would clasp my hand lovingly and warmly, and would quietly ask of me:

"Are you tired enough, Ustyna?"

XLV

One evening we were all sitting about: the Muscovite on the bench holding his pipe, the landlady by a window and I with Prokip at some distance from them. We all sat in silence. Just then someone knocked at the door and shouted: "Greetings, all!"

Would you believe it — it was Nazar!

He entered and stood before us, his head almost touching the ceiling, his pipe clenched between his teeth, his curly hair flecked with gray.

"God bless the lady of the house and all the rest of you!"

"Thank you!" said she, "You are welcome!"

"Where have you come from, Nazar, so suddenly, as if out of the blue," asked Prokip.

"I come," he said, "from the journey that all good people want to take."

The Muscovite gave a twitch and looked at the door.

"Why are you twitching, sir Muscovite? We are all of the same faith, stop shamming."

The Muscovite continued to look at the windows and at the door.

"You don't say! Look how hard to hold he is! Listen you! Are you trying to catch the wind on the steppe? I see that you, too, are a steppe-dweller. So don't even try it — you don't stand a chance of catching it. You had better give me a light for my pipe. And how goes it with you folk here?" he asked us, changing the conversation. "Are the young city ladies expensive?" he asked, winking at me.

"And how is it back home?" I asked him.

"How is it, you ask! The same doom as ever — still the same two choices open to folk like us: whichever you choose — it's ruination beyond recall!"

"What a calamity! What a black hour!" the landlady sadly exclaimed.

The Muscovite twirled his moustache.

"And how is granny?" I asked.

"She is still alive. Granny can stand up to anything. She sends you her good wishes."

I asked what the mistress had to say about me.

"Ehe! The lord got it on account of both of you after you left. 'Because of your slackness,' the mistress told him, 'we have lost two laborers! Who was made a fool of?' And I tell you, the way he was standing there before her — he looked like a downright fool!"

Meantime, the landlady announced that supper was ready. Nazar drew a bottle of whiskey from inside his shirt and set it on the table.

"Let us drink a bumper," he said, "for our life is short! Here is health to those who have dark brows!"

"What sort of whiskey is this?" said the Muscovite. "One might as well drink water as this stuff!"

"Every man to his taste. Water, if one so prefers," replied Nazar.

"The whiskey seems all right," said the landlady.

"May the life of the man who sold it be like his whiskey!" snapped back the Muscovite, but, in between spitting and swearing, he kept on drinking it.

The landlady wondered at him, shaking her head, until at last, unable to contain herself, she burst out:

"Why are you calling it down so?"

"Mind you own business, woman!" he shouted. "One drinks anything to please one's friends."

"Good health to you, then!"

"That just goes to show what good fellows you Muscovites are!" added Nazar.

Supper and conversation continued. The Muscovite kept drinking and drinking. He grew pale and slumped forward on to the table. He looked at me and my husband and said:

"See here, you young love birds! You won't have it long together. But, it's not all that bad! Don't worry. You lived for a while in clover — that should do you. Some people have less. People often know no such thing as happiness at all; one spends one's life in abject slavery constantly under the rod. Try that for a way of living! . . . No family, no home, no one to welcome you, or give you advice. . . ."

"Where are your kinsfolk, my good man?" asked the landlady. "Where do you hail from?"

"I have no family I have ever known of. My kinsfolk belonged to the people who, as you may have heard, perished in the plague."

"What about your mother?"

"As I said: I do not know! . . . Why ask such pointless questions!"

"I have no kinsfolk either," said the landlady, sobbing.

"Hark to her tale of woe!" shouted the Muscovite, "Some misfortune you have! . . . A mere spit! Would you like to know what real misfortune is? It is where no one thinks of you, and you have no one to think of. It is when you have nowhere to go, nowhere to stay. . . . You have nothing of your own and no one to call your own. . . . You said that I am a steppe-dweller," he shouted to Nazar. "Yes indeed, brother! I was taken from those steppes. For all I know they were perhaps glorious! . . . Give us more whiskey, woman! Let us drain our glasses to the very bottom — our young days are there!"

He laughed and drank, while the tears rolled down his cheeks. Finally he slid down on the bench and fell asleep.

"Well, safe home, all," said Nazar, "and goodbye to you, Prokip — my brother! Oh, I almost forgot. I brought a little bit of money for you: five rubles. Keep well!"

"Thank you, brother! I do not know when I will be able to pay you back."

"There is no hurry! It is not a hand-out from a lord, but from a friend. Don't let it worry you! I will earn some cash for myself: now I am free, for at least half a year; even with dogs they won't catch me!"

And he took his departure. That was the last that was seen of him.

XLVI

O God! What a life we then had togehter! So lovely, so blessed by God, even though it was spent in poverty and worry. We could breathe, think, and look around us freely! What I earned was mine, and mine alone; I could sit and talk without fear of anyone; I could work or not, without being forced to do either. For the first time, in soul and in body, I felt I was alive.

In the spring it was rumored that the Muscovite troops were marching out.

"It could not be true," I consoled myself, but my heart felt immediately that it was true. And then the marching orders came.

Prokip tried to comfort me, to convince me that it was only temporary and, when he came back, we would both be free.

"Yes, yes!" I said, "yes, my dearest!"

But my heart ached, and the tears flowed.

The day for the march-out was already posted. We went to our native village to say goodbye. The lords were not home; just granny all by herself on the estate. Dear, dear granny! — I recognized her from a long way off, and recognizing her began to cry. It was only her soul that was still alive. I ran to her and embraced her as I might have my own mother.

"Why are you crying, my darling?" she asked quietly.

"You are actually staying on in this hell!"

"Yes, dearest! Here I was born, christened, and left an orphan . . . and here I'll die, my child."

"So you'll put up with it, till you die?"

"I shall indeed, my dearest."

She blessed us both and gave us what she could, as if we had been her own children. We said goodbye and took leave of her, turning to look back many times. There on the doorstep stood granny. Silence reigned around. Everything was so bright! A wind wafted from the fields; the cool air was blowing from the meadows; water was trickling somewhere; and the whole scene was overspread by the sun's golden radiance.

XLVII

I saw my husband off as far as Kyiv, and remained there myself to work while he went with the army — somewhere far — to Lithuania.

"Don't wear yourself out with weeping, sweetheart!" he commanded me, "I'll come back . . . I am looking forward to it, and you should do the same. Wait for me!"

I waited. What a long tour of duty it was for him! Seven years went by from the day he left me. Would I see him again? I had not been to my native village in all that time. I heard through certain people that everyone was alive there and that things had not changed. Granny was still alive and standing up to it, but there was not a scrap of news regarding Nazar. I worked away and earned my living. It was money earned by the sweat of one's brow. Just the same, from time to time I was happy in the thought that I could stop working whenever I liked. The thought gave me strength to carry on, and another year would pass by. "This sort of life," I would tell myself, "will not last forever!"

How could I even for a minute forget my husband? He was the one who freed me from the hell of slavery! May God forget me if I ever forget Prokip! He is a good man! Protect him, Mother of God! I am free! I talk, walk, and look around me, and whether there are lords in the world or not, is no concern of mine!

THE SLACKER

Our mistress was not in the prime of life, yet she was not very old either. She was tall, stout, and spoke rapidly and loudly. She dressed meticulously, with every thread and button exactly in place; she would walk about so, like something out of a picture.

It was pleasant in our living quarters too. Everything was spotless, polished, and freshly-painted — a little chair, a little table — everything just as it should be, in a noble household. The place was crowded with all kinds of statuettes, and glass bowls, plates, and bottles in green and red. None of it, I suppose, was of much worth, but the total effect of it, as it glittered and dazzled, caught one's eye. The most expensive item hanging on the wall was the portrait of a man dark-haired and beetle-looking, gloomy as night and with gold rings on his fingers — it was our mistress's late father, a noble prince. Whenever anyone came to visit the mistress, she would point at it and declare: "This is my late father!"

In this matter, she knew how to handle different types of people: how to talk, how to look, and how to sigh at the right moment. If some poor wretch came on the scene, she would proclaim in a loud voice: "This is my father — a prince!" To another, if he happened to be a rich man, she would say, sighing: "When my dear father was alive — this is a portrait of him — I never knew grief." To some sincere youth she would say: "What is the use of worldly wealth, possessions, and ranks? My late father was a prince and he rose to a very high rank."

One way or another, she never lost an opportunity of letting everybody know that she was the daughter of a prince. Of course, no mention was ever made of how the beetle-looking prince squandered his wealth with riotous living and left her only a modest house in the city, with a yard and a small orchard — these he could not squander simply because they were his wife's property.

The house consisted of four little rooms. The windows were finished in a peak at the top, and the porch had overhanging eaves. Behind the house, there was an old overgrown orchard. The yard was deep in tall green grass and, from the gate two narrow paths ran through it: one led to the house, the other to a cottage. In the middle of the yard stood an apple tree, heavy with branches.

The mistress rented half of the house to young gentlemen boarders — that was how she made her living. Her husband, we heard, was employed in some distant place; we never saw him; as for the mistress, she was not the least concerned.

The young gentlemen did not give the mistress time to be bored: every day and every evening, they amused her with card-playing and sing-songs.

Nothing pleased the mistress better.

II

I had been given to her as a present. I was born in the village of Hlushchykha, where at one time I had been the property of Ivankovsky's landowners. I was living in the beginning at home with my parents — how well I remember my life there! One day our master got married, and he took me into his household to serve his young wife. My present mistress, who was a friend of hers, would visit and stay with her about a month or so. One day she began complaining:

"What am I to do? I have no servant! Perhaps there is someone you can give me?"

"Why, certainly. Take any one you like."

So she selected me and took me from my kith and kin. After I was taken from home, my father and mother died, and I was left all alone in the world.

I lived at my present mistress's house for about five years. At first I was the only servant, but later on, when the number of boarders increased, the mistress brought in her own two serfs, a woman and her daughter. Up till now she had kept them somewhere with her friends because, apart from the house, she had neither farm nor land: everything was sold. That's how well her father, the noble price, had managed things for her! These two serfs had been left in a far away place and, it took the mistress a long while to decide to take them into the household. You see, they were descended from free Kozak stock, and somehow the beetle-looking prince had come by them dishonestly, so the mistress — poor soul — had to hide them; she was afraid to take them to town in case the townsfolk might tip them off about their right to freedom, and she might lose them.

The serf woman was called Chaichykha Horpyna; her daughter's name was Nastya. Chaichykha was neither the talkative nor the friendly type. A sadness of some sort permanently enveloped her. The mistress might scold her, or hit her (the mistress was not so bad, but she sometimes hit us) or might make her the present of a skirt or a kerchief — Chaichykha would accept it all in silence, and depart. She seemed to be the hard-working and obedient sort, until you took a look at those dark brows drawn together, and those flashing, deep-set eyes.

One day I was a bit depressed. I was sitting on a bench, crying. You know how it is! Even a happy person has sad moments now and then — imagine, then, how things were with us serfs! You will get used to it, folk say! Oh, no, you don't! One can get accustomed to suffering all right and, somehow, learn to tolerate it, but one bitter word is sometimes enough, to remind you of how things really are. That's the way it goes! There are times when one can forget a beating soon enough, but a harsh word spoken at the wrong moment pains the heart for months, even for years.

I was depressed. I wanted to hear a sincere word of comfort. Chaichykha was busy at the stove.

"Horpyna," I said, "here I am grieving and crying, while you are always the same. That is, perhaps, just the way God made you! Surely you, too, must have known misfortune?"

She threw a glance at me with her dark eyes, as if querying what was on my mind, and replied:

"Why shouldn't I?"

"Dear Lord," I said again, "how good I once had it, in my childhood with my parents!"

"And I have spent my life," she said, "dragging my way from one manor to another."

At that we lapsed into silence.

"Were you left an orphan in your childhood, Horpyna?" I asked her again.

"No. I was taken as a child from my family. I hardly knew my father and mother. It is unlikely that they would have recognized me, if they had seen me! However, they never did see me again — they died."

"But your late husband, where was he from?"

"He also was from Horievka. He was in house service with the same landowner as I was."

"Were you a long time married?"

"Half a year."

"Dear Lord! You hardly had a chance to enjoy life together! What happened to him?"

"He drank himself to death."

With that she walked out and, from then on, I never raised this subject again.

III

When our work ended in the evening and the mistress would go visiting, we sat by the gate, passing the time talking to our neighbors. Chaichykha usually sat in silence. Nastya would be chatting with an orphan girl called Kryvoshyenkova, who lived across the street. She was such a nice girl with her bright eyes, her long light brown braids, and her cheeks rosy-red like an apple! No matter when you saw her she was constantly gay and the sound of her voice was like a fast flowing brook. She and Nastya were very fond of each other; they were like sisters —

always together. Nastya, being still in her early teens, did not have a great deal to do — so they talked away to each other, the dear little chatterers. As for Horpyna — she was always alone and always silent.

"Horpyna," I said, "why don't you, at least, talk to your daughter? It will cheer you up."

"How can I talk to her? She is still a silly little thing — let her learn how to think first."

"If I were you," I said, "I would talk even to a child, if only for the sake of having someone — anyone — to hear me out! I would speak about my troubles, I would cry a little, just to ease my grief."

"But a child would blab about your troubles to this, that, and the next one."

"Of course, because she is still young. But does that matter?" I said. "Some good soul she blabbed to, would, perhaps, sympathize with you."

To that Chaichykha made no reply.

Her girl was really beautiful, like a flower. She was somewhat high-spirited and sensitive. If she worried, she even took ill; when she was merry, her merriment knew no bounds — she would joke and sing and be so full of witticism. She was dark-haired, slender, agile, and graceful. As for her eyes — they had a language all their own! Some people weep silently and sigh; when they are happy, they smile — and that would be all there is to it. Not she! When she was sorrowful — she cried her eyes out! When she was happy — her whole being laughed! When she felt sympathetic — she threw her whole heart into it. That's how it was with her as she was growing to maturity.

IV

With each day Chaichykha grew more sullen — just like a black cloud. I began also to notice that from time to time she would go off somewhere. Certain people began calling on her late in the evenings, and she would talk with them for a long time. I kept my peace and asked no questions. Then one day I saw a red-collared, heavy-featured, and moustached Muscovite coming into the courtyard. He asked whether the mistress was at home. "Yes," I said. "She is!" I glanced quickly about. There was Horpyna standing in the doorway, white as a sheet, following the Muscovite with her eyes. I became frightened. "What is the matter with you, Horpyna?" I said to her. She just made a hopeless gesture with her hand to me.

The Muscovite gave some sort of paper to the mistress. When she read it, she became angry and rather alarmed. She wrote something down and gave it to the Muscovite, who took it away with him. Soon after that, a fat individual arrived and began to confer with her. She was talking rapidly, wiping her eyes from time to time with a handkerchief, and striking her hands together now and then. She gave him some money too. He was listening to everything she said, raising his eyebrows the while, and rapping with his fingernails on the chair. He took the money and put it in his pocket. "Have no fear," he said. "You don't have a thing to be afraid of!"

The mistress thanked him, saw him to the gate, and thanked him once again. I went and told all that to Horpyna.

"What is it all about?" I asked.

She clenched her teeth and moaned: "I knew it, I knew it!"

I could not make head or tail of it. The two men came from the Court of Justice.

They sat down and ordered Horpyna to stand before them.

When the one had sniffed some tobacco, and the other had wiped his face with his handkerchief, they asked her:

"Are you the one who is aiming to get your freedom?"

She said:

"Yes, I am!"

"You will get into trouble, foolish woman! You are better off serving your mistress and sticking to your work."

She made no response.

"Do you hear? Do you understand? Watch your step! Behave! Don't make trouble for yourself! We don't want to hear about anything of this sort from you again."

They took their departure.

I wanted to say something to Horpyna, but when I looked at her I could not utter a word. She sat down and lowered her head on to her arms. She did not cry or burst into lamentation. It looked as if life had come to a stop in her?

Nastya was standing there too. She was deep in thought. Her face kept changing color.

V

Lord, how the mistress railed at Horpyna! She could not even set eyes on her for a couple of weeks or so.

One day Nastya said to me:

"That is why my mother was always so sullen! This is what she worried about! When I was small, she used to tell me about our forebears who were free, and how she wanted to be free herself! She was merrier then," said Nastya and, as she said that, she became meditative and sad. "She was not at all as she is now. She would be spinning and would tell me stories about how our forefathers, the free Kozaks, lived along the Dnipro, and she would sing sweet songs about those olden times."

I said to her:

"So that is what you, too, are always thinking about, Nastya?"

"Yes, that's it. I dream of that ancient freedom and, somehow it upsets me. I am always waiting for something to happen, I don't know what . . . and my thoughts are sometimes confused, and sleep does not come to me; then when I do fall asleep — I always dream of being free!"

VI

Nastya was going on sixteen. The mistress was teaching her embroidery and sewing. Nastya was bright and lively. She learned quickly, but to her own disadvantage. The mistress was happy about it and started to bring in outside work for her to do. If anyone approached her with something to be done, she would say: "I have a young neighbor here, she sews well!" and she would pass on the work to Nastya. The mistress got good money for it, and they supplied her with lots of work. You sit and keep at it, Nastya! And Nastya was so young, still a slip of a girl, full of the joy of living. Her thoughts were still those of a carefree girl! She would have loved to pass her days in green orchards, gazing at the stars on quiet evenings, hearing words of love in the moonlight. But what could one do about it! Anyone else would just have cried and got reconciled to the situation. Nastya was not like that. God alone knows how many tears she had shed! She wasted away like a candle. Her bright eyes grew dim and she became sullen like her mother.

VII

One day the mistress went visiting. None of the boarders was at home. Chaichykha and I tidied up the house, and then we went to Nastya, who was sewing in the mistress's room. We walked in and there she was, her face covered with her hands, almost choked with weeping.

"What is the matter, Nastya?" I asked.

Chaichykha glanced at her daughter, and, without saying a word, sat down.

"What is the matter with you?" I asked again.

Nastya pointed to the window, nodding her head in the direction of the street.

"What is out there, my little dove?"

"There are people out there!" she shouted. "They are living, walking about; they are looking at God's world, and here am I, wasting my life doing somebody else's work."

"Oh, my little bird!" I consoled her. "Don't those people have sorrows too?"

"Sorrows? I am not afraid of sorrows! I have worse things to cope with. Here I know neither sorrow nor joy! Here am I, changing to stone! I am like a stone!"

I looked at Horpyna. She was sitting, listening, as if to a familiar song, without even moving her head.

Nastya heaved a heavy sigh, then she wiped her tears and said:

"Sit down, nearer to me, mother! And you, aunt, talk to me, speak a consoling word."

All I could say to her was:

"Nastya, don't worry, don't cry."

Paying no attention to my words, she threw herself at her mother and grasped her by the hands:

"Mother, mother! Say one word to me, say something! My soul has been in agony. My heart is pining away!"

"And what can I say, daughter?" said Chaichykha gloomily. "There is no advice that one can give for that."

Suddenly someone was heard coming! "It is the mistress," I said. "It is the mistress!"

And there she was, in the doorway.

VIII

"What sort of get-together have we here?" shouted the mistress. "I have only to step out of doors and work comes to a stop."

She took the shirt from Nastya and glanced at it:

"It looks to me as if you have not done a single stitch, huh?"

"I have a headache," replied Nastya with a downcast look.

"But gaping doesn't give you a headache, does it? You lazy good-for-nothing! You are just like your mother. Perhaps you, too, wish to be free? I will give you freedom — just you wait!"

And she stood in the doorway so that Chaichykha and I could not pass.

"I feed her, I dress her, I keep her alive, and look at her — the slacker! She has no inclination to do any work for me!"

"Perhaps, then, I am working for myself!" Nastya exclaimed bitterly. "Have I, perhaps, earned something for myself?"

"You dare to answer me like that! You have not yet learned your lesson!" And she began to beat her.

"All right, beat me," cried out Nastya. "And, perhaps, you would like me to thank you for that too!"

"Shut up! Shut up, I tell you! Or you will be sorry for the rest of your life!"

"Well, let me!"

I looked at the mistress — she was livid with rage. I looked at the girl — she was pale, menacing, in a panic of despair. I looked at Chaichykha — she was a black cloud!

As luck would have it, the boarders appeared on the scene. The mistress then pushed Nastya out the door.

"What a life I have here!" she lamented. "Did you ever see such a good-for-nothing slacker! Just imagine her talking back as rudely as that to me! And why? Because she did not get the right treatment; she was not beaten enough as she would have been in other places. Oh, my dearest father!" — she glanced at the prince's portrait, and her eyes took on the same look as his, and the same wrinkle appeared between her eyebrows. "Did you ever think, could you ever have guessed, that your daughter — the daughter of a prince — would have to wear her nerves out and trouble herself with such trash!"

"Stop troubling yourself!" said the boarders. "Is that slacker worth your trouble! Let us have our supper!"

That is how serfs live! You work in your youth, and wind up in poverty and disgrace in your old age. What is there of one's youth to look back on?

IX

In our part of the house there was now no talk, no conversation. The only laughter, talking and joking that could be heard came from the mistress's quarters.

The mistress would be reading the boarders' fortunes from cards, or telling them yarns. Sometimes she would sing. Her singing was always about some dear friend: "Why does my friend not love me, why does he forget! Why does he not visit me." She was probably thinking of her husband, who can tell?

But in our quarters silence reigned. The fire would be burning in the stove. I would be sitting in one corner, Nastya would be sulking in another. Chaichykha, gloomy as a thunder cloud, would be working at the stove.

The girl next door would sometimes drop in on Nastya.

"Nastya dear, come to our place! Let us have a chat. Why are you so sad? Don't worry about the mistress not letting you go out. Whenever you have a free hour, come and have a merry time to make up for what you have lost!"

"I cannot make up for lost time, dear sister!" she would say. She would say it in such a bitter tone of voice that even the happy chatterer from next door would bow her head, sigh, and grow silent.

Then this started to happen: by nightfall, Nastya would disappear. And it did not happen on just two or three occasions either.

One night we went to bed and she was still out. We did not see her the following day, she worked in the mistress's quarters; nor did we see anything of her during the evening of that day. Chaichykha sat up waiting for her. I was not sleeping either. The whole thing saddened me so! Mother of God, have mercy on us (I thought)!

It was sometime after midnight when she returned. She walked in and her mother met her.

"Where were you, daughter?" she asked. And her voice was like a broken string.

"Don't ask me, mother! Don't ask!" replied Nastya, and her words rang through the house, like a lamentation.

Chaichykha went on:

"What are you up to, daughter? What is on your mind? Is this meant to bring trouble on my unfortunate head?"

The daughter went to bed. She lay there motionless, as if dead.

"Where were you? Where were you, daughter?" Her mother's exhortations and pleas were of no avail — she turned a deaf ear to all of them.

X

Next evening Chaichykha was waiting by the gate. When her daughter came rushing out, she seized her by the arm:

"Where are you going? Get back into the house!"

She took her back into the house, and, all evening, Nastya sat in a corner, with her hands crossed and with downcast eyes, not saying a single word.

And it was like that from then on: whenever the mother was not watching — the daughter escaped. No matter how we asked or pleaded — she refused to listen. We watched her movements, even followed her. There she would go, looking about her and, on seeing that she was being followed, she would run as fast as the wind. She was young and ran so fast that even a young person could not catch her, least of all her worn-out mother or myself. She paid no heed to our tears or our entreaties.

How sad it was in the house! How quiet and forlorn! For weeks sometimes not one pleasant word was uttered. There were times when I wanted to speak to the mother or to the daughter — but a look at them was enough to put me off.

One evening Chaichykha and I were sitting in our quarters. Everyone else had gone to sleep and all was quiet. Nastya was out. We sat for a long time. Only the wind in the orchard stirring the branches and rustling the leaves and the notes of a nightingale could be heard.

Suddenly we heard Nastya's guffaw. We gave a start. I got frightened. There she was, throwing the door open noisily, standing laughing in the doorway. The night-light was turned down to a peep. She stood there, her face so red, her eyes flashing. Her mother went up to her and stared at her. Then Nastya began to speak. She spoke in such a hilarious way that it made me so, so sad.

"My dearest mother!" she said. "You were waiting for me, perhaps? Here I am! Your daughter has come home. Why are you staring, mother! Don't you recognize me? It is I . . . I am happy."

She stepped forward staggering. My God! She was plain drunk! She staggered to the table and sat down.

"Well, my dear mother! I have found a man who will get me my freedom. . . . I tell you for certain that he will free me. . . . We will be free! We will live and work for ourselves, and remember him in our prayers. . . . Even though he has now no respect for me, and gives me no protection . . . let it be! I am thankful to him just the same, mother; I bow down humbly before him. . . . He will write me a paper. . . . The mistress has no claim on us! She has no land, he says. . . . We are Kozak stock, mother, therefore free. . . . They had no right to condemn us to serfdom. . . . Oh yes, he will free us. . . . And he will free her (pointing at me). I am so happy, dearest mother! . . . When I am sad, he gives me money . . . and with it I buy myself some whiskey . . . and my head then is full of stars!"

So she went on talking and laughing, and Chaichykha just listened, never taking her grim eyes off her.

Nastya fell asleep, bent over the table. The nightlight went out. The dark night covered them.

XI

From that time on, Nastya was drunk every evening, and, whenever she had a free hour in the day, she got drunk in the daytime as well. The mistress found out and got furious; she shamed her and her mother:

"You are her mother. Why don't you put a stop to it?"

Nastya would be kept under lock and key — yet she would escape anyway, if not by the doors, then by the windows. The mistress scolded and beat her, but she would say:

"All right. Let her beat me! I will get drunk and will forget all about it! I will have a good time!"

The mistress tried everything in her power. At the times when Nastya was sober, she would deliberately shame her before the boarders: "What a girl! What a treasure! What a slacker!"

Nastya would act as if she had not heard her. They would laugh and she would even smile. The mistress became tired of getting angry at her. "At least you do your work well in the daytime, you good-for-nothing! To the devil with you!" she said.

XII

A child was born to Nastya. How small, puny, and weak it was!

"O, my child! My grief!" she moaned on seeing it. She covered her face with her hands and began to weep, which she had not done for a long time. I was afraid that Chaichykha, who now did not look at her daughter, would not welcome the child, so I held it up gently to her.

"The Lord has given us a child!" I said.

She took the child in her arms and gazed at it steadily with a sad, sullen look. She looked and looked at it, then the tears began to flow. "What a grief," she said, "what a misfortune! What a grief!"

"A grief, indeed!" I said, weeping along with her. This is how we greeted the new-born — with sadness and with weeping!

The child's growth was difficult and painful. It was always sick and ailing. Nastya began to drink more than ever. When she was drunk, she would talk to me and fuss over the child, consoling it: "My child, why doesn't your father come to see you? It's no use waiting for him! He won't come! What does he care? He never even asks about you. And you, my little angel, do not forsake me!" That was the way she talked, smiling to the child and clapping its hands together. It was pitiful to look at: the child barely alive, and her playing with it. When she was sober, she would never go near the child, or as much as look at it — she ran from it. We were the ones who gave the ill-fated little thing its milk.

One time Nastya was confined to the house for two days or so. Good Lord! She fought, she shouted, as if she were being branded with a hot iron: "Oh, let me go, please let me go! Or else behead me! Have pity on me! Why do you torture me? I am an incurable drunkard. Have pity on me, let me go! I shall get drunk and forget my troubles. When I am sober, grief is ever with me, staring me in the face!"

Still the mistress would not let her go, and complained to the boarders: "What sort of people are these drunkards! They have, I believe, a different constitution from ours. Look at her — so young, and drinking so much! She is a slacker all right! Phew! She has completely neglected her child — it is fading away too."

And the boarders retorted: "It is frightful! These people have no shame, no conscience, no soul!"

So they would pass judgment as they enjoyed their supper or entertained themselves.

XIII

The child passed peacefully away. One morning I came to fondle and feed it. I entered the room. It was overcast outside and the room was dark. Thunder rumbled in the distance; the wind had dropped and all was still.

I noticed on entering that the child's eyes were already dim.

I rushed to it and blessed it. It gave one sigh and its soul departed. Neither Chaichykha nor Nastya were at home. I washed and dressed the child, prepared the table, and laid the body on it. I ran and bought a candle, lit it at her head — and crossed her arms.

Horpyna arrived. She crossed and kissed her granddaughter cold in death, and for a long time stood looking at her. Nastya arrived next — happy and drunk.

"What is this?" she asked. "My daughter has died? My daughter, my little daughter! My dear little cold hands! My dear little withered face!" She took the child's tiny hands and kissed them, then she kissed her head. "How mute she is now! At least it used to whimper so — but now it is so quiet. . . . So, you have died! . . . It is all right, my daughter! It is all right, indeed!"

As she spoke, the tears poured from her eyes as though in sorrow and in joy at the same time.

Then suddenly she gave an abrupt start:

"Get some whiskey, we need it! The people will be here to bury my daughter!. . . . Will they come? Whether they do or don't — we need whiskey just the same. . . . I will go and get it!"

Off she went, and did not come back till night. We had already obtained a coffin, laid it out, and covered it with herbs. At night Nastya returned. Once more she took the child by the hands and kissed her head again. She collapsed beside the coffin and fell asleep, repeating over and over: "It is all right! Indeed it is!"

When she awoke in the morning and saw the coffin — she shuddered and went pale.

"She did die!" she exclaimed, as if she did not know or had forgotten this. She tried to approach the child, but I held her back!

"Nastya! Nastya!"

"Let me go!" she screamed. "Let me look at her! I have never really seen her until now."

She kept looking at the child, calming down gradually, then she left the house.

She was not present when we buried the child. When she returned that night, sober, tired and white as a sheet, she asked no questions. After that, she drank still more.

XIV

This sort of life did not last for only a day or two. My God! It went on for two years! Then all of a sudden Nastya stopped drinking. She looked very troubled and never went out of the house! Her face kept changing color; she winced and trembled — as though she was waiting for her death, or maybe . . . her freedom! I quizzed her — there was no response. It was like this for three days. On the evening of the third she burst out: "He has betrayed me!"

"Nastya, my dove," I said to her, "what is the matter? Tell me, my ill-fated one!"

"What am I to do! I will go to him. I will either blot him from the earth, or do away with myself. He assured me that on Monday my freedom would be delivered to me. I will go to him, I will strangle him. . . . Perhaps that may bring me relief. . . ."

She tore herself away from me and ran off. I ran after her, shouting to her mother: "A tragedy is about to take place!"

But the mother merely nodded her head, as if not expecting anything else.

I ran after Nastya calling out: "Nastya, Nastya! Wait for me! I want to go with you . . . I will help you in everything."

She just ran on without paying any attention. There was nothing left for me but to return home.

Nastya stayed away all that night and all the next day. The mistress sent us to look for her. We searched but could not find her.

Then, on the second day around noon, she turned up with two Muscovites leading her.

I rushed up to them.

"My good fellows! What are you planning to do to her?"

"You have gone mad, woman! Perhaps your whole breed is mad!" a wretched looking, yellow-skinned Muscovite said to me, waving a paper in his hand. "This one is mad as well," he said, pointing to Nastya. "Here is her freedom, she should be rejoicing, but instead she is losing what sanity she has left."

"What freedom?" I asked, not understanding what it was all about.

"She is free now! That's what! It has already been agreed on. And what a fine, young, handsome gentleman pleaded on her behalf!"

The other Muscovite added:

"Ehe! Nobody would plead for the old woman! Away and drown yourself, old one!"

They were having their little joke this way. Nastya was white as a sheet, she was neither sad nor happy — she looked as if she were made of stone.

Chaichykha ran out. I told her what had happened. She did not believe me, and did not even want to listen. The mistress became frightened and appealed for help to some of her friends; she wept and begged them for advice, and we waited for the outcome — what would it be for us poor souls — death or freedom? The wrangling went on like this for a week. Even after the final decision to set us free, the mistress still did not want to let us go. At the end, however, she had no other choice.

They gathered us together for the last time to explain that we were free, and handed us the documents. As soon as we got outside the gates Chaichykha began weeping bitterly! My God! How she did sob! She exclaimed repeatedly: "God be praised! God be praised!"

The neighbors came out on to the street, gathered round, and congratulated us. They wept with us, comforting us at the same time.

"My sisters, my brothers, my family!" Chaichykha cried to them. "Don't stop me — let me weep! I have not wept for twenty years!"

She said this in such a way that everyone burst out weeping again.

Now when I looked at her, I saw for the first time what kind eyes and what a sweet smile she had. She seemed quite different from the withdrawn and sullen Chaichykha I had known.

When she finally calmed down and looked at her daughter, she became sad and morose once more.

Nastya was standing right there looking at everything and everyone, whispering to herself:

"I have had a drink today already — my head is spinning."

"Good people!" she moaned. "Am I free, or am I just drunk?"

XV

Nastya's old friend, Kryvoshyenkova, invited us to stay at her house. A few other good neighbors had gathered there and we were working out what we should do next. Nastya was the only one who took no part in our discussion. She sat in a corner with her head bent, and stayed that way as if turned to stone.

"Nastya," we called, "come into the group, join the consultation."

"I have a headache!" she replied.

The next day she became seriously ill and never got well again. Her life burned out like a candle. She could no longer recognize anyone; her eyes had a terrifying look. She clutched her head continually.

"My head is on fire!" she would say.

On the fifth day she rose and looked for her kerchief with the intention of making a break and running away.

"Nastya, where do you want to go?"

"I want whiskey. I will go and get it! I will go!"

Her mother began to weep, and pleaded with her:

"My daughter, come to your senses!"

"Let me go, let me go!"

"Where can we let you go? You cannot even stand on your feet.... Lie down!"

"Kill me then, kill me!" she screamed, wringing her hands.

We got her back into bed again. She began to thrash about, to pant, and scream:

"I am free, I am free! ... That is great! ... I am free, I am a drunkard and a good-for-nothing slacker! ... Where do I now belong? Is there any place I can go to? Is there! Any good master will throw me out. 'She is a drunkard!' he will say, 'She is a slacker, we must get rid of her!' That is what he would say and do. And he would be right!"

By nightfall her strength was completely gone. She just moaned and pleaded:

"Do not throw me out — let me rest a while! Mother, I am your child — do not drive me away!"

She was imagining that she was being thrown out. She was also remembering her child:

"Bury my child, bury it!" she whispered. "It died so long ago!"

At midnight, she raised herself up on her bed.

"How cold the winter is!" she exclaimed. "Where are you driving me away to?"

And she fell back on to the bed.

Those were her last words.

TWO SONS
Dedicated to M. O. Maksymovych[1]

My husband died and left me with two little children, two sons. I had to work to support them, but my earnings alone were not enough. I sold this and that — soon I sold everything I had. It is difficult for us poor people to part with things earned by the sweat of our brow! But I parted with everything.

From day to day worries and work filled up my life. There was never time to enjoy my children, who, in the meantime, were growing up. There they were, my little nightingales, clinging already about me, chattering constantly.

II

Andriyko was full-faced, bright-eyed, and curly-haired; he was a happy and sprightly little boy. Throughout the day he would bother me a lot with his nonsense, and yet, he livened things up to me.

Vasylko, the other one, was quiet and gentle, his presence never felt inside the house or out. From his very youth he was somehow contemplative. Could it be attributed to the critical hour of his birth that came soon after my husband died, or was it just the will of God? I really cannot tell.

Andriyko would dash through the village and return flushed, full of joy and out of breath. The other one would sit quietly beside the house somewhere and think. He would potter about in the soil or search for various herbs. He would rake out a worm here or catch a butterfly there, looking them over and contemplating them. If Andriyko called him at such times, he would be startled. Sometimes he would spend a whole day in the orchard, lying motionless, as if listening to something.

---

[1] M. O. Maksymovych — well-known Ukrainian ethnographer and historian of the nineteenth century.

"What," I would ask, "are you meditating about, my son?"

"How large this world is, mother!"

Even as a boy, he knew all about the various herbs, where and when they bloomed, and what color they were. He knew at what time of the year the birds migrate to the warm countries, and when they come back again. Of all these things he had full knowledge.

"This is God's gift to him," people would say to me. "Let him be! This is God's gift!"

III

During the long autumn evenings when my work had tired me out, I would take both of them on my knee and try to instruct them to the best of my ability. I explained this and that, and had discussions with them. My Andriyko got bored very quickly, became impatient, rubbed his eyes, yawned, and sighed. "Let me go now, mother!" he would beg. And when set free — he took full advantage of his freedom! He would create a noise and cause mischief until he became sleepy. But Vasylko would sit up the whole night through, if need be, listening attentively and concentrating on everything I said. Even after we all fell asleep, he stayed awake, unable to sleep.

"Why are you not sleeping, my son?"

"Because . . . I don't feel like it! . . . Mother, why is the night so dark?"

"Because God made it so, my child. Go to sleep!" I would tell him. "Go to sleep!"

He would get quiet. . . . But still for a long time, he would toss about restlessly.

When the moon began to shine through the window, he would not take his eyes off it. And I had heard that it is not good when the moon's rays shine on sleeping children — so, I would cover them and warn Vasylko: "Do not look at the moon, Vasylko! One should not!" He would sigh at that. There was seldom a night that he got a quiet sleep. He might have no sleep at all, or, if he did sleep he had distressful dreams.

Andriyko was not like that at all. The morning sun would be high in the heavens and he would still be sleeping, sprawled out and getting all warm and rosy in his sleep. It was as difficult to waken him in the morning as it was to put him to bed at night. As soon as he awoke, the little imp made so much noise as nearly to raise the roof! He ran about and hummed or shouted for joy until everything got into a state of disorder and confusion! How happy, gay, and carefree he was then! In the end, I would put a stop to his pranks, even though I felt sorry to do so. I would scold and raise my voice at him a little.

Vasylko was younger, but would admonish his older brother. Andriyko was impulsive and as fervid as a spark. Several times a day he would quarrel or fight with the children on the street, on the slightest provocation.

"Why are you so sad, Andriyko?" his little brother would ask.

"I was fighting, that's why!"

"So now you see, Andriyko, it is all because of your naughtiness. If you did not get yourself into these things, you would not be sad now and ashamed of being defeated!"

Andriyko would give him his side of the story:

"Well, it is so boring just sitting around doing nothing."

And again he would tear out of the house, without leaving a track.

Vasylko was quiet and serious-minded. God knows who was to be thanked for such behavior. Whether he went to a friend's place or somewhere else, he soon returned. He would never stay too long nor become engrossed in his play. And that was how he grew up, mostly on his own, taken up with himself. He did not talk much, and he was not inclined to jocularity. I really do not know whom he took after!

Andriyko was friendly with all the girls in the village. He always applied himself conscientiously to his work, but he also took time off for amusement. But the other one — when he took on anything, he would not take his eyes and his mind off it — he got totally absorbed in it.

IV

My children, my children!

A rumor had come to us that this year there would be recruiting for military service. When I heard this, a cold shiver came over me. I looked at my two young lads — how handsome they had grown! How very young they were!

One morning — and I would not wish anyone to experience a morning like it — word came that it was Andriyko's turn to go into the service.

I packed his things to get him ready. It is not easy for a mother to send her son away to military service! If anyone does not know what this means, let him just ask me! As for Andriyko, a change came over him — I could already see him withering before my very eyes. Where was that undaunted look in his eyes? Where was that radiant smile?

At his departure I was not the only one to lament for him, breaking his heart with sorrow. There were also certain young eyes that wept bitter tears for him and his good looks! He was known throughout the village for his beautiful voice, and many a time his singing could be heard in the warm starlit night. And perhaps — who knows? — it was through this that he won the heart of a lovely, affectionate girl. In the summer, during the warm, quiet nights, I would lie for a long time, sleepless — thinking and worrying, listening sometimes to their quiet lovers' talk. I had hoped for a daughter-in-law to be my joy. The recruiting service dashed all my hopes.

V

New recruits were supposed to leave on Wednesday afternoon. I was sitting awaiting that hour, when Vasylko came running in, breathless and pale, followed by two men.

"Get them both ready," they said. The master has given orders to take Vasyl as well!"

I did not believe them.

"It cannot be so!" I said. "Surely the master is himself a creature of God!"

"No mother, it must be as they say!" replied Vasylko.

They all started to talk me down. My heart sank. Although I heard what they were saying and saw all of them clearly, their words were not getting through to me.

VI

A team of three wagons drove away, all carrying the young recruits. Their relatives were seeing them off. I also sat between my sons in the wagon. The road flickered past, the fields and groves came into view.

And something had come over me: like a small child, I could not comprehend, or get a word out, or remember anything. There was only fear gripping over me whenever I glanced at my children.

We came to a receiving place where all the new recruits were gathering. The young men were led away and we were left waiting. All that time I was as if half asleep, awakened from time to time by sounds of crying and sobbing around me. My sons were the first to come out. Lord God, who are all-powerful and merciful! I would rather see them dead and buried!

VII

They led me into a sort of dark little shack. Whether this was a mud hut or a cellar or something else I cannot really say. A Muscovite was sitting there, unkempt and unwashed! With the growth of stubble he had all over his face, he looked like a hedgehog. He was the one who was to be in charge of them.

I bowed and begged: "Please, sir, be good to my sons!" I gave him what I could afford: a little money, some linen material. I also gave him something for my children.

"Do not worry, old woman!" he exclaimed in a gruff voice. "Your sons will be a little lonesome at first but, after all, this is quite natural; soon, though, they will like it here; and at the end, they will become good soldiers, like me, for instance!"

I looked carefully at him then: he had a red face, and was all kind of puffed up. His eyes were rather faded. Oh my God! And my sons, my little gray doves! My sons with their souls so pure and holy; with their loving faces like flowers in bloom — would they become like him?

VIII

We said goodbye. My children saw me off. To this day, when the weather grows hot and suffocating in the summer, I recollect our

departure. Here we are, going through the town. All the buildings are closed, and everywhere the windows have their drapes tightly drawn. On the outskirts of the town dark fir trees overshadow the sandy road; a squeaky wagon pushes forward in front of me, and, the sun high in the sky, beats down.

IX

I was left all alone in poor health. I knew no sleep, no rest or peace. I had to force myself to work, and was oblivious to everything.

One year passed, then another, and a fifth.

A dark cloud had enveloped me, and the only light I could see was my children — the two stars in a desolate dark night.

One night after Christmas, I was sitting up late, spinning. Outside a violent storm was raging. It was pounding against the window and causing the light to flicker.

All of a sudden — Knock! Knock! I opened the door and there stood Vasylko.

"Vasylko, my son! And where is Andriyko?"

"Andriyko is gone, mother! Andriyko has lain down and will not get up again!"

It was as if I already knew it. I prayed for him each day and cried for him every night! He was so young and had all of his life before him! His physique, his strength, and his looks resembled those of his father: so, it was that he followed his father into the other world!

"You have aged, mother! How has life been for you here? Did you have much hardship to put up with?"

"This has been the extent of my life: waking up crying and going to sleep crying. That is how I have lived!"

"I have come to you, mother, to die!"

I took a close look at him — woe is me! For he was still young and already his health was ruined!

"My dear son, I wish I had not lived to hear these words from you!"

The words he said were true.

My Vasylko was burning up like a candle. He was bedfast for a while. He grew weaker. By spring he was no more. It was impossible for him to live! He had no great health as it was, and the military training and expeditions drained even that strength out of him.

"I was not born, mother, to kill people in war!" he would say. "War is not for people like me, and I was not a very enterprising soldier!"

As he was lying gravely ill, he pondered continually.

"Oh God!" he would say. "What a wonderful world is yours! And I have not lived long enough to learn and understand anything!"

In his last hour, he declared:

"I have never lived in this world, mother. I was merely preparing to live!"

So he was cut down, as by a scythe, in his youth. And I was left.

X

The only joy I have now is when I dream of my children. I always dream of them as they were when they were little; never, as they were when they were grown up. Life-like, they stand before my eyes: Andriyko with his curly hair, running happily and careering about the house — the house so bright and gay — and Vasylko sitting deep in thought amongst the flowers and herbs.

I wake up — nothing but work awaits me. I must live. I must attend to my work. I must put up with my sorrow. So, I live.

I watch my house crumbling into dust, and feel that I myself am gathering dust, somehow becoming gradually stupefied and losing touch with reality. It is as if while still alive, I were sinking into my grave.

MISMATCHED

Misfortune will dog your footsteps no matter how you live. Such is God's will! Such is the fate allotted to all of us.

I had a niece. Being an orphan from her childhood, she grew up under my guidance. I saw her father and mother laid to rest and mourned their loss bitterly. I brought her up to be a smart, sensible girl, and looked after her property. She had a fine house with a large parcel of land; and so deep were her clothes-chests that, even by bending over, one could not reach the bottom of them.

She lived happily with me! Lovely she was, so dark-browed, bright-eyed, red-lipped, and shapely. And how blythe and jocular!

She was a good, hard-working housekeeper. As she matured I had no problem with her, for she was in every way reliable and considerate. Her presence really livened up the house.

II

So we lived together in heartfelt happiness. Then, all of a sudden, I began to notice that Parasya had something on her mind. She spent a lot of time thinking, she lost weight, her voice was seldom heard in the house, and her happy laughter ceased.

She did not confide in me, and I did not question her. She used to go to merry gatherings in the evening, and, before leaving, she would usually say: "Darling auntie, I am going to see the girls," or something like that. Now, she would flit out of the house without mentioning it.

III

One evening Parasya came home quiet, but happy. It seemed as if she wanted to tell me something, but she hesitated.

"Parasya, my dove, something good must have happened to you. What is it?"

She still hesitated to tell me; she just darted glances at me, blushing all the time. I kept insisting: "Tell me, tell me!"

At last she said:

"My dear aunt, I . . . I am going to be married very soon."

"God bless you! May the Mother of our Lord grant you a happy life!"

I asked her whom she had in mind.

"Semen Paliy," she said.

"Oh, my child! Is that a good match?"

"Oh yes, a good match, and to my liking!" she replied proudly.

IV

Semen Paliy was known to the whole village as a weird, peculiar person. Although a rich man, he lived as poor people live, and somehow could not make headway in this world. Whether he bought or whether he sold, the profit was never on his side. Everyone who wanted to cheat him, could easily do so. This did not mean that something was actually wrong with him. He was intelligent, could handle people, and carry conviction, but, for all that, he was still a strange man. I have never seen anyone like him in my life! From time to time something would come over him; he would then lie for a whole day in the garden as if he were sick, or at night he would wander over the fields. No one could figure out what was bothering him!

V

So I kept impressing all these things on my niece. Being in love, however, she did what every girl in her case would do — she paid no attention to anything I said to her. She was in love and that was all she cared about — her future was of no immediate concern to her!

I pleaded with her and advised her. As she listened to me, she wept, but her heart was still drawn to Semen Paliy, like a moth to a light — impossible to prevent it, or chase it away. I did not have the heart to part them, so I gave them my blessing.

VI

Seeing the happy, loving married life they had together, I was happy too. I would go visiting to their place — there they sat, so much in love and so beautiful! The more I got to know him, the more I liked him; I came to regard him as my very own. What eyes he had and what a voice! What a good-looking man he was!

Parasya would often come to visit me for a few minutes. Oh Lord, how blissful and happy she was!

"How is everything, Parasya?" I would ask.

"Everything is good, dearest auntie, everything is so good for me! He loves me very much. He will not have me away from him for a moment, always asking me to sing: 'Sit down beside me, sing for me, my nightingale, sing!' So I sing and he listens and looks into my eyes. What beautiful eyes the Lord has given him!"

"And how are things on the farm?" I asked.

"They're also going well. Everything is going well. I try to do my best to please him! And he, my aunt, he doesn't let me do my work, honestly he doesn't! For instance, I am busy by the stove or elsewhere and he will say: 'Why are you taking so long, Parasya!' 'For you, my dove,' I will answer, 'so that you will enjoy your meal.' He might respond: 'It makes no difference to me, my love! I'd rather you came and sat beside me and embraced me. Let us talk about life and how people live in this world.' And when he begins to talk, auntie, I forget everything I started to do and how to do it. When I come to my senses I feel ashamed of myself! What kind of a housewife am I? Now I have grown wiser; I houseclean, wash, sew, but he, I notice, at such times grows sad and gloomy and does not want to eat or drink. I beg him over and over again: 'At least taste it; put your lips to it! It is delicious!' At that he answers: 'It is delicious! It is exceptional! How could it be otherwise — you cooked it with your little hands and added a sprinkling of your thoughts.' It is as if, in saying this, he were mocking me. Then I start kissing him and he is happy again."

VII

I was delighted as I listened to her cheerful talk. It never occurred to me that one day all this happiness could change into great misery. Although Parasya no longer visited me as often as at first, I still thought: "It is because she is all wrapped up in her happiness, and for the happy person the rest of the world does not exist!"

One Sunday I went to visit them. The house was closed. I went next to the orchard and saw them both sitting down, somewhat sad and silent.

The greenery of their orchard ran along a hill down to a wide river that flowed beneath. On the other side of the river the ripened grain could be seen; the grinding of the mill and the rustling and creaking of the willow trees could be heard. A gentle breeze filled the air.

They were sitting under a pear tree. He was looking into the distance and she was looking at him. I approached them. They both started.

"Good day! How are you?"

"Please, join us!" they said.

Even though they greeted and talked to me, I had a feeling that there was something missing — everything was different from what it had been before.

I sat with them for a while and, as I got ready to go, said: "Parasya, will you see me off?"

She did so.

"Parasya," I said, "what is the matter with both of you today? What has happened?"

"Nothing, auntie! Honestly, nothing!" she replied.

And she did not tell me. So we said goodbye.

As I walked the rest of the way home, I thought: "Why has she grown so uneasy? What is going on between them? Maybe they just had a little tiff? They will probably make up soon, my little doves."

VIII

I waited and waited for her to come over, but she did not come. When I chanced to see her at work, it was only for a moment.

"Why don't you come over, why don't you visit me?"

"I will come, I will, auntie!"

But still she did not come. I had noticed that she was becoming increasingly thinner.

Again I went to see her. By this time we were in the freezing grip of winter. I entered the house. She had kindled a fire in the stove, and was sitting on the floor, her head bowed and her hands hanging down helplessly. Was she alive or dead? "Grief and misfortune have befallen my Parasya!" I thought.

"Parasya!" I called.

She got to her feet and turned pale and downcast.

"Tell me, my child, tell me what has happened!"

She stared at the fire without answering. In tears, I went on begging her to tell me, but she just kept staring at the fire. For a long time I pleaded with her, and she just kept on staring. Then she turned her head to me.

"He does not love me!" she said.

"God preserve you! ... He does not love you? What do you mean, Parasya?"

"He does not love me!" she repeated. And the way she said this, so sincerely from the depths of her soul, I could not but believe her.

"At first he loved me, now he does not."

"Why? Does he abuse you?" I asked, "He beats you, maybe?"

"No, he does not beat me, he does not abuse me — only, he does not love me. He does not look at me, does not comfort me, does not smile at me."

"What exactly has happened between you two?" I said.

"I don't know myself," she said. "I pleased him, I loved him, but such is my fate!"

"Maybe he is angry with you for something you have done?"

"Done what? Did I not listen to him? There were times in summer when we would sit in the orchard and he would point saying: 'Look how clear the water is! How the reeds rustle — listen!' At first I did not want to look or listen. 'Better that I should kiss you!' I would say to him. 'Why should I look there?' Then I saw how he would gather his brows into a frown. So thereafter, I did look and listen. I began to look, so intently, as though I had never before seen anything like it, just to please him. Again, when old Lysenko died and his widow was selling the cattle, I begged him: 'Buy some! She will give them to you cheap.' And he replied: "Do you want to get rich on a widow's misfortune, Parasya?' I tried to convince him that, if we did not buy, other people would. 'But not us!' he exclaimed. I saw him grow very bitter on hearing those words coming from me, so I fell silent. No, auntie, I listened to him. This is just my bad luck!"

IX

Just then he entered the house. He took off his cap and greeted us, but maintained a sullen and proud reserve.

"I am freezing!" he said.

How Parasya attended to him! She stoked up the fire; she brushed the snow off his coat and coaxed him tenderly.

And he, handsomer than ever, stretched out his hands and warmed them over the red flame. When his sad, proud eyes met Parasya's, which were fixed upon him, he quickly diverted his glance.

I wanted to say something, to give advice, but somehow I could not say anything and took my departure.

How many times after that I wanted to go to them, but when I recalled what happened, how he stood there, so proud and aloof, I changed my mind about going. No, I would not go there! For nothing would help anymore.